ONE SHOT

Brandi Easterling Collins

LUMINESCE
•PUBLISHING•

Luminesce Publishing books may be ordered through booksellers or by contacting:

Luminesce Publishing
www.luminescepublishing.com

LUMINESCE
•PUBLISHING•

Illustrations:
Designed by Freepik
Designed by Dashu83/Freepik
Designed by macrovector/Freepik
Cover and interior design © Luminesce Publishing
Author photos © Jonathan Collins

ISBN: 978-1-7322289-6-2 (paperback)
ISBN: 978-1-7322289-7-9 (ebook)
Library of Congress Control Number: 2020952620

This novel is dedicated to my late father,
Douglas Wayne Easterling,
and my late stepfather,
Ronnie Anthony Campbell.

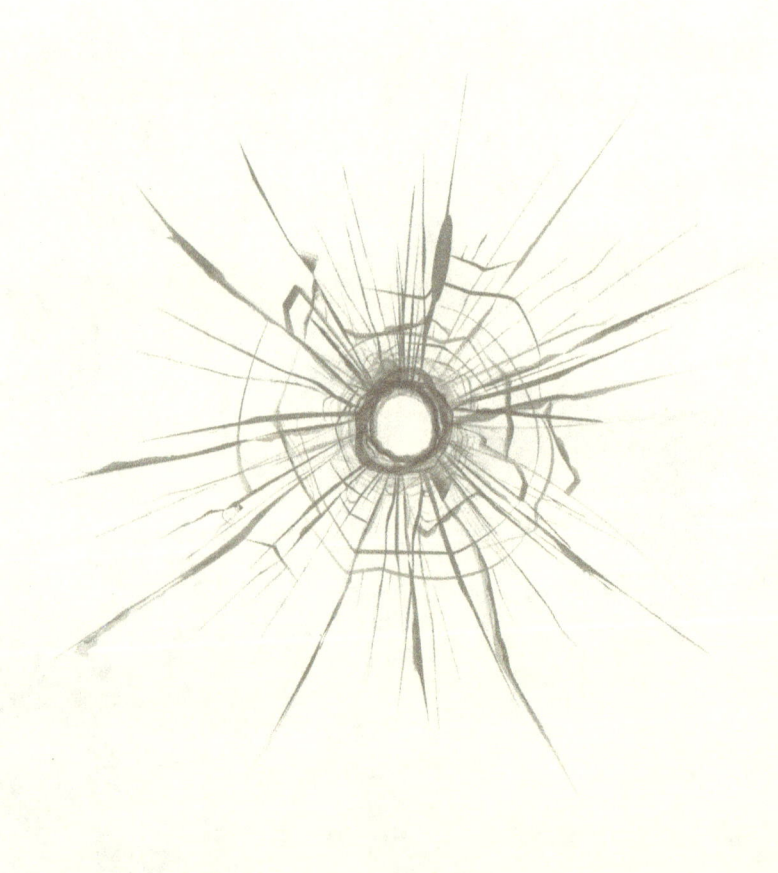

Acknowledgements:

Thank you to my husband, Jonathan, for being generally awesome, supporting my dreams, and offering opinions from a male perspective. Thank you to my children, Drew and Meredith, for allowing me time to write and read.

Thank you to my wonderful friends and beta readers, Alisha, Devin, and Melissa for their valuable feedback and support of this story.

Thank you for the continued support of my family and friends.

Thank you to the #amwriting and #writingcommunity Twitter communities for the continuous support and encouragement of independent authors.

Thank you to my favorite mutts, Peanut, for being a captive audience during my read-aloud editing sessions, and to Roscoe, for bringing perfect doggie kisses from the moment I met him at the animal shelter in December 2020. And special angel dog hugs to my Buddy, who crossed the rainbow bridge in September 2020.

Prologue

December 23, 2015
YouTube Video transcript
Charlotte

"It doesn't really matter what town we lived in or who my parents were in our community. Our family wasn't as famous as the Kennedys or the Clintons or the Obamas, but we were well known all the same. Known well enough that when a tragedy struck our family, it felt like the whole country was praying with us. We were a political family in the United States. My dad had always been in some sort of progressive campaign for as long as I could remember. And I hated all of it—the cameras in my face when I wasn't prepared, the fancy fundraising dinners, and the constant expectation to be seen as perfect but not heard.

"I had to take things into my own hands, albeit anonymously at first, to call out the guilty parties when my sister was kidnapped on her way home from babysitting earlier this month. We lived in a nice community where things like that didn't happen...until she was just gone. My mom was a wreck, and my father seemed to care more about turning on the tears in front of cameras for his campaign.

"You already know what happened since a trial of epic proportions was avoided yesterday when the biggest player involved pled guilty. Spoiler alert: It's safe to say that shit's hit every single political fan now."

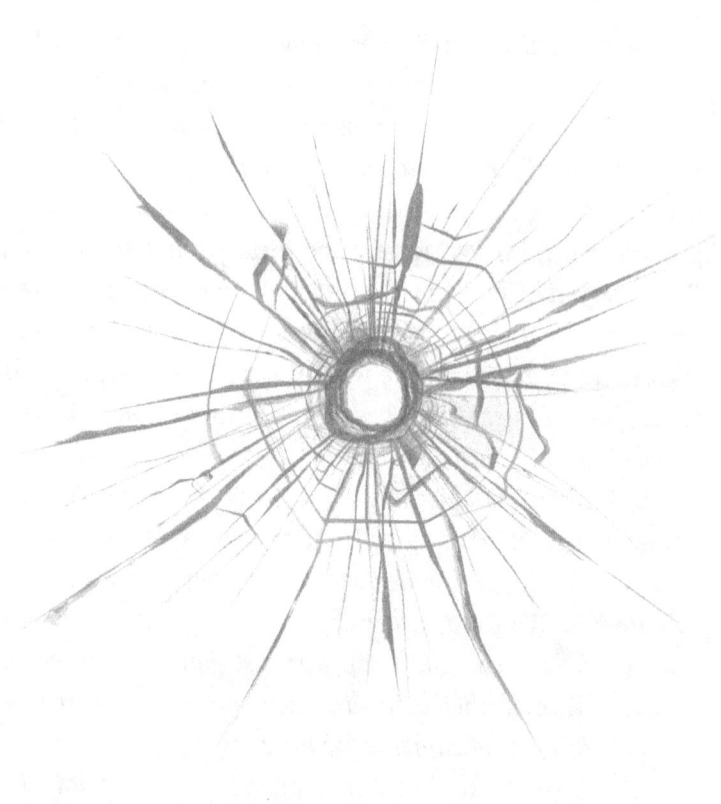

Three Weeks Earlier

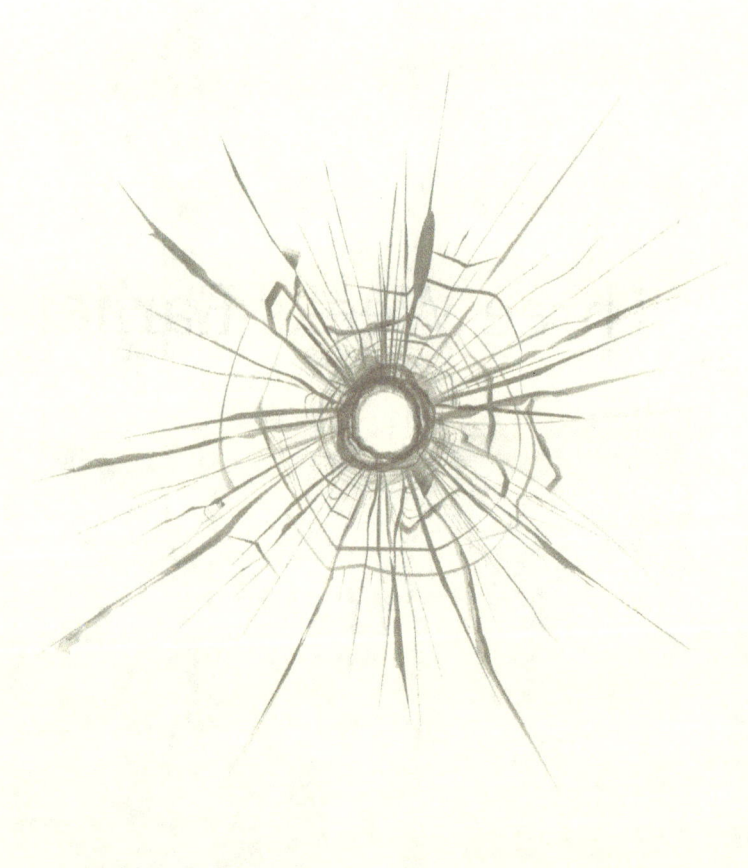

Chapter 1
Wednesday, December 2
Vincent

Out of all the girls at prep school, Vincent Rowlands had fallen for Charlotte Manchester. Her looks had captured his attention first—an unconventional beauty with long red locks and inquisitive eyes—and then the moment she'd opened her mouth in debate club, he was done for. A gorgeous girl with brains; how'd he get so lucky? And how weird was it that his girlfriend's dad was now a high-performing candidate in the primaries to run for president in 2016?

Vincent was daunted by Charlotte's father the night of their first official date two years ago when they were both sophomores in high school. Tall himself at just over six feet, Vincent had to look up to meet Mr. Manchester's eyes as they shook hands. After that first meeting and chat, Mr. Manchester was everywhere and nowhere all at once. Sure, he was in commercials and televised debates, but Vincent couldn't recall having had more than five actual conversations with Charlotte's dad the whole time they'd been dating.

He knew Charlotte's mother quite well since his mother served alongside Gina Manchester in various clubs and organizations staffed entirely by the rich women in their neighborhood. And Charlotte's sisters were great. Her older sister, Olivia, was away at college, and their younger sister, Julia, was a fun kid who'd been dancing since she could walk.

"Vinny," Charlotte said. "Snap out of it. You're all spaced out again."

Vincent smiled at her as he closed his book. "Sorry. It's hard to concentrate on calculus when you're all sprawled out there." He got up from his desk chair and walked to the side of his bed, where Charlotte was resting with her books, her dark green sweater complementing the red and navy plaid of his comforter.

Charlotte rose to her knees and kissed him. "I should go then. I can't be responsible for ruining your grades right before the next wrestling match." She plopped down and grabbed her boots.

"I'm more worried about making weight."

Charlotte stopped zipping her boots and looked up, concern wrinkling her brow. "I thought you were feeling better after last week?"

"A little, but food still doesn't taste good. I'm still down five pounds." Vincent hated his illness, but at least Charlotte could empathize. Having ulcerative colitis as a teenager was hard enough without having to explain everything to friends who thought you were flaking out on them all the time.

"Any blood or mucus?" she asked.

"I love it when you talk sexy to me," Vincent said, stealing another kiss.

"Vinny..."

"No, I promise. I just need to take it easy for the rest of the week. I'll be fine by the match if I don't get benched for not making weight."

Charlotte was content to stay in during the weekends Vincent didn't feel well and never complained about it, just like Vincent never complained about staying in when Charlotte didn't feel well. Charlotte understood better than anyone because she had UC, too—though she'd not had it as long as Vincent.

"You'll get there," Charlotte said. "It wasn't so bad last week, so technically it was just a small setback. You're still in remission."

It was true; Vincent knew he'd be okay this time...or the time after that. "Come on," he said, pulling Charlotte to her feet and embracing her in a tight hug. "Let me drive you home." She ran her hand under the back of his sweater and felt Vincent's ribs. He winced from her ice-cold hands. "I promise I'll hit the protein shakes hard this week."

Charlotte broke their embrace and grabbed Vincent's hands. "With extra frozen yogurt," she said. "We can't have you getting too skinny, Vinny." She kissed him and then pulled away, flashing her warmest smile.

"Kind and beautiful, and she rhymes too," he said before kissing her again.

A former child model, Charlotte always seemed to have the right kind of smile to warm anyone's heart. But it wasn't just her physical attributes and intelligence that had stolen Vincent's breath as he'd fallen in love with Charlotte. They'd bonded while serving the community away from the camera flashes of the charity events they'd been dragged to by their families. Charlotte—whose father seemed to value appearance over anything else—genuinely cared for others while no one else was watching. She'd logged the most hours volunteering at the State Children's Hospital last year, second only to Vincent—also a patient there since his family had moved the summer before tenth grade.

As they pulled through the gated entrance to Charlotte's two-story grey colonial-style house five minutes later, Vincent pointed to the unfamiliar black car in the driveway. "Who's that?"

"Probably Dad's campaign manager, Byron Saks. He reminds me more of a greasy used-car salesman than a political wannabe. He talks to me and Jules like we're seven."

"Don't you mean sleazy?"

Charlotte chuckled. "No, I mean greasy. You should see the amount of product he uses in his comb-over. Dudes should just go bald gracefully, you know—like, who does he think he's fooling?"

"I imagine it's hard to accept for some men," Vincent said. "Would you still find me attractive without my hair that you enjoy running your hands through so much?"

"It's mainly for your sweet ride." Leaning over the center console of Vincent's hand-me-down red sedan, Charlotte took handfuls of Vincent's shoulder-length brown curls and pulled him closer. "I'd still think you're a hottie with no hair at all." One last lingering kiss and she bailed out of the car before Vincent could walk her to the porch. He sighed and waved to her as she slipped through her front door.

As Vincent pulled away, he saw the man who had to be Byron Saks judging by how the outdoor lights gleamed off the hair product. Through the rearview mirror, Vincent watched Byron snap several photos of the back of his car.

Chapter 2
Charlotte

Charlotte ducked into the half bath off the entryway to avoid having to speak to Mr. Saks. He'd only been around the last few months, but the man gave her the creeps. It was nothing he'd said really; it was just the way he looked at her and Julia. Liv wasn't around much now that she was in her junior year of college, so she hadn't met Saks and couldn't offer her younger sisters any support when Charlotte had brought it up to their mother over some hot chocolate one evening.

"He's just a campaign manager," Mrs. Manchester had said. "Byron's a little more high-strung than some of the others. Just stay out of his way."

"How can I, Mom? He's two steps away from choosing my clothes for me, which is hilarious considering that he dresses like some little boy playing dress-up in his father's suit. Thank God we wear uniforms to school."

Breathing a sigh of relief as the front door closed, Charlotte slipped out of the bathroom and dashed to the main staircase, just past her father's den.

"Young lady." Her dad's voice stopped her in her tracks, echoing off his bookshelves full of thick law volumes he never seemed to read.

Charlotte stuck her head in the half-opened door. "Hi, Dad."

"Good day at school?" he asked.

"Yeah, it was fine." She hovered in the doorway, hoping to avoid another lecture.

"Don't go slacking off now. The early-admit colleges will still look at your grades this semester." Mr. Manchester flipped through the pages on his computer screen.

Charlotte sighed. "Dad, I just came from studying. My grades are perfect."

"Make sure they stay that way. I don't want to see a 'B' on your senior transcript."

"Yes, sir. Goodnight."

As she stomped up the stairs, Charlotte glanced at the family portraits hung along the wall—a new one was taken each fall for as long as she could remember. No one saw the yelling and tears it took to get everyone picture-perfect for her dad's latest campaign when the girls were younger.

In the latest photo, thirteen-year-old Julia stood a head taller than twenty-year-old Olivia. Charlotte, at seventeen, was the tallest of the three but not for long if Julia kept growing at her current rate.

If it hadn't been for the strong resemblance to her maternal grandmother, one might assume Charlotte had been plucked from an unguarded hospital bassinet the day of her birth—a redhead in a family of brunettes. Charlotte was always the focal point in every family portrait shared with the media, as others couldn't help being drawn to her hair.

Hell, many of the constituents—at least the ones who had no understanding of genetics—probably assumed she was adopted anyway because of her appearance, not that it mattered. Still, Charlotte seriously doubted any of the voters gave a damn that she'd gotten a "B" in advanced placement chemistry last year.

Later that evening, while at the dinner table, Charlotte picked at her roasted chicken and plain baked potato while Julia gushed to their mother about her fabulous day.

"I never thought I'd actually win class president for next semester!" Julia beamed as she turned excitedly between her mother and Charlotte. Her dark brown hair was separated into two braids that reached her waist.

"That's wonderful, baby," Mrs. Manchester said. "Your father will be so proud of you."

Charlotte looked at the grandfather clock along the back wall. Dinner had been late every night that week, trying to accommodate Mr. Manchester's busy schedule, but he was still absent each night. "But not so proud that he could tear himself away from the campaign long enough to have dinner with us," she muttered.

"Where's Daddy tonight?" Julia asked. Charlotte found it cute that her thirteen-year-old sister still referred to their father that way.

"Another conference call ran late," their mother said. "It takes sacrifices from all of us for the greater good."

It was always about the greater good with Mr. Manchester. Charlotte couldn't remember a time when her father hadn't been preoccupied with something in the political realm. While she admired his enthusiasm, she often wished he was more present for their family for real, not just for the photos. Hoped that when he'd grilled Vincent before their first date that it had been out of concern for Charlotte's wellbeing. Not because of what their potential relationship might look like to the public since Vincent's mother was a prominent neurosurgeon and his father owned a large engineering firm. The Rowlands immediately fit in to the charity circle to which the Manchesters were already card-carrying members.

At least their mother cared. Charlotte could count on her mom for hugs and reassurance in ways that her father never provided. The "C-minus" on the chemistry final last year—a non-issue for Mrs. Manchester, who was sure Charlotte had done her best, landed her a one-hour lecture from Mr. Manchester. She'd busted her ass studying for every single test for AP chemistry and wasn't feeling well the day of the final. Of course, that was never good enough for her father. It didn't matter that she'd still squeaked through with "B" in the class. And Charlotte really had done her best. Even her biggest debate club rival had only managed a "B-plus" on the test.

"I can tell him about it later," Julia said, turning to her Charlotte. "Who won class president for your class?"

"Umm, Martin again, I think..." The truth was, she'd found herself daydreaming about college and the future during assembly while holding hands with Vincent. She sometimes wished she were older and closer to having a career and marrying Vincent. Anything to get away from all the politics in her family. Of course, she hadn't exactly said the M-word to Vincent, but she hoped their love would last a lifetime. It was hard to know everything with complete certainty at seventeen.

"Oh," Julia said. "He's nice. His sister, Maggie, is my VP."

"That's awesome," Charlotte said. "I'm so proud of you, Jules. You'll be a great president."

"You should have run, too, Charlotte," Mrs. Manchester said. "It would have looked great on your college applications."

"Mom," Charlotte groaned. "You know I've already been accepted at my top-three choices pending my grades this year. The schools were all fine with volleyball, debate club, yearbook, and the hundreds of hours I've logged at the hospital. I didn't need anything more, and I don't want to get into politics of any kind."

"Your father has a very important job ahead."

"We know that, Mom," Charlotte said, glancing at Julia. "I'm glad Dad does what he does, even if I don't want that life for myself."

Mrs. Manchester shoved her half-eaten salad to the side of the table. "I'm just tired," she told her girls. "And not very hungry. Ask Hannah to pack away my dinner for tomorrow." She got up and left the girls alone in the formal dining room.

"Is she okay?" Julia asked.

"She's been pretty busy with all the fundraising lately," Charlotte said. "I wouldn't worry too much about her." But Charlotte did worry a little about her mother. Makeup could only hide some of the dark circles that had become more apparent each day since the big campaign announcement earlier that fall. Even in her exhausted state, no one could deny that Gina Manchester was a beautiful woman—more than just the perfect trophy wife after retiring from her Broadway acting career in favor of philanthropy and motherhood.

Mrs. Manchester was the lead fundraiser for the State Children's Hospital long before Charlotte became a patient there at age fourteen. While her mother looked at Charlotte's illness as a problem to be solved, Charlotte's father saw the inconvenience as an opportunity to get on another soapbox. Mr. Manchester had successfully rallied for more funding for inflammatory bowel disease research, but Charlotte never felt like he'd done so for her. She didn't want anyone feeling sorry for her, but for once, she'd just like her dad to hold her and acknowledge the shitty set of genetic cards she'd been dealt to have such a disease. Maybe him making her the poster child for his fundraising and awareness efforts was his way of showing love.

The Manchesters' long-time housekeeper, Hannah, came in and carried out the task of putting away the extra food. It seemed that Mr. Manchester would not make it to the dinner table after all, and Charlotte wasn't surprised. Hannah, a plump woman in her 60s with cropped grey hair, had been with them since Julia was born. At the time, the family needed more help because Mr. Manchester's higher political positions had become more time-consuming. First, he'd been on city council in his free time from his law office, and then he'd progressed to mayor, state representative, and state senator before setting his sights higher. After several years as a US senator, he was now vying for a bid in the next presidential election, and it looked like it might happen this time.

Charlotte was thrilled that her father's ultimate career goal hadn't come to fruition until she was getting ready to leave for college. She hated the thought of leaving Julia behind, but at least her younger sister would love the opportunity to finish her adolescence in the White House if their father won the election. Out of the three Manchester sisters, Julia was definitely the best suited for the political spotlight, having started her own debate club at their prep school at the tender age of nine, refusing to wait for the opportunity to join the school-sponsored team in middle school.

Julia was the favorite child who wanted to follow in her father's footsteps, Charlotte was the rebel who had dared to bring home a "C" on an AP test, and Liv was the perfect oldest daughter who'd never disappointed her parents. But Charlotte knew something about her older sister that her parents didn't know yet. Liv was coming home for dinner tomorrow with big news for her family that would change everything.

Mr. Manchester would soon lose his shit when he found out what Liv needed to tell him. Only Charlotte knew so far, but Olivia Manchester—the unmarried twenty-year-old daughter of Simon Manchester, the front-runner for a presidential campaign—was pregnant. How would that work out for his traditional (i.e., marriage-before-babies) family values campaign?

Chapter 3
Thursday, December 3
Olivia "Liv"

Confiding in Charlotte was one thing. Telling her parents might be a different story with her father's campaign underway, but she had to tell them eventually. Liv had always wanted children, but being pregnant at twenty hadn't been part of her plan. By the time the baby arrived, she'd be twenty-one—legally old enough to buy alcohol, not that it interested her at all in her current state of perpetual nausea.

Telling her boyfriend, Eric, about the baby had been easy. He was wonderful about the whole thing, even if it wasn't in his plans right now either. They'd taken every precaution—well, almost every precaution. Liv had to believe that this baby was meant to be since she had taken her birth control pills religiously since the age of sixteen, and Eric had always worn a condom. The one time Liv was a couple of hours late taking her pill coincided with the one time the condom broke, and it was enough for her to get pregnant.

Whoever or whatever was to blame didn't matter—they were having a baby. It was one thing they'd agreed on right away. Their choice was to be a family. Eric had a decent job as a junior associate in an engineering firm, and Liv could take online classes next semester to stay on track with her mathematics degree. They were young, but they could make it work—they loved each other fiercely. There was room in Eric's rented townhouse for both Liv and the baby; she certainly didn't plan to move home upon leaving the dorms at the end of the semester. Although Liv was adamant about not marrying Eric until she'd finished college, with the baby coming, it made sense to move in with him for the help.

Her dad would be furious about the lack of a wedding band, but Liv was an adult—even if she felt like a little girl in the towering presence of her father. As a slight man himself, Eric was clearly intimidated by Mr. Manchester at first, but Liv knew Eric was the man for her. Anyone could see how his eyes lit up every time Liv entered the room. He adored Liv, and she felt the same about him.

At the table, Liv broke her roll into four pieces—one for each member of her family sitting with her in their dining room. It was Thursday, and Charlotte had already told Liv that it was the first time all week that their father had managed to join them. Mr. Manchester seemed a bit stressed as he bumped his cuff link against his water glass while reaching for his bread. Liv began to wonder if she should have brought Eric with her for moral support.

No one had spoken yet when Charlotte nudged Liv's foot under the table. Liv looked at Charlotte and then at Julia across the table. It was time. She cleared her throat. "Mom, Dad, there's something I need to tell you."

"What is it, dear?" Mrs. Manchester asked.

"Well...Eric and I have decided to move in together at the end of this semester."

"You know how I feel about living together before you're married," Mr. Manchester said gruffly. "Think about our morals. How will this look for my campaign?"

"Dad, hardly anyone thinks like that anymore. I'm an adult."

"Liv, let's think about this..." Mrs. Manchester picked up her glass and then set it down without taking a drink. Realizing her mistake, she picked it up again and brought it to her lips.

"Mom, Dad, I'm pregnant."

The glass slipped from Mrs. Manchester's hand and clattered against her plate, spilling water all over the table and into her lap. She jumped up and let the water drip onto the floor. Mr. Manchester's jaw locked into place, and his nostrils flared as he slammed his open hand against the table, sending his fork flying across the room. Julia was startled at their father's reaction and again upon the fork's impact on the floor.

Charlotte patted Liv's hand. "Congratulations," she muttered before leaving the table. Julia followed her sister out of the room into the kitchen, leaving Liv with her parents.

"Oh, Liv," Mrs. Manchester said, sitting down hard in her soaked chair.

"How the hell did this happen?" Mr. Manchester asked.

"The usual way..." Liv rested her head in her hands.

"Don't be a smartass with me, young lady," snapped her father. "We raised you better than this. How can I preach morals when my own daughter doesn't have any?"

"Seriously, Dad? You think I planned this to screw with your campaign? This wasn't in my plans either. We took every precaution, and this baby happened anyway."

"Except abstinence! Waiting for marriage! Did you forget about those options?" Her father's voice seemed to make the windows rattle.

"Dad! It's obviously too late for that. And don't be a hypocrite. I seriously doubt you and mom walked down the aisle as virgins!"

"Is it too late for other solutions?" her father bellowed.

"Simon," Mrs. Manchester scolded her husband. "How can you even suggest that? This is our grandchild we're talking about, and we have the means to help out financially."

"No. Hell, no. Eric and I can raise this baby. That's not an option for us at all, and it sure as hell isn't your decision! I'm twenty years old." Now, Liv was fuming. She stood up and placed her napkin on the table, noticing her mother staring at her abdomen. "Not showing yet, Mom. I'm fourteen weeks, according to the clinic on campus."

The soon-to-be grandmother sat stunned, and Mr. Manchester got up and left the room, slamming the door to his den a few moments later.

"I should probably go now," Liv said to her mother, whose only response was to burst into tears.

Later, Eric met Liv at the door to his townhouse, taking her coat from her as she stepped inside. The moment Liv looked into his eyes, all the tears she'd suppressed broke through.

"I wish you would've let me go with you," Eric said as he led her inside.

Liv wished he'd been there, too, but it was all over now. She sat with Eric on the sofa and let him hold her. "It went about as bad as I expected," she said. "Dad thinks I did this deliberately to mess up his campaign."

"No," Eric said. "*We* did this; we made a baby. It isn't a bad thing. We'll show him that. If it makes him feel any better, we could go ahead and get married now."

Liv pushed Eric away. "No. You know I want to wait. I can't believe you'd even suggest that again!"

"Hey, it's just a suggestion to make things easier for your dad. You know I love you, and we'd already talked about getting married right after your graduation, anyway." Eric ran his hand through his blond hair, which snapped right back into place.

"I love you, too, but my dad doesn't deserve to have things be easier after the way he behaved tonight. All he cares about is his damn politics."

Eric brushed away Liv's tears. "I'm really sorry it went down that way. Everything's going to be okay."

"I hope you're right. I'm scared." Liv fell back into Eric's arms.

"I'm scared, too, but as long as we love each other and love our baby, everything will work out. I know it will."

Liv still had doubts. She needed her parents—her mom, especially—to be involved in her baby's life. Her mom would come around, and her sisters would be involved in their niece or nephew's life. There'd still be a void without the support of her dad.

Charlotte activated her webcam and launched her voice-altering software. She turned on a feature that darkened her face to conceal her identity as she prepared for her weekly live broadcast. Her dad would stroke out if he knew what she said each week, but Charlotte loved her huge following and had an opinion on everything. Only three other people knew who the person was behind the filter—Vincent, Liv, and Charlotte's best friend, Rachel.

In the past year, she'd gone from two to over two million followers. The whole thing had started as a joke, a parody of all the ridiculous laws and regulations politicians had made up throughout the years. Soon, she'd committed to a weekly live broadcast of at least five to ten minutes and gained more views each week.

YouTube Video transcript:

"Tonight, let's talk about money and taxes. You work and get paid, right? Then the government takes some of your money to fund projects that are supposed to be for the greater good. There's money taken out for federal taxes, state income taxes for some people, Medicare, Social Security, and whatever else comes out. Then you have sales taxes in most states and personal property taxes.

"So, most people are buying things with money that's already been taxed, paying sales tax on the item, and then

having to pay personal property tax just for owning a big-ticket item like a house or a car. Isn't that supposed to be the American Dream? Aren't we supposed to want to work to make our dreams come true here? How can some people do that if they're being taxed to death?

"I'll be the first to admit that I live a privileged life. I want for nothing materially. But when I volunteer my time and resources, I see people who are struggling. They're trying so hard to provide for their families, but they just can't get ahead. At least, that's what I hear when they chat with one another while picking up grocery boxes from our local food pantry. For anyone out there wondering—that's what I do with the money I make from this channel. It all goes to charities like the food pantry and the homeless shelters where I live.

"I live in probably the wealthiest country in the world, and there are people in my city who work and still don't have enough money to feed their families. It's disgraceful and just plain sad. And so many people are beaten down in this crazy world we live in. Some of the politicians tell us to pray for these people and to help them by any means possible, and others ask us to cut off the freeloaders. I don't care what your political affiliation is, really, if you can't see that our great American system is broken.

"Until we can all work together to do something about it, everything will stay broken, and what a sad, sad world we'll leave for future generations. I don't know what the answer is, but I bet we can come up with one if we all look out for each other and work together for a solution instead of making more problems by arguing about who's a Democrat and who's a Republican, and who's right or wrong. Maybe nobody's right."

Charlotte shut off her broadcast and rested her head on her desk as she pulled her wavy red hair from her messy bun. She always kept her hair pulled back to avoid being recognized by a super-sleuth, rabid fan who might try to figure out her identity. Charlotte wasn't embarrassed by her opinions and had no shame from expressing them, but she knew her father would kill her if he found out. Well, not actually *kill* kill her, but make her life a living hell.

A knock on her door startled Charlotte, then Julia bound in and plopped down on the bed, still wearing her ballet gear.

"How was class?" Charlotte asked, joining her sister on the bed.

"Boring," Julia said with a sigh. She took down her bun and shook out her hair. "It's just the same thing over and over again until the recital, and I already know the whole routine—I could do it in my sleep. I'm ready to learn something new."

"You'll get to learn something new soon, and you'll be the best dancer out there as always since you already know the routine. You can perfect all your moves."

Julia huffed as she left the room. "My form is already as perfect as it can be."

Charlotte shook her head. Her little sister took ballet about as seriously as Charlotte had taken modeling at Julia's age, encouraged by her mother. Julia had no real desire to be a serious ballerina despite her slim frame and graceful persona, just as modeling wasn't really Charlotte's idea; it was her mother's dream for her since Charlotte was already a head taller than most of her peers at twelve. Going through the motions was all Charlotte could do until she stopped altogether at fifteen. Julia enjoyed dance and had committed to dance through high school, but that was as far as she'd be willing to go.

Getting diagnosed with ulcerative colitis as a young teen had a lot to do with Charlotte's decision to drop modeling. Having already been labeled anorexic by some of the other girls when she lost too much weight at her sickest, Charlotte became tired of explaining herself. Anorexia and colitis were both serious illnesses—not things to be mocked. Every now and then, she contemplated returning to the scene to show the world that UC hadn't slowed her down; but her real dream wasn't modeling anyway. Getting behind the marketing side of it—that was something for which Charlotte was enthusiastic.

Marketing and the idea of fame had always fascinated her. She often thought of the marketing that had gone behind her mother's fame as a young woman. And now, many people became internet famous, seemingly overnight. It had happened the same way with Charlotte's YouTube channel. She'd posted a few anonymous videos, and once a couple of influencers shared them, the number of subscribers began to double each week. People were soon asking for Charlotte's thoughts on many things, anxious for her next weekly post.

Sure, there were some haters, but Charlotte ignored them and focused on the positive. Because of her, teenagers and adults alike were intrigued enough to seek more information on political topics before voting. While she had her opinions, Charlotte preferred to remain independent of affiliation with a particular political party. Both major sides were making mistakes in her opinion, including her father.

Dwelling on any of it for too long depressed Charlotte, so she tried to let things go after posting her videos. Something about getting it out there just made her feel better. She figured her disease would stay in remission longer if she limited her stress and obeyed her doctors with her medication and diet regimen. She missed indulging in popcorn at the theater with her friends, but it was worth missing out to avoid days of feeling awful for the half-hour of mouthwatering goodness.

Still, even with her UC in remission, there were days when Charlotte would curl up in bed and cry from the pain. Her lower abdomen would ache so much she'd imagine reaching inside her body to rip out the offending organ. From her time volunteering at the hospital and the food pantry, Charlotte knew that some people were much worse off, and she tried to avoid feeling sorry for herself too often. Her heart broke for the children and families she encountered while volunteering who had to make decisions about affording food or medicine some months. She wanted to do anything she could to lessen their burdens, which was why she donated all of her profits to charities with Liv's help. She looked forward to turning eighteen so she could handle the financial aspects of the donations herself.

Chapter 5
Saturday, December 5
Julia

The alarm woke Julia on Saturday morning, although she usually woke up long before the current time for school during the week. Ballet class had worn her out since she was getting ready for the Christmas program. Now that she was older, she would take part in several scenes of her studio's production.

After a quick breakfast of oatmeal, Julia was ready to walk two streets over to babysit for the Smiths. They had an adorable three-year-old son, Aiden, who was quite the handful, and he had taken a liking to Julia during church. Ever since then, Julia had been Aiden's favorite babysitter.

Hannah had the day off from managing the Manchester household, and Charlotte was still sleeping. Julia figured her parents were out on their morning jog before they would leave for their charity event out of town, so she left a note on the dry-erase board on the fridge to remind her family she'd be home by ten, after the movie with her friends. Her mother knew about the babysitting job and the movie, but Julia doubted her father remembered with his obsession with campaign stuff.

Last night, when her bubble bath had grown cold, Julia begrudgingly drained the water and got out of the tub. She'd pulled on her favorite pink terrycloth robe and combed through her dark, waist-length hair. As she looked in the mirror, she turned her head to each side to examine her profile. Now that she was getting older, her face had lost its childhood roundness and was now the face of a young woman. Julia looked more like her beautiful mother every day, though she sometimes wished she had red hair like Charlotte.

Julia had no self-consciousness about her own beauty; she knew she was pretty. Because of that fact and her family name, she was popular at school too. Ballet kept her tall frame lean and graceful, though she knew she didn't want to continue ballet after high school. It was fun, but she had no real passion for it. She'd yet to find her dream, but Julia knew she had time to pursue many things before making a career decision someday. For now, she was content to enjoy her friends and learn from her older sisters.

The idea of becoming an aunt thrilled Julia because she loved babies. She'd been babysitting with Charlotte several times and had always enjoyed infants and toddlers. Now that she was able to babysit by herself, she felt a little more nervous about it. Though she'd never had a problem while sitting with her sister, just having someone else there who was older had been comforting. Her first solo job was coming up the next morning, but Charlotte had agreed to be on-call if Julia needed her.

After slipping into flannel pants, a sweatshirt, and her favorite rainbow-striped fuzzy socks, Julia had returned to her room to chat with friends before bed. She'd pulled out her phone—covered with a glittery pink case decorated with her initials in rhinestones—and sent a photo of her socks to her two best friends. She waited for each of them to respond while checking out the rest of her social media world. When neither had responded five minutes later, Julia began to worry if she'd offended them in some way.

As if they'd heard her unspoken pleas, the two girls responded at almost the same time with hearts and cries of "CUTE!" Julia reminded her friends not to let her die of boredom during the toddler's naptime on Saturday since she'd be there all day. Both girls promised and confirmed plans to go to the movies after Julia's babysitting gig. All was right in her world again when Julia had finally put away her phone and settled into her soft bed, dragging her down comforter up to her neck as she turned over to her stomach.

Julia walked for twenty minutes to get to the Smiths' house, and while they were glad to see her arrive fifteen minutes before they needed to leave, they chastised Julia for not calling one of them to give her a ride. Soon, they departed for their date day and left Julia to sit with Aiden. All the phone numbers and instructions were on a notepad near the kitchen phone. She could also call Charlotte, who would be just across town at Vincent's wrestling tournament at the high school in the afternoon. But Julia didn't want to call anyone. She had to prove that she could handle the job on her own.

"Juwie!" Aiden called, getting Julia's attention. "Pway bwocks."

Julia grinned at him. It was impossible not to love the little curly-haired, blond boy. "Sure, buddy," she said. "I'd love to play blocks with you. Let's go."

Aiden took off, running toward his playroom, and Julia followed him while wondering what Liv and Eric's baby would look like.

After a whole morning of playing with Aiden, Julia was exhausted, and her head ached. She ended up falling asleep on the sofa after lunch while Aiden napped on a blanket in front of the fireplace in the large house. Aiden had claimed he was too scared to sleep alone in his room. When Julia woke up two hours later, her head still throbbed, and Aiden was already awake and playing quietly on the floor with some cars. She joined him, hoping he'd stay calm until his parents returned home.

Moments later, the garage door rumbled. "Mommy! Daddy!" Aiden cried as he jumped up and ran over to the door. The Smiths came in with their hands full of packages. Julia breathed a sigh of relief. Since they had returned early, she could go home and rest for a while before her evening out. They dropped the packages on the breakfast table and greeted Julia and Aiden.

"Julia, thank you so much," Mrs. Smith said. "We enjoyed an early movie and had a nice late lunch and some shopping. We both just missed our little guy so much that we were ready to come home early."

"We'll still pay you for the full day, of course," interjected Mr. Smith as he carried Aiden on his shoulder into the living room. He dropped Aiden on the sofa and tickled the boy's tummy, making him dissolve into giggles.

Mrs. Smith handed Julia some cash from her purse. "Thank you," Julia said as she grabbed her phone and backpack off the recliner. She slipped the money into the outside pocket of her bag and threw it over her shoulder.

"Do you need a ride home?" Mr. Smith asked. "It's freezing out there, and the wind's picking up."

Julia's head was hurting so much by then that the thought of riding in a car made her feel sick. "No, thank you," she said. "I'm going to go to my friend's house. She's just two houses down." It was a lie since Natalie wasn't home and planned to meet Julia and their friend, Makayla, at the movies later, but a white lie that would work.

"Oh, Natalie? She's such a sweetheart. She's babysat for us before when you and Charlotte weren't available," Mrs. Smith said.

"Yes. We're in the same ballet class." Julia walked to the front door.

"Thank you again, Julia," Mrs. Smith said, opening the door.

It had been a few months since Julia's last migraine, but once she was outside in the light, she could tell that her headache was turning into one. She walked quickly, both to get home to her medicine and to stay warm. As she approached the gate near her house, Julia pulled out her phone and texted Natalie and Makayla to cancel going to the movies with them. She had stopped walking to read their sad reactions when a black SUV with tinted windows pulled up beside her and slowed to a crawl. Julia started walking faster, and the car sped up. She was only a few feet away from her gate when the passenger side doors on the car swung open.

Startled, Julia dropped her phone as two masked men burst from the car. She took off running, leaving her phone behind. Before she could scream for help, the men caught up with her and grabbed her from behind, shoving a damp rag against her nose and mouth. Julia tried to hold her breath to avoid inhaling in the fumes from the wet cloth, but she couldn't hold out long while kicking her legs, trying to make contact with either of the men. Her chest ached for oxygen and her eyes watered. Desperate for air, Julia took a shaky breath through the rag, and then everything faded to darkness.

Chapter 6
Charlotte

Watching her boyfriend wrestle was one of Charlotte's favorite hobbies lately. Vincent's thin, muscular body inside the high school's regulation uniform was a thing of beauty— at least to Charlotte. She loved him more than what should be possible at her age, but it was how she felt.

They'd been each other's first kiss, first make-out session, first everything—including their first awkward sexual experience only a few weeks ago. The second encounter wasn't much better, truthfully, but Charlotte had enjoyed the third time. It was an intimate secret only the two of them shared because she'd told no one—not her mother, her sisters, or even her best friend, Rachel. It was more special that way.

Of course, they'd been careful. Charlotte took birth control to help control her UC symptoms around her time of the month, and Vincent was prepared with condoms. Charlotte knew she was taking a risk anyway, considering that Liv had gotten pregnant while on the pill, but it was a small risk worth taking to go to the next level with Vincent. She couldn't imagine ever being with someone else and was happy to have shared so many firsts with him.

She watched and jumped to her feet as Vincent won his match. "Way to go, Vinny!" she called. "Woo! Baby!" He grinned and waved to her in the bleachers.

"Girl, you've got it bad," Rachel said from beside her. Charlotte had forgotten her oldest friend was even there while in her Vincent-inspired fog.

"I know," Charlotte admitted. "I never thought I'd be one of those girls married in high school, but here I am."

"At least you got a good one and didn't get some player like my brother," Rachel said. "That boy collects broken hearts like some dudes collect baseball cards."

"That's so true." Charlotte remembered very briefly having a crush on Rachel's older brother but had luckily come to her senses before she could let it crush her soul. Marcus was still devastatingly handsome. Too handsome for his own good. And now, with the modeling contract, he had a big ego to match.

"I need a drink," Rachel said, standing up. "You wants?"

"Yeah, get me something with no caffeine, thanks." Caffeine upset Charlotte's stomach like nothing else. Besides Vincent, Rachel was the only friend Charlotte felt comfortable talking to about her colitis symptoms. Rachel wanted to be a doctor, so nothing grossed her out. Charlotte reached into her purse for money, but Rachel waved her off and headed to the concession stand.

Charlotte wondered how Julia was doing with her first solo babysitting job. She sent her sister a quick text and wasn't surprised when Julia didn't respond immediately. Aiden Smith was a handful to babysit, even for two teenagers. Julia was probably swamped just keeping the kid from climbing the fireplace mantle or swinging from the ceiling fans.

Rachel came back and sat down so fast beside Charlotte that the beads at the ends of her braids smacked Charlotte in the face. "Watch it there, little girl hair," Charlotte said with a laugh.

Rachel didn't care that she was a senior in high school; she loved wearing her hair in braids. The braids protected her hair, and she loved the pops of color from the rainbow plastic beads she'd worn since she was a little girl. Some of the kids at school made fun of her for it, but Rachel turned away with a shake of her head and moved on. She had no time for such childish behavior.

"There were these two chicks from the other school talking about your boy," Rachel said. "I told them to shut their faces." She handled Charlotte her soda.

Charlotte felt her stomach sink. "Thanks."

"You're welcome."

"What were they saying?"

"They were talking smack about the tall anorexic guy needing to be disqualified."

"People are so damn mean. He guzzles protein shakes just to keep his weight up to qualify...he's had such a bad couple of weeks—"

"Char," Rachel interrupted. "I know you and Vinny have trouble with food. Those bitches had no reason to be talking about anybody. Neither one of them had any curves to speak of anyway."

"Thank you for standing up for him."

"I got your back, always," Rachel said, draping her arm across Charlotte's shoulders. "And Vinny's too, as long as he doesn't hurt you. If he does, I'll kill him. He may be a skinny white boy who's a foot taller than me, but I'll take him out with my car if I have to."

"Down, girl." Charlotte chuckled. "Put away your homicidal tendencies for the afternoon."

Both girls laughed and cheered when another guy from their school won. Rachel watched the next wrestler closer than she'd watched anyone else. Charlotte figured her friend had a crush on LaShawn, who'd only been at their school since the beginning of senior year, but Rachel had yet to act on it.

"Sadie Hawkins is coming up, you know," Charlotte said, nudging Rachel.

"I've never gone to any of the other dances. Why would I start now? I don't wanna hang out in a gym with a bunch of other kids who can't dance."

"LaShawn wasn't here for any of the other dances either."

Rachel desperately tried to hide her grin, but Charlotte knew her too well. "I know...am I that obvious...and is LaShawn that oblivious that I exist?"

"He'd know you exist if you'd ask him to the dance. You're beautiful and so much fun. He'd be crazy not to go with you."

"He's so pretty, though. Oh, God, what if he's gay? That would end my life right there. But he could be bi, I guess. That, I could work with."

"You won't know until you ask."

"Wait. What? Just walk up and ask him if he's into dudes at all?"

Charlotte slapped Rachel's knee. "No! Go up and ask him to the dance and then get to know him better. If he's not interested in you romantically, then maybe you'll get a good-looking friend to hang out with. Besides me, of course. I am pretty good-looking."

"And pretty crazy," Rachel said.

LaShawn pinned his opponent and won the match. Charlotte dragged Rachel to her feet and cheered, "Go, LaShawn! Way to win!" LaShawn looked up at the girls in the stands and waved to them. He locked eyes with Rachel and grinned. Charlotte elbowed her. "See, now he knows you're alive."

Rachel collapsed in her seat as LaShawn returned to the bench. "I think I'm feeling those homicidal tendencies coming back," she muttered, covering her face. After a few seconds, she turned to Charlotte. "I don't know why I'm hiding; it's not like I turn bright red when I'm embarrassed like you do with that pale, freckled skin of yours. But I still think I might kill you."

Charlotte grinned. "Nope. You love me." She pulled out her phone and sent a quick text to her boyfriend.

Rach likes LaShawn. Any hope there?

Vincent didn't respond, but Charlotte could see that he'd read her message. She figured they could talk later during their dinner date at their favorite burger place.

After the matches were done, Charlotte waited in the stands for Vincent to get out of the showers so they could go out for burgers. Rachel was just standing up to leave when Vincent walked up to them.

"Hey, babe," Vincent said, greeting Charlotte with a quick kiss. "You mind if LaShawn joins us at the burger place? His parents had to work today, too, so he's on his own."

Charlotte stood up and grabbed Rachel's arm. "That's great," she told him. "Rach is coming with us, too, if that's good with you."

"Sure." Vincent pulled his phone from his back pocket and sent a text. He waited for the reply and then sent a response. "He'll meet us there."

"I shouldn't go," Rachel said. "LaShawn isn't expecting me to be there. I'll just walk home like I planned." Rachel lived only two houses down from the school, but Charlotte wasn't ready to let her friend go without a fight.

"No, you have to come, Rach. Don't leave me alone with two guys who just dominated a tournament! They won't talk about anything but wrestling if you aren't there too."

"LaShawn knows you're coming, Rachel," Vincent said. "I told him in the text. Let's go."

Rachel leaned against Charlotte's shoulder as they followed Vincent to his car. "Dear God," she muttered as they waited for the doors to unlock.

"Chillax, girl," Charlotte said with a chuckle as her friend jumped into the back seat. She grinned at Vincent as he started the car and winked at her. She hoped Rachel and LaShawn would get along well because Charlotte wanted her best friend to be happy. She always worried about leaving

Rachel out or making her feel like a third wheel since she'd been with Vincent.

Rachel never complained or said anything, but Charlotte could sense her friend's loneliness at times. She was among the prettiest girls at their school, and her smile was the most genuine. If Rachel smiled, it was for a good reason. Otherwise, she wore a blank, but not unpleasant, expression on her face for everything else as she studied her way through high school. As standing valedictorian, Rachel had already been admitted to pre-med programs at all the Ivy Leagues on her shortlist.

Charlotte's best friend was so impressive that most of the boys in their school were intimidated by her. Except for Martin, who was desperate to move up from his position as second in the class to take Rachel's place as first. Rachel stood barely five feet tall, but her personality was at least twice that. Despite her small stature, she could instantly put someone in their place if she felt they were mistreating anyone. Bullying was something Rachel wouldn't stand for at all.

LaShawn was standing beside a yellow Mustang in the burger place's parking lot when they arrived. Charlotte glanced in the review mirror to check on Rachel just in time to see her take a deep breath. The one thing Rachel liked more than a hot guy was a hot guy in a sports car.

Once introductions were made, which Rachel survived without passing out, the four teens went into the diner— reminiscent of 1950s America—and occupied Vincent and Charlotte's favorite red vinyl-covered booth. It was the same one they'd sat at during their first date, which felt like years ago and yesterday all at the same time.

Going to Daisy's Burgers on a first date was a rite of passage for most of the kids in their private school. Charlotte secretly hoped it would be the first of many dates for Rachel and LaShawn.

The last thing Vincent wanted to do was turn full-on matchmaker for his friends, but when Charlotte had texted about Rachel liking LaShawn, he had to do something. In the locker room, LaShawn had already asked him about the hot girl sitting beside Charlotte. How could he ignore the potential of double dates that would make his girlfriend so happy? Since dating Charlotte included Rachel in the package-deal, Vincent had gotten to know her. Rachel was a great girl and a perfect match for the extremely studious LaShawn.

After they were seated, Vincent realized no one was talking. He had sat on the inside of the booth with Charlotte to his left. LaShawn had followed suit, with Rachel having no choice but to sit on his right, across from Charlotte.

"What did you ladies think of the tournament?" Vincent asked.

"Your whole team did really well," Rachel said softly.

Charlotte didn't answer because she was watching two younger teens who had come through the door with a woman who looked to be the mother of one of the girls. "Excuse me for a sec," she said before getting up to approach them.

LaShawn and Rachel were making small talk about sports statistics as Vincent watched Charlotte talk to the girls and the woman. After a couple of minutes, Charlotte returned to the table, pulled out her phone, and sent a text. She stared at the phone for a second with her eyebrows scrunched up like she did when she was worried about something.

"What's wrong?" Vincent asked her.

"Julia was supposed to be out with them tonight. She cancelled because she said she had a bad headache. She didn't call or text me to come help with babysitting, and she's not answering my texts now."

"So call her," Rachel interjected. She turned back to LaShawn. "Julia's her little sister."

Charlotte tried but had no luck. She left a message. "Hey, Jules, call me back, please. Right away." She made another call. "Hey, Liv, have you heard from Julia?" Vincent could hear the panic in her voice. "Yeah, you're probably right." Charlotte placed her phone face down on the table.

"Everything okay?" Vincent asked, putting his arm around Charlotte.

"I don't know. Liv hasn't heard from her either."

"That's their older sister," Rachel told LaShawn.

"I'm sorry," Charlotte said, unable to hide the shakiness in her voice. "I'm being so rude. It's just...my mom and dad are out of town for the evening for some kind of campaign bullshit, and Julia was supposed to go out with her friends tonight, and now she's not answering her phone."

"Did it ring or go straight to voicemail?" Rachel asked.

"I don't know," Charlotte said, redialing her phone. "I'm trying the house phone."

Rachel pulled out her phone and clicked on a name from her contacts. After a few seconds, she and Charlotte both put down their phones. "It rang before going to voicemail," Rachel reported.

"No one's answering at home," Charlotte said.

"Is Hannah not there?" Vincent asked.

"She doesn't work Saturdays," Charlotte said, standing up. Vincent could tell she was on the verge of panicking. "I need to go now. I'm sorry, guys."

Rachel stood up and grabbed Charlotte's hand. "Julia probably just went to sleep to help her headache and left her phone on silent. I doubt she'd even answer the house phone; you know how much she hates taking messages for your parents."

Vincent got up, too, and put his hand on Charlotte's shoulder. "Let's go," he said. "We'll just go check on Julia."

Charlotte's phone rang, startling them all, and she stepped away to take the call as LaShawn stood up.

"I'm sure everything's fine," Rachel said, not talking to anyone in particular.

"That was Liv," Charlotte said. "She called the Smiths, and they said Julia left their house about two hours ago. She refused a ride home and said friends were picking her up. That was right around the time Julia texted her friends about the headache."

"Let's just go straight to your house, and I can take Rachel home after that," Vincent said.

"You guys go," LaShawn said. "I'll take Rachel home."

"That's perfect," Charlotte said, not giving Rachel a choice in the matter. "Thanks." She grabbed Vincent's hand and pulled him toward the door.

"Charlotte," Vincent said once they were outside. "Slow down. I'll get us there fast enough."

"I'm just really worried. It's not like Julia to not answer her phone or let me know what's going on. She knew I wouldn't be home until later tonight. And she knows that I would come home early if she were sick."

Julia had grown up quite a bit in the couple of years Vincent had known Charlotte. Even though Julia was still a young kid, lately she had begun to assert herself more from what he could tell. But, having no siblings himself, Vincent wasn't sure about the dynamic of being the youngest child in the family—especially in one like the Manchester family. He didn't find it at all odd that Julia might want to have the house to herself for a while. Vincent loved having his house to himself when he didn't feel well, so maybe Julia did too. She was probably just fine. Nothing terrible happened to people in their neighborhood, especially to anyone in the Manchester household.

Chapter 8
Julia

Her head throbbed in time with her rapid heartbeat, and her stomach churned as she moved. Julia forced open her eyes and took in her unfamiliar surroundings. She was sprawled out on an old, striped mattress that was placed on a concrete floor. Two windows close to the ceiling above her were covered in dark paper to block out the light, but it was dark outside now anyway from what she could tell. Those were the only windows in the room, and the only light came from a single fluorescent light fixture near the opposite wall. One of the bulbs was blinking in time with what should have been a normal resting heart rate for a healthy teenage ballerina, but Julia's heart was still pounding.

Even without the ceiling-level windows, Julia could sense she was in a basement somewhere. But where? The last thing she remembered was the black SUV pulling up beside her. No…wait, there were men…two men. They had grabbed Julia and put a cloth over her mouth. Then the darkness came—a deep sleep that had left her groggy.

She took a deep breath and sat up slowly on the mattress. She was still wearing her coat, but her scarf and hat were gone. There was no other furniture in the room. Two doors—one grey and heavy-looking and the other an unpainted wooden interior door that clashed against the white cinder block walls—seemed to be the only exits from the room. Julia's knees buckled as she tried to stand up. She couldn't; her head ached too severely. She crawled to the grey door and got up on her knees to turn the knob, but it was locked.

She crawled to the opposite wall to the wooden door and pushed it open.

Behind the door was an old washer and dryer sitting beside a utility sink stained with decades' worth of paint drippings. In the back corner, behind another wide-open door, sat a toilet that looked brand new and completely out of place in the room. Julia managed to get to her feet long enough to get to the bathroom before emptying her stomach. Soon, her nausea dissolved to nothing more than painful dry heaves. After flushing the toilet and struggling to stand long enough at the sink to wash her face and rinse her mouth, Julia sensed she was not alone.

"Ah, you're awake," said a woman's voice from behind her. Startled, Julia gripped the side of the sink and turned around slowly. A short woman, no taller than Julia's sister, Liv, stood in the doorway. She wore a dark ski mask over her face and thick winter gloves and boots with coveralls. Through the mask's eyeholes, Julia could see that the woman was white with light eyes—green or blue maybe.

"Please don't hurt me," Julia said. "I just wanna go home."

"Do what I say—when I say it—and we won't have problems," the woman said.

"Please, just let me go."

"I can't do that till your daddy pays up. He's got the money, or your mother does. Once we have it, we'll let you go."

Julia's heart sank. Her parents weren't even supposed to be home until Sunday. Could they even get money over the weekend? How much was her life worth to these kidnappers? Julia whimpered and sank to the floor. The woman grabbed Julia under the arms and dragged her back to the dirty mattress. Julia didn't have enough strength left to scream or fight; she sobbed as the woman left and locked the heavy door behind her.

The room's musty scent was now mixed with the aroma of chicken noodle soup in a microwavable can sitting on the floor near the mattress. Julia's stomach still ached and felt worse with the soup nearby. She picked it up, took it back to the laundry area, and dumped it down the utility sink. The soup was probably drugged with something anyway. Her head still throbbed, so anything she tried to put in her stomach would come right back up; eating was pointless. Julia tossed the empty soup container into an empty trash can and went back to the mattress. She hadn't noticed before that there was a heavy, navy flannel blanket folded on the end of the mattress. Wrapping it tightly around herself, Julia pulled the end of the blanket over her face to block out the blinking light and curled into a fetal position. She had to get out of this place.

L iv hoped her baby sister was just home, sleeping off her migraine. She didn't want to worry their mother, but something in the back of Liv's mind told her she might need to call anyway. She'd been more emotional since getting pregnant, all the hormones coursing through her veins to her heart. But, of course, Mrs. Manchester would never commit the social sin of having her cell ring during a charity dinner. Even so, Liv could leave her a message.

"Hey, Mom," she said to her mother's voicemail. "Charlotte called me about Julia being sick with a migraine, so I just wanted to let you know that I'm gonna head to the house to stay with her and Charlotte. I'm sure everything's fine, but I just wanted to let you know. Call me back when you get this. Love you. Bye."

"Do you want to wait to hear back from Charlotte?" Eric asked. Liv hadn't realized he'd followed her into his bedroom.

"No. I'm going now."

"Babe, I'm driving you there," Eric said as he wrapped his arms around Liv from behind.

Liv leaned against him, letting him hold her tighter. "That would be great," she said with a sigh. "I'm so tired."

Liv checked her phone constantly during the drive to her parents' house. She pulled up Julia's social media to see if her sister had been tagged by anyone recently. Her pregnancy-related brain fog had kept her from thinking about doing so before. Maybe Julia had just ditched her friends and would get ratted out by someone else. There was nothing except a photo of a large pile of blocks that Julia had posted hours earlier with the caption, "What took me 20 mins to build, the toddler I'm watching destroyed in 2 secs."

"What was I thinking?" she said aloud to herself. "Julia wouldn't do that to her friends. She's not rebellious."

"What's that?" Eric asked, turning down the volume on the radio.

"Nothing," Liv said. "Just checking Jul's profile again."

"I doubt she'll post a play-by-play of her headache. Doesn't she puke with them? Nobody wants to share that—even these kids who share almost everything else."

"I know…it's just…I've got a bad feeling in my gut right now."

"It's not the baby, is it? Are you okay?" His voice shook as he spoke.

Liv held out her hand for Eric to take. "Our baby is fine. I'm not feeling as sick as I did a couple of weeks ago, and the nurse at the university clinic said he has a good, strong heartbeat."

"Or she."

"I've already told you this baby is a boy."

"We'll see." Eric chuckled.

"That's right; we will. Now you're just trying to distract me from Julia by getting me into a heated discussion."

"Maybe."

Liv's phone rang, and she nearly dropped it before answering. "Charlotte, is she okay?"

Chapter 10
Charlotte

As Vincent pulled into the driveway, Charlotte looked up at her house. There were no lights on at all—not the porch light and not the flicker of blue light coming from Julia's window on the second floor.

After unlocking the house, Charlotte rushed to type in her code on the alarm system—it was still set to "away" as she'd set it before leaving the house earlier that afternoon. A cold sweat broke out on her forehead as she ran up the stairs to her sister's room. Without knocking, Charlotte burst through the door and flipped on the light. The room was empty. So was the bathroom. Vincent came up behind her a minute later.

"Julia! Where are you?" Charlotte called. Nothing but silence answered. "Vinny, help me check the house, please."

"On it," he said. "I'll check downstairs."

Charlotte checked her room and peered into Liv's old room and through the connecting bathroom with no sign of Julia. The media room was also empty. She shivered as the heating system kicked on. Judging by the temperature in the house, the occupancy sensor on the thermostat hadn't detected movement inside since she'd left that afternoon. She heard Vincent downstairs calling out for Julia.

Next, Charlotte checked her parents' bedroom, bath, sitting room, and walk-in closet. Everything was pristine and vacant, just as her mother always left the suite each morning. It was no use. Julia hadn't been back home, and she wouldn't have gone into their parents' room anyway.

She met her boyfriend on the stairs on her way back down. "I checked everywhere," Vincent said. "Even the garage. She's not here."

"Get my laptop and post as me asking if anyone's talked to Julia tonight. Tag her. I need to call Liv and my mom."

Vincent went upstairs while Charlotte sat on the stairs where she called Liv, who answered quickly, "Charlotte, is she okay?"

"I don't know where she is," Charlotte said, finally letting herself cry. "She hasn't been home. Vinny's checking online now, but I think I need to call Mom and Dad."

"I already did. I left a message for Mom, and we can call her back together. Eric and I are almost there. Just sit tight. I'll check in with Hannah, too, to see if she knows anything. Do you know of any other friends to check in with?"

"I don't know." Charlotte pushed her hair off her forehead and wiped the tears from her cheeks. "I'll see what I can find."

She ended the call as Vincent came back down the stairs carrying the laptop. "Let's go downstairs and check for messages on the landline," he said.

Charlotte got up and followed him to the kitchen. A glance at the phone showed no messages, and the only missed calls for the day came from hers, Rachel's and Liv's numbers. There were no notes on the dry-erase board by the phone other than the one about Julia's babysitting job for the day, and the Smiths didn't know where Julia went after she left their house. It was Charlotte's first time to be responsible for staying with Julia without an adult present, and it wasn't working out as smoothly as she'd expected. The whole situation was making her feel sick.

Vincent looked up from the laptop screen as Charlotte sat beside him on one of the bar stools. She leaned on the countertop and rested her forehead against the cold granite. "Has anyone answered yet?" she asked without raising her head.

"Lots of people have," Vincent said, placing his hand on Charlotte's back. "But no one's seen her today."

"What did you write?"

"I wrote 'Hey, I think Julia Manchester's phone died. Who's with her? Let me know or tell her to call her sister.'"

"That's perfect." Her boyfriend always had a way with words.

Vincent shrugged. "I didn't want to scare anyone."

Later, when the front door slammed, Charlotte jumped up. Liv and Eric met her in the entryway. "Shit," Charlotte said, hugging her sister. "I hoped you were Julia."

"Hannah doesn't know where she is either," Liv told her. "She said we should call the police, and she's on her way over."

"This can't be happening…" Charlotte moved away from Liv and collapsed on the sofa.

"What about the pool house?" Eric asked, looking around.

"I checked in there and also in the garage," Vincent said, running his hand through his hair. "There's no sign of her anywhere."

Liv handed her phone to Eric and walked toward the kitchen. "I'll call the police from the landline. Eric, please keep trying my parents."

Charlotte watched Eric starting a call as he followed Liv into the kitchen. She bit her lip and turned to Vincent.

"Char, I'll call my mom and have her come over, too, if that's okay. She should be home from work by now."

Charlotte nodded, and she felt Vincent's warm hand on her cheek just as tears spilled from her eyes again. He pulled Charlotte into a hug against his chest as he spoke with his mother on the phone. Hannah was already coming but having Dr. Rowlands join them as well would be comforting. But maybe they were all making a lot out of nothing. This could all be a misunderstanding. Still, though, it wasn't like Julia to drop off the face of the earth.

Drying her eyes, Charlotte checked her phone to see if anyone else had responded to Vincent's post. Several of Julia's other friends had responded, but none of them had seen her. Remembering the name of the banquet hall where her dad's event was, Charlotte did a quick Google search and found a number for the venue. After one ring, a curt voice answered, "East Banquet Hall, how may I assist you this evening?"

"Hello, this is Charlotte Manchester, and I need to reach my parents immediately."

"Miss, is this a prank? I assure you, I have no such time for childish things, as we have a significant fundraiser happening this evening."

"This isn't a prank!" Charlotte growled. "I must reach my parents right now. They're at the important fundraiser. My father is Simon Manchester, and my mother is Gina Manchester. Now, please, have someone go find one of them right now and tell them to call their daughter!"

"I'll see what I can do. Would you like to hold?"

"No!" Charlotte ended the call and got up to check on Liv.

In the kitchen, Liv was still on the phone, pacing back and forth as she spoke. Charlotte caught her sister's eyes as she leaned against the bar. Eric put Liv's cell phone on the counter and met up with his fiancée mid-pace. Leading her to a chair in the breakfast nook, he made her sit down to finish the call on the landline. Charlotte loved the way Eric took care of her sister. He was the first guy Liv had dated that Charlotte could imagine having as a brother-in-law someday.

"Any luck reaching my parents?" Charlotte asked.

"Not yet," Eric said. "What's the name of the event they're at?"

"Thank you," Liv said. She ended the call and placed the cordless phone on the table. "The police are sending someone to get a report from us."

"I called the banquet hall and asked that the front desk find Mom or Dad," Charlotte said.

"That's good," Eric said. He looked at Liv, who had laid her head on the table. Leaving Charlotte alone at the bar, Eric went to the cabinet and pulled a glass down. He filled it with water from the refrigerator and took it to Liv, insisting that she take a sip.

"Hannah should be here soon," Charlotte said, unsure if she was speaking to Eric and Liv or herself. "And Vinny asked his mom to come over."

The doorbell rang, and everyone froze. As Charlotte got up to answer the door, Hannah burst in from the garage. Eric went around Charlotte and headed to the front door.

"Any word?" Hannah asked. Charlotte shook her head. "I've been trying to reach your mother the whole way here."

"We've tried too," Liv said. "The police are on their way."

"And I called the banquet hall," Charlotte said as Eric came back into the room.

Behind Eric, Vincent rushed in with his mother, who was carrying a phone in a sparkly pink case. "Look what my mom found," he said. "I think it's Julia's."

"I saw it when I was driving over," Dr. Rowlands said. "It was on the sidewalk. I just happened to see it shining under the streetlight. When I saw the 'J' and "M" on it, my heart just sank. We need to call the police right now."

"They're already on the way," Liv said from her spot at the table.

Charlotte's heart thumped madly in her chest as she took the phone from Dr. Rowlands. It was Julia's phone, and the screen was busted. Charlotte could no longer deny that something was seriously wrong.

In what seemed like only minutes, an hour had passed since the police had descended upon the Manchester house. Seconds after Dr. Rowlands and Hannah arrived, Liv had answered a call from her mom. Frantic after the discovery of Julia's broken phone and suspecting foul play, Liv had begged her mother to get home as soon as possible.

Returning from her second restroom break during the police questioning, Liv sized up the man in the expensive but ill-fitting suit standing near the counter talking to a short female detective who had cropped blond hair. From the looks of the man, complete with the greasy comb-over, she assumed he was her dad's new campaign manager, Byron Saks. She'd figured Charlotte's description of Saks was an exaggeration, but it had been dead-on.

She sat down beside Charlotte at the table to continue the questioning. A photo of Julia lay in the center of the table. It was from school, so she was dressed in her burgundy blazer embroidered with the academy's logo.

"You're certain Julia doesn't have a boyfriend or girlfriend she might be with right now?" asked the lead detective as he studied the photo. Detective John was an older black man with a full head of hair greying at the temples. While John's counterpart—a young Asian man who sported a short ponytail—carried a tablet computer to take notes, John wrote out his notes by hand in a stenographer's notebook.

"She's thirteen years old!" Charlotte said. "She was supposed to be with her best friends tonight and cancelled just like I told you. You have their numbers and their parents' numbers. Between all of us, we've called every single contact on her phone and posted on her social media accounts. No one's seen her since she left the Smiths' house. She wouldn't just run away."

"John," said the ponytailed detective who had strolled in from the family room. He carried Julia's iPad, which was still in its purple leather case. "There's nothing in the girl's online presence to indicate she met up with anyone. Nothing suspicious at all in the last six months I've checked. All ballet and crush-related messages with some boy named Josiah, who is apparently a fellow seventh-grader."

Liv sighed. "Josiah Frazier is a boy I used to babysit. He lives next door in the grey house."

"Check that out," Detective John barked to the female detective and then turned back to Charlotte and Liv. "Let me get a few more details from you two while we're waiting on your parents. Do you have any more recent photos of Julia?"

"No," Charlotte said. "Just that and whatever she's posted online."

"Do you know what she was wearing today?"

Liv looked at Charlotte. She despised feeling so helpless when her baby sister was missing, but she hadn't lived with her sisters since starting college.

"She was wearing a long purple sweater—one that she borrowed from me this morning—and black skinny jeans with grey boots," Charlotte said. "She has a black wool coat and a bright pink scarf. She wears a hat with a furry pink poof on top and black gloves. She hates carrying a purse, so she usually carries her pink canvas backpack everywhere she goes. She's about five-seven, and she's slim and strong because she's been dancing since she could walk. Please, you've got to find her. Something's really wrong."

Detective John made notes as Charlotte spoke, and Liv wrapped her arms around her sister's shoulders. Charlotte was putting on a brave face, but Liv knew her sister would likely fall apart soon. Charlotte and Julia had always been close. Byron Saks crossed the room to go outside onto the back patio, his cell phone in hand, and Liv shuddered as he passed behind her. Something about Saks made Liv uncomfortable, but she couldn't determine what.

"I don't understand why you're not issuing alerts to find her," continued Charlotte. "Do something! Everyone's just sitting around. What about those Amber Alerts I always see?"

"I assure you we're not sitting around," John said. "We're monitoring the phone and knocking on doors and canvassing the different routes Julia could've used to walk home. Before we can issue any alerts, we have to confirm that an abduction has occurred. Amber Alerts have a certain set of criteria that just haven't been met in this case. No one's witnessed an abduction with any vehicle description to go on."

"But what about the phone?" Liv interjected. "Julia wouldn't just throw her phone on the sidewalk. You know who our parents are, and you know they have money. Someone could've taken Julia, hoping to score some ransom money or for human trafficking. Oh, God." As she spoke the words, Liv hoped that if someone had taken Julia, they'd done it for money and not for reasons more sinister.

John nodded. "We're doing everything we can."

All they could do was wait.

Detective Ernest John's Notes: 12-5-15

Missing child. Julia Marie Manchester. White female. 13 YO. BR Hair. BR Eyes. Approximately 5'7" tall, 115-125 pounds. Slim build. Last seen in purple sweater, black jeans, grey boots. Black coat. Pink hat. Pink scarf. Carries pink canvas backpack.

Abduction or runaway? No witnesses yet.

Sisters: Charlotte Anne and Olivia Lynn Manchester, ages 17 and 20.
Young women adamant that Julia was abducted— would not run away
Social media searches not consistent with runaway
Girl's broken phone was found outside home on the sidewalk. Glass is shattered, but Techs can recover data?

Others present. Eric Benjamin Jacoby (24), Vincent Rowlands (minor?—mother present, did not check ID) boyfriends of sisters.
Victoria Janine Rowlands (45), Hannah LeAnne Butler (63), Byron James Saks (47)

Questioning: Mr. Franklin Smith and Mrs. Jennifer Smith—Julia babysat for their toddler son earlier today. Smiths questioned separately. Both said Julia left their house on foot approx. 3:30-3:45 p.m.

Natalie, Makayla—Julia's friends—need to be questioned.

Josiah Frazier, 12—Boy Julia was messaging on social media. Questioned with parents present. Innocent, genuine in concern about Julia. States that Julia has tracker on her keys. Techs checked the signal—last known ping outside downtown 300 block approx. 4:30 p.m. Sending patrols to canvass the area.

Parents Gina Anne (48) and Simon Wells Manchester (51)—at political charity event two hours away. Check witnesses.

Parents are wealthy—mom is retired entertainer, dad is trying to run for president. Could be a ransom demand coming in. Get authorization to tap phone lines.

Vincent sat on the sofa beside Charlotte in an attempt to comfort her. She was curled into a fetal position and resting on some uncomfortable-looking decorative pillows with her eyes closed. She stirred as Vincent rubbed her shoulder and then moved to lean against him instead of the pillows. He wanted to do something more, but there was nothing he could do but hold her. He looked at his mother, who watched him from an armchair near the fireplace.

He'd never felt comfortable in the formal living room at his girlfriend's house. Its dark hardwood floors were beautiful, but the room didn't feel cozy without an area rug to soften the floor under his feet. He preferred the media room upstairs. Its comfy, suede overstuffed sofas had been perfect for debate club practices back when Charlotte had hosted. And the plush carpeting, though staticky, was comfortable to the club members' socked feet during long practices. The projector flashed controversial articles upon the large screen, and the twenty or so team members would split off into groups to weigh the pros and cons of different scenarios. Already friendly with Charlotte from volunteering at the hospital, Vincent had always been the last to leave—insisting upon helping Charlotte return the room to its pristine unoccupied state.

It was on one of those overstuffed sofas that he and Charlotte had shared their first kiss. At fifteen, he'd never kissed anyone before and wasn't sure if Charlotte had either. Vincent didn't really want to know if she had because the thought of her kissing someone else made him feel sicker than he had in the few moments before he finally worked up the nerve to kiss her that night. They'd watched a movie—Vincent couldn't for the life of him remember which one because Charlotte's leg was touching his—and he'd managed to put his arm around her but mostly resting on the back of the sofa. Charlotte had responded as if Vincent's move was natural and scooted closer, securing a spot for her head on his shoulder.

When the movie ended, Charlotte stretched her arms over her head and smiled at Vincent at the exact moment he'd blurted out, "I want to kiss you." Thinking he'd die right there in his seat if she refused him, Vincent could still feel the echoes of his pulse pumping in his head from the moment Charlotte's lips had met his halfway.

Now, helpless, Vincent leaned down and planted a kiss on the top of Charlotte's head. "I wish I could do something to help."

"Just don't leave," Charlotte said.

Meeting his mother's eyes from across the room, Vincent silently begged her to let him stay. As if she heard his plea, his mother nodded. "He's not going anywhere."

"Thank you," Charlotte said, her voice muffled in Vincent's sweatshirt.

Vincent's phone buzzed in his front pocket with a text from Rachel to check on Charlotte. He'd silenced the notifications while talking with the police earlier. He texted her back that there was no other news since the last update. "Rachel's checking on you again," he said.

"I'll call her later."

"She knows. Don't worry about it."

Eric came into the room and sat in the chair beside Vincent's mom. "No news, I guess?"

"Nothing," Dr. Rowlands said. "How's Liv feeling now? Poor dear looked so pale."

"She's okay. I got her to eat a granola bar and lie down in her old bed. She's asleep now. The baby is draining all her energy."

"Oh," Dr. Rowlands said. "I didn't realize she was expecting. Congratulations." She looked over at Vincent. "Babies can drain the energy out of you even when they're on the outside."

"Gee, thanks, Mom," he said, closing his eyes in shame.

"I've heard that," Eric said.

"Will Liv finish school?"

Leave it to Vincent's mother to ask the invasive questions. Embarrassment overpowered his guilt. "Mom—please. It's none of your business."

Eric didn't seem to mind. "She'll finish spring classes right before the baby's due, and I think she wants to do a completely online semester next fall so she can stay home with the baby. I'll support her whatever she wants to do. My place is big enough for the three of us to stay there for a while after we get married."

"How wonderful." Dr. Rowlands stood. "I smell coffee in the kitchen. Would you care for some, Eric?" She was mostly out of the room before Eric could answer.

"Sure," Eric said to her. "Thank you. Black."

Vincent shifted and realized Charlotte had fallen asleep against him. He tried to move carefully to avoid disturbing her, but his leg had also fallen asleep. He managed to move Charlotte to the pillows and cover her with a blanket without waking her. "Sorry about my mom," he said to Eric. "She can be nosy."

"It's fine, man. I have nosy parents too."

Something told Vincent it was better to have nosy parents like his rather than preoccupied ones like his girlfriend's parents.

Chapter 13
Sunday, December 6
Julia

Light streamed in across the room from a tiny tear in the paper covering the windows. Julia closed her eyes again and reopened them, hoping the whole ordeal was just a dream. It wasn't a dream, though; it was a living nightmare. She'd spent the entire night in the cold, damp basement in her makeshift bed on the floor. She longed for her fluffy, pink down comforter and pillowtop mattress. She wanted her bedside table with the phone dock so she could wake to classical music like her usual Sunday morning routine. The post-workout shower was a luxury she desperately craved now since she knew her yoga mat and workout gear sat unused in her bedroom at home.

And she was missing church. Charlotte would have taken her while their parents were out of town. Julia knew her father didn't care much for all of the sermons since he sometimes complained on their way home. But going to the largest church in their neighborhood looked good for her father's campaign. Julia always enjoyed the children and teen group activities so at least she was getting something out of it, even if her father didn't. Her mother was active in the women's choir, and Charlotte was also actively involved in the youth outreach that volunteered at hospitals. Julia couldn't remember much about their sporadic church attendance before the last few years.

Julia sat up slowly on the mattress, feeling her hip bones sink to the cold, cement floor. Thankfully, the bottle of water that had accompanied last night's soup was still factory sealed. She opened it and took small sips to stay hydrated. Her stomach was still upset from the previous evening and felt tight and crampy. She also had no idea when or if her captors would bring more food or water. Who knew if the water from the tap in this place was safe to drink? Julia hoped to be back home before having to contemplate such things.

As she stood, Julia felt dampness and realized she'd gotten her period. "Great," she muttered as she walked to the bathroom. Once there, Julia cleaned herself as best she could with toilet paper and water. She made a makeshift pad from folds of toilet paper and some paper towels she found in the laundry room. It wasn't ideal, but it was the best she could do. She washed her hands and face and then returned to the other room wearing her damp pants. At least they were black, and the stain wouldn't show. Julia inspected the mattress, relieved to find no blood on it. She plopped down and leaned against the wall.

Did her family know she was missing yet? What about her friends? Or Josiah? She was planning to ask him to the dance at school. Her friends had lightheartedly teased her about him being several inches shorter than her, but Julia didn't care. Josiah would probably grow more as he got older, and she likely wouldn't. Julia's ballet teacher had said that most girls didn't grow much more in height after starting their periods, and Julia had suffered through hers for a grueling six months now. It wasn't as exciting as her mother claimed it would be. As far as Julia was concerned, the whole thing just got in the way of dance—even if exercise made the cramps feel better. What she wouldn't do to have access to a box of tampons or pads now. Using tampons made her feel weird during dance classes, even though Charlotte had assured her that virgins could and did use them all the time, but it was better than broadcasting to the whole class that she was having her period. Way too embarrassing. The whole thought of sex sounded scary anyway, despite how cute Josiah was.

A shiver rippled through Julia. What if the men came into the room to hurt her? Surely not. Those types of things didn't happen in her neighborhood. Of course, kidnappings didn't happen in her town either. Not that she'd heard of before now. Crap. She'd been kidnapped. How had that happened? What if she didn't get to go home?

Fumbling noises outside the heavy door startled Julia. She backed into the corner and pulled her knees to her chest, feeling the mattress sink below her onto the concrete floor. The door opened, and the woman walked in. This time, she was wearing dark sweatpants and a hoodie to hide her hair, along with dark sunglasses. Julia quickly glanced through the open door to see if she could tell what was behind it, but the woman blocked most of her view. All Julia could see was another old fluorescent light fixture on a cinder block wall lighting the end of what looked like a rickety wooden staircase. The door quickly slammed closed and made Julia jump.

"Don't get any ideas," the woman growled. "We won't hurt you as long as you cooperate." She tossed a box of granola bars and two bottles of water onto the mattress.

"Breakfast and lunch. I'll bring you something hot for dinner. Any requests?"

"I wanna go home," Julia said.

"As soon as your daddy pays, we'll send you on your way. Answer me now, or it's granola for dinner too."

"I don't care about dinner."

"Suit yourself," the woman said.

"Wait! Please, I need something...I started my period. I don't have anything in here, but there's some stuff in my backpack."

"Your backpack's gone," the woman said. "We'll pick up something when we can. Just use toilet paper for now since I don't have anything to help you." She turned and walked back through the door, locking it behind her.

Julia sighed and picked up the box of granola bars. They were factory sealed as well, much to her relief. Her stomach rumbled as she tore open the box and took out a bar. Not realizing how hungry she was, it was the best granola bar she'd ever eaten. She'd dropped her phone in the shock of being grabbed, but she was sure her backpack had stayed on. The kidnappers must have dumped it somewhere after they'd taken her.

Dear God, would anyone remember she had a tracking device not only on her phone but on her keys as well? Surely, someone would remember. Josiah! Please let him remember. He helped her set it up when he had an extra one in his kit. It was linked to Julia's email account, but Josiah didn't have that password. Her tablet! Her tablet was still at home and signed in. If the police got involved, they'd find it, right? Her sister or her parents would give the police her tablet, and someone would find her.

After finishing the granola bar, Julia stood up and slowly examined the room. She couldn't find any indication of cameras watching her. She walked into the laundry area and searched for any possible way to escape. The only windows above the washer and dryer were barred from the outside based on the shadows she saw, and they were covered with the same paper used in the other room. Julia hoisted herself onto the top of the dryer and pulled back a corner of the paper. She couldn't see anything except the thick roots of a shrub.

Hopping down, she walked into the bathroom. There were no windows in the room except for a thin row of glass bricks above the tub and shower combo. The tub was beige with heavy rust stains down from the faucet, which was still actively dripping. Drip. Drip. Drip. It was almost the same rhythm as the strobing fluorescent light in the other room. Geez, these people never changed lightbulbs. This wasn't a place that was used regularly. The house was old. Like 1960s or 70s old. Unlike any of the houses in her neighborhood, which were heavily remodeled colonial homes. She wasn't in her neighborhood. Where was she? How long had she been out? How far away from home was she now? Even if she could escape, how would she ever get home?

Julia's heart started pounding, and she began to feel dizzy. Panicking, Julia dropped to the floor and crawled back to her makeshift bed, desperate for air. As she lay on her back, staring up at the ceiling, Julia recalled every prayer she'd ever heard, begging God to send her enough air and strength to survive. After a few minutes or maybe even hours—she wasn't sure because time had no meaning to her now—Julia could breathe again.

As much as she hated to, as darkness fell upon the room, Julia could barely keep her eyes open and drifted off to sleep.

L iv's professors understood when she emailed them about her younger sister's kidnapping, each of them responding even though it was Sunday afternoon. With the baby coming, taking incompletes in her classes wouldn't be the worst thing in the world anyway. Going to class would be pointless since she could barely think without crying. She could make up the work when Julia was home safe and sound. Liv tried to silence the voice in the back of her mind that told her Julia was still unsafe for now and tried to focus on what she could do, which was share Julia's story to everyone who would listen.

Using every social media account she owned, Liv shared the news stories about Julia's disappearance. Someone had to have seen something. A thirteen-year-old girl couldn't possibly vanish in broad daylight without someone knowing something. A neighbor could have noticed another neighbor acting suspiciously, such as getting groceries delivered when they usually didn't, or a strange car in a neighborhood. Strange noises. Something.

She urged everyone to look at Julia's photo. To share it. To pay attention to what was going on around them. If they didn't save Julia, they might just save someone else in the process. Typing until she thought her fingers might crack open and bleed, Liv finally stopped when her laptop started to run out of battery, and she was too tired to get up for the charger. Just after that, Eric forced her to lie down on his sofa so he could rub her feet. He'd been with her all day, forcing her to take breaks that weren't bathroom-related and to eat and drink every now and then since they'd arrived home early that morning after sleeping in their clothes at Liv's family's house.

"You can't single-handedly find your sister, Liv," he said. "And it's no good for our baby if you worry yourself to death."

"I know…" Liv's eyes filled with tears.

"The police are doing everything they can, and your parents were talking about bringing in extra forces with private investigators if need be. The best thing you can for everyone involved is to rest."

"You know me better than that; I can't just lie here and do nothing."

"You're not doing nothing. You've shared the story everywhere, and now you're going to take a nice warm shower with me before you go to bed. You're crashing here until all this is over, and then we'll go back to your dorm to get your things. I don't want you out of my sight until Julia is home safe. Just in case."

"You're worried they might come after me or Charlotte still, aren't you?"

"Of course, I'm worried about that. This whole thing is crazy." Eric leaned back on the sofa but continued rubbing Liv's feet. She wasn't even showing yet, but her feet already hurt and felt larger from swelling. And the baby was definitely affecting her bladder, considering she had to pee every hour.

With everything crazy, Liv wanted to be with Charlotte and her parents more than anything. Her parents' house would probably be safer than Eric's place with all the heightened security.

"I should go home until Julia's found. I should be there for Charlotte. She's beating herself up for letting Julia babysit by herself; I just know it."

"Not tonight, though," Eric argued. "You're exhausted. Shower, then bed. I'll drive you there first thing in the morning."

"I can drive myself. What about work?"

"Are you kidding me?" Eric stood and pulled Liv into his arms, moving her toward the bathroom. "There's no way I'm going to work this week. I've already called in."

"I already took a shower when we got here this morning."

"Then you'll take another one. It'll help you sleep."

Liv breathed a sigh of relief as Eric started the shower. He was the only person able to keep her calm right now.

She hoped the last two days had been a nightmare, but the number of police officers who'd paraded in and out of her living room confirmed the worst night of her life had, in fact, happened. Answering the same series of questions multiple times had left Charlotte exhausted and frustrated, but at least the detectives were finally taking Julia's disappearance seriously. She'd vanished without a trace except for her broken cell phone. No one connected to Julia on social media had heard from her since early afternoon on Saturday.

Josiah, the boy from next door, had told the detectives about a tracking device that he'd put on Julia's keys for her earlier in the semester after she'd lost them for the third time. He'd pulled up the tracking information, but unfortunately, the last known location the tracker had picked up was downtown on Saturday evening. According to the police technicians, the tracker wasn't updating anymore. It was destroyed during a scuffle if Julia was abducted or the battery had died or been removed by someone. Searches of the businesses and apartments in the downtown area had turned up nothing. It still infuriated Charlotte that the police would even consider that Julia hadn't been abducted. There's no way her little sister would have run away.

Now it was Monday, and Charlotte had stayed home with her parents. Liv and Eric had also arrived early that morning, having spent the night at his townhouse and gathered some things to stay until Julia was home. Vincent had stopped by briefly after school to drop off Charlotte's assignments for the day, but schoolwork was the last thing she could focus on with Julia missing. The police seemed to have no leads at all. The canvass of the neighborhoods between the Smiths' house and the Manchesters' house had turned up nothing substantial. Two or three people had maybe remembered seeing Julia walk by, but no one could be certain. And no one had come forward seeking ransom. Charlotte had overheard the detectives speaking to her parents about kidnapping and sex trafficking. The very thought of either made her heart ache for her baby sister.

When the phone rang, everyone in the house stopped what they were doing to run into the kitchen. The lead detective had the phone tapped, so Hannah was instructed to answer the call like any regular day.

Charlotte watched Hannah's hands shake as she reached for the phone. Hitting the speaker button, Hannah maintained control in her voice as she answered, "Hello, Manchester residence, house manager speaking."

The entire room was silent—two police officers, a police technician, Liv, Hannah, Eric, Charlotte, and her parents—as everyone waited for the caller to speak.

Feedback blared from the speaker before a distorted voice said, "We have your daughter. She's alive. We'll call with instructions on Wednesday." A loud click cut the air in the silent room before the line went dead.

Mrs. Manchester dropped to the floor. "These people have my baby!" Charlotte and Liv went to their mother's side and looked to their father for guidance.

Mr. Manchester began frantically pacing the room. "Money's not an object," he said to the police officers. "We'll give them whatever they want; we just want our daughter back unharmed."

"That's not always the best way to deal with these situations," Detective John said.

Charlotte's heart was pounding. Her sister was alive. It was a kidnapping for ransom money. That meant Julia wouldn't be hurt. Unless the police didn't let her parents pay the ransom.

"The only good way to deal with this is to get our daughter back!" cried her mother. "Thank God, she's alive!"

"Everyone needs to calm down while we review the case." Detective John made some motions to the other officers. "Let's go in the other room to discuss this so the officers can work."

Instead of staying with her family, Charlotte slipped upstairs to get away from everything. She went to her bedroom and fell into the bed, pulling her knees to her chest. She cried as she pulled out her phone and texted Vincent and Rachel.

Please come over.

Soon, her boyfriend and best friend were with her in her room. Charlotte felt like she was out of tears for a while. Now she was just angry, and so was Rachel.

"How could anyone do something so evil just for money?" Rachel twisted one of Charlotte's pillows in her lap. "These stupid jokers are gonna get caught. Do they not watch movies or TV?"

From across the bed, Charlotte reached for her pillow and pried it from Rachel's hands. "I'm angry, too, but I don't know what else to do. The police were telling my parents not to pay the ransom."

"Why wouldn't they?" Vincent asked, spinning around in Charlotte's desk chair. He held Charlotte's laptop and turned it for them to see the screen. Flashed on it was a press release from the police department with an alert about Julia.

Charlotte gasped and reached for the laptop. "When did it go out?" The timestamp was an hour ago. "Seriously? All they did was issue a press release stating that she's missing."

Rachel took the computer after Charlotte was finished reading. "At least this is something. It doesn't say anything about suspected kidnapping, though. What about those Amber Alerts? Why didn't they do one of those?"

Charlotte took back the computer. "It didn't meet the criteria. Those are used when someone witnesses a kidnapping, and there's a description of the suspect or vehicle, but no one saw Julia get taken." She pulled up social media again to check Julia's profile. Hundreds of messages were posted now, and the number seemed to be climbing.

"Up until an hour ago, the police still thought Julia could've left on her own," Vincent said. "I saw an alert earlier that said to be on the lookout for her as an endangered runaway."

"What?" Charlotte closed her laptop and handed it back to Vincent. "Why didn't you tell me?"

"You have enough going on without having to deal with all the misinformation," Vincent said, moving to Charlotte's side on the bed. He put his arm around her shoulder. "We all knew something was wrong because we all know Julia."

Rachel reached for Charlotte's hand. "Everything will be okay. The police—they'll figure this out and get Julia home safe."

"But what if they don't? The robo-voice on the phone said we'd get instructions on Wednesday. What else could happen to her in that time? She must be terrified." Charlotte was terrified.

"And why Wednesday?" Rachel asked. "That seems odd to me that they waited that long to contact you in the first place. Why would the kidnappers want to keep her for another two days before even giving instructions? It seems like they would want to tell your parents now how much money they want right away."

"I seriously doubt these people took 'Kidnapping 101' before planning this scheme," Vincent said.

"I don't know," Charlotte said, tears forming in her eyes. "I don't know how any of this works. I just want my sister back." And she did. All the sibling squabbles of the past seemed so trivial now. Charlotte vowed to never fight with Julia again if she could just make it home safely.

The tiny strip of light that shone through the paper-covered window wasn't as bright as the day before, but Julia figured it was daylight. Her neck ached from sleeping on the hard mattress without a pillow for the second night in a row, but she was glad to feel warm finally. Judging by the strange-looking streamer flapping from the vent at the top of the wall, at least some warm air was flowing into the basement. Still, the painted brick walls and concrete floors made everything seem cold and damp.

She stretched and walked to the bathroom. Julia finished her business as quickly as possible to avoid being caught in the other room if the woman should come back. By her count, she'd been gone from home at least a day and a half now. Her family had to be looking for her, and the police had to be looking for her. It was only a matter of time before her family would pay the ransom, and she'd be back home in her own bed.

But those thoughts of going home weren't enough to comfort Julia. She was like a caged mouse waiting to be fed to a snake. She still felt the men's hands over her mouth and on her body, and the coldness in the woman's voice wasn't hard to discern. There was no guarantee these kidnappers would let her go, so she had to work on a way to get out.

Standing on the dryer again, Julia peeked out the window and saw water pooling around it as raindrops dripped around the shrub roots. Great. Even if she could find a way out, she'd be in a strange place in the cold rain. As cold as the glass felt, the outside temperature was probably only a few degrees above freezing.

Looking up at the dropped ceiling tiles in the laundry area, Julia lifted her arms over her head to move one of the tiles. She coughed as dust fell on her head. In the recess above the tile was nothing but electrical lines and other pipes that might have been plumbing. Julia wasn't sure. The only thing she was sure about was that escaping through the ceiling wasn't an option.

There were a couple of rusty toolboxes on the shelf beside the washer and dryer, but both were empty. The rest of the shelf held old paint cans that looked useless as well. Julia doubted she could overpower anyone with a paint can like that kid in the old Christmas movie, but she made a note of their location all the same. What she'd hoped to find was a crowbar or something else she could use to pry open the window, or in a worst-case scenario, use to defend herself. There was a metal folding chair behind the washer. It was old and heavy, so it wouldn't help her much for hitting someone, but she might be able to jam the door with it.

Giving up on her quest for escape tools or weapons after turning up empty-handed, Julia went back to the main room for water and another granola bar. Although she was hungry enough to eat more than one bar, her still-rumbling gut told Julia to conserve her food supply.

It occurred to Julia that it must be Monday. She was missing school for the first time all semester. She'd been lucky to avoid illness so far and had looked forward to the idea of getting out for the holidays early if she were exempt from finals with her good grades and perfect attendance. She figured she might get a pass for having been kidnapped. Even though she didn't particularly care for her Algebra class, she'd give anything to be sitting in class figuring out the value of X rather than trying to figure out where the hell she was and how to get home.

Detective Ernest John's Notes: 12-7-15

Missing child. Julia Marie Manchester. White female. 13
YO. BR Hair. BR Eyes. Approximately 5'7" tall, 115-
125 pounds. Slim build. Last seen in purple sweater,
black jeans, grey boots. Black coat. Pink hat. Pink scarf.
Carries pink canvas backpack.
Last seen approx. 3:30 p.m. Saturday

Now considered a kidnapping or endangered runaway—
Call came in Monday. Caller said to expect instructions
on Wednesday.
Line cut off before tracing could happen. Voice altering
device used. Caller ID blocked. Possibly a burner cell.
Could be a hoax, but my gut tells me it's not in this
case.

Julia's phone came back clean. No suspicious texts.

Natalie, Makayla (minors)—Julia's friends—questioned
separately with parents present. No knowledge of Julia's
whereabouts. Neither girl exhibits personality traits

consistent with deception. Both girls willingly handed over phones to prove no contact with Julia.

Parents Gina and Simon Manchester—at political charity event two hours away. Check witnesses. —Follow up proved alibis. Multiple witnesses place Manchesters at event. Security cameras and timestamped social media posts confirm as well.

Simon: Agitated...looks to Saks for confirmation...Deceptive...about what?
Gina: Distraught and emotional

Byron James Saks—Home alone—no alibi—further questioning needed. Seems too invested for a campaign manager. Has worked for Manchesters for less than 6 months. Acts like long-time family friend. Charlotte and Olivia clearly uncomfortable around him. Was present during phone call.

Hannah—home with husband and grandchild— confirmed.

Eric, Olivia: drove in—live 30 miles away

Charlotte, Vincent: At HS wrestling match at time of suspected abduction. Confirmed with wrestling coach and teacher working ticket booth.

Chapter 17
Tuesday, December 8
Vincent

What Vincent hated more than anything else was feeling helpless. Having UC made him feel vulnerable enough, and now he could do nothing for Charlotte except hang out at her house after school to answer the hotline phone they'd set up for any information about Julia. The Manchesters and the police were keeping quiet about the phone call from the kidnapper. They still held out hope that the call was a hoax, but Vincent's gut told him it wasn't.

Charlotte told him the police were pitching scenarios in which Julia had run away to get attention and had a friend call to impersonate a kidnapper. The whole idea was ridiculous. He'd known Julia almost as long as Charlotte, and he was certain someone had snatched her. There's no way she would put her parents or her sisters through so much pain. Julia got plenty of attention as the doted-upon baby in the family. She was a cheerful and friendly kid. Sure, Charlotte claimed her sister had bratty moments, but Vincent had never witnessed it.

Having spent the last two hours answering and cataloging calls from crazies and wannabe psychics, Vincent was about to give up for the evening and let someone else have a shift. Just as he stood up to call for Eric in the living room, the phone rang again.

"Eric! Your shift's up next!" Vincent grabbed the receiver and prepared to take notes one more time. "Manchester hotline, Vincent speaking."

"Hey," the caller said. "I saw the news and thought I should call. I work at Marzano's downtown, and I found a backpack in the dumpster behind the restaurant that looks like the girl's bag in the photo I saw on the news."

Vincent's heart began pounding as Eric walked into the breakfast room. "What's that address?" The caller told him. "Let me put you on hold for a sec." He pushed the mute button and called for a detective.

Detective John came running into the room and took the phone from Vincent. "What's going on?" he asked.

"She thinks she's found Julia's backpack in a dumpster."

After requesting that the officer in the kitchen get a team dispatched to the restaurant location, Detective John picked up the call.

"Ma'am," he said. "This is Detective Ernest John. There will be officers arriving soon at your location. Has anyone moved the backpack?"

Oh, God, please don't let Julia be dead in that dumpster, Vincent prayed. He had to tell Charlotte, but he was also compelled to stay until he knew more.

"That's great," Detective John said. "Just stay there, and don't let anyone touch it or throw anything else into the dumpster. Thank you for calling the hotline. Goodbye."

"Detective John, could she be...well, you know, in the dumpster too?" Vincent held his breath while waiting for a response. Eric leaned forward and put his hands on the table.

"No, son. The dumpster was emptied recently, so the bottom is still visible. It's just the backpack."

Vincent exhaled. "Thank God."

"But what does this mean?" Eric asked the detective.

Detective John looked back and forth between Eric and Vincent before answering. "I don't know."

Waiting was the worst part. Vincent stayed with Charlotte while she and her family waited to hear back from the police. Well, most of her family was there. Mr. Manchester was in his office on the phone as usual when Vincent visited. Mrs. Manchester was knitting or crocheting—Vincent didn't know the difference—while sitting in the uncomfortable-looking chair near the front window.

Liv and Eric were sitting on the floor beside the coffee table, working on a puzzle with tiny pieces that Charlotte had dragged out. Occasionally, Charlotte would half-heartedly place a piece into the puzzle from her spot perched on the edge of the sofa. Vincent couldn't concentrate at all. He'd rechecked the social media accounts, hoping for some news, and he'd texted Rachel with an update. LaShawn had texted for an update, too, since Vincent had chosen to skip wrestling practice to be with Charlotte. He wanted to text his friends some good news, but the longer Julia stayed missing, the worse Vincent felt.

He was scared for Charlotte and her family, and his gut was showing signs of his stress as well. He'd already excused himself to use the restroom twice since the news of the backpack came through. Vincent wasn't sure whether he hoped the bag was Julia's or had belonged to someone else. If it was hers, it meant someone had dumped it and that Julia might not be alive. Of course, there was no guarantee Julia was still breathing even if the bag wasn't hers. Kidnappers weren't exactly known for their integrity. And if Julia wasn't found safe, Charlotte would be devastated.

Mr. Manchester came into the room, his cell phone in his hand like another appendage—as usual. "Any word from the police?"

Mrs. Manchester dropped her project to the floor. "Not yet. Shouldn't they be back by now?"

"I'm sure they're just being thorough," Eric said from his spot on the floor. "Checking for fingerprints and such."

"I doubt there's anything useful on a dumpster," Mr. Manchester said. "Imagine how many people have touched it."

"I'm sure the people who would have reason to touch it and are innocent would have no problem submitting their fingerprints for comparison," Eric said. Vincent had noticed Eric being more combative with Mr. Manchester lately, despite Eric being a smaller man in stature.

Mr. Manchester glanced at his two daughters, who were now looking at him expectantly. "I'm sure that's it, Eric." He walked over to the other chair near his wife and sat down, looking down at his phone.

"Something important?" his wife asked.

"I'm working on scheduling a press conference about Julia."

Charlotte and Liv stood up quickly and said in unison, "Dad, no!"

"It's the best thing to do under these circumstances," he argued. "Getting the public to look for Julia and see that we're a real family here."

"What about the phone call?" Charlotte asked. "The people who called could see you and hurt Julia. They're supposed to call tomorrow."

"Dad, it's not a good idea," Liv interjected. "The police are already spreading the word like she's a runaway. The public knows. It's all over the news and social media."

"Simon," Mrs. Manchester said. "I agree with the girls; a press conference isn't the best idea right now."

"Gina," he argued. "It's the best way for us to find Julia. Even the police will agree that it'll help to see us as real people and not just a political candidate and a former Broadway star."

"We don't give a damn what people think right now!" Charlotte said as she left the room. "We just want Julia home safe!"

Vincent left the tense room to follow Charlotte upstairs.

Her hands were shaking as she flipped on her light and began to slam her door. When there was no satisfying slam behind her, Charlotte turned and found Vincent standing there. He gently eased the door closed and approached her. She wasn't supposed to be alone with him in her bedroom with the door closed, but her parents had more important things to worry about than her non-existent virginity.

"I'm so angry and scared," she said, letting her boyfriend hold her.

"I know, babe. I know." He led her to the bed where they both sat, their hands intertwined.

"Tell me something about school. Anything to get my mind off things while we're waiting to hear back from the police."

Vincent grinned. "You sure you're ready for this?" Charlotte answered with a smirk, urging him to continue. "There's a new couple forming in our grade."

"What! Who? Do I know them well?"

"Pretty well. Some might even say we were the matchmakers."

Matchmakers? "Wait...you don't mean..."

"LaShawn and Rachel are getting close. After we had to leave them, they ate dinner and then hung out at Rachel's house to watch a movie. Rachel even went to church with him on Sunday. LaShawn's little sister was teasing him in the hallway this afternoon about bringing over his new girlfriend for dinner tonight and said her name was Rachel."

"That's awesome!" Charlotte was thrilled for her friend, and she was confident LaShawn was a good guy if Vincent thought so. Vincent was a good judge of character, and he and LaShawn were both liked by most of the people at their school. "I wonder why she didn't tell me?" She looked down at her lap and picked a piece of fuzz off her pants.

"You're kidding me, right?" Vincent turned Charlotte toward him by her chin. "Talking about herself while your sister is missing? You know her better than that. She'll talk to you all about it and give you all the details when Julia's home."

"You're right." But still, Charlotte couldn't help but feel the sting of not being the first to know about her best friend's new romance. She sprawled out on her bed and pulled a pillow into her arms. Vincent stretched out, too, leaving his feet hanging off the end. He faced Charlotte and brushed her hair out of her face as he kissed her forehead.

"It's gonna be okay," he said. "I love you, you know."

Charlotte nodded, fighting back tears. "Love you too. Julia has to come home, Vinny. I can't stand not knowing where she is and that she's okay."

"These jerks just want money. They won't hurt her. They'll try to get their money and get caught in the process after they give Julia back. They always get caught sooner or later."

"I just can't stop thinking about it. The whole thing is weird with the waiting..."

"It's just a sign they don't have their shit together. It's their first kidnapping, and they don't know what they're doing."

"I don't know if that's supposed to make me feel better that you don't think they're experienced kidnappers. It means they could screw everything up too."

"Shit. Bad way to put that. Their mistakes—that's what'll get them caught, not cause Julia to get hurt."

"But she's already scared and hurt, Vinny." The tears Charlotte had been holding back all day came out at that point.

Vincent threw the pillow out of his girlfriend's arms and pulled her into his. "I'm sorry; I'm a jerk. I just mean that the police will find Julia, and she'll be okay."

Charlotte continued to cry. "But what if she's not?" she whispered. She hated even thinking that way, but there was a possibility that Julia would never come home again. There was a chance she wasn't alive anymore. Her baby sister could already be dead.

She lay there in silence with Vincent, acutely aware of how much time was passing as she listened to his heart beating in his chest. She moved up to kiss him, and as her lips touched his and he started to respond, the doorbell rang and stopped them both. Charlotte jumped up and looked out her window down to the driveway. The detective's nondescript black car was there, now joined by a marked police cruiser.

Downstairs, everyone assembled in the living room as Hannah led in Detective John and two police officers, a young blond man and an older Hispanic woman. The male officer carried a pink backpack in a clear bag marked "Evidence." Charlotte gasped as she saw it because it wasn't just any backpack; it was Julia's. It still had the little plush monkey dressed in a tutu and ballet slippers hanging from the zipper—a gift she'd given Julia for her thirteenth birthday.

Detective John turned to Charlotte. "It's hers, isn't it?"

Charlotte nodded and grabbed Vincent's hand. "I gave her the monkey keychain." She pointed to the bottom of the bag.

The female officer lifted the bag and looked at the keychain. "A ballet dancer," she said.

"Julia is a ballet dancer," Mrs. Manchester choked. "And a gymnast. We always called her a little monkey when she was little. Excuse me." She held her hand to her chest as she walked to the side table to grab a tissue.

"This isn't confirmation," Mr. Manchester said. "Was her name in the bag?"

"Um," the male officer said, looking at Detective John. "No, sir, but I do have the contents for the family to identify as well." He held out a set of bags Charlotte hadn't noticed before. "There were two books with no names written inside, lip gloss, a few ink pens, a pink notebook, some grey pants—size small, and a purple makeup bag with some, um, female hygiene...tampons inside."

"It can't be hers then," Mr. Manchester said. "Julia's too young for that."

Dumbfounded, Charlotte had to correct her father. "Dad, it's Julia's backpack. The makeup bag was mine that I gave her, and she is old enough for that stuff. And the books…" she sat down on the sofa. "The books would be *The Diary of Anne Frank* and *The Hunger Games*, right? Jules was studying Holocaust literature in school and reading the other book for fun."

The officers looked at each other and then at Detective John. "She's right," the female officer said, taking the books from her partner to pass to Detective John. Charlotte watched her mother collapse into the chair near the window.

Instead of comforting his wife, Charlotte's father pulled out his phone and made a call. "We need to do this press conference tonight," he said before hanging up. He looked at the officers. "There will be news crews here within the hour to hear a statement. Be ready to speak."

"This is a bad idea, Dad!" Liv said, jumping up from her spot on the sofa. "A horrible idea."

Charlotte got up and went to her mother, who was crying softly into her tissue. She sat on the floor and placed her head in her mother's lap. Mrs. Manchester stroked Charlotte's hair. "It's going to be okay, baby," she said. "We'll find her."

"I'm sorry, Mom. I should've been there with her, and this wouldn't have happened."

"Don't say that," her mother said. "If you'd have been there, they might have taken you too." Charlotte hadn't thought of that, but at least Julia wouldn't be all alone if they'd both been taken.

True to his word, Charlotte's father brought news crews into their living room within the hour. He ordered Charlotte and

Liv to dress in their campaign best. Their mother was already wearing a stylish pantsuit. She dressed up so often now that Charlotte barely recognized her mother during the rare occasions when she happened to get up early enough to catch her in yoga pants after early morning workouts.

Detective John had reluctantly agreed to give a statement on camera when Mr. Manchester wouldn't back down on going through with the press conference. Charlotte understood her father well enough to know that he would go through with it with or without police cooperation.

Mr. Saks showed up minutes after the news crews, making sure they all had copies of the Manchester campaign promises he'd printed out. Charlotte rolled her eyes at the sleazy campaign manager. Like anyone cared about the campaign promises when the man's daughter had been kidnapped. Of course, the media didn't know that with any certainty. Sure, there was speculation based on some of the articles Charlotte had looked at with Vincent earlier, but only their family, close friends, and a few people in the police force knew about the kidnapper's call.

Mr. Saks seemed to be in his element running between the reps from the three stations who now stood in the living room. "We're ready to go live in thirty seconds," he barked. "Everyone but the Manchesters and the lead detective can wait behind the cameras."

Vincent squeezed Charlotte's hand before joining Eric behind one of the cameras. She met his eyes and took a deep breath. Charlotte hated being in front of a camera without her standard disguise. Unable to smile, she kept her face as blank as possible, terrified that the kidnapper would see their message and harm Julia.

Mr. Manchester turned on the charm as soon as the stations went live. "This is Simon Manchester, here in my living room with my family tonight. One member is noticeably absent in our household." He placed his arm around his wife, who sniffled. Charlotte grabbed her mother's hand. "My thirteen-year-old daughter, Julia Marie Manchester—whose picture you should see on your screens—has been missing since Saturday evening. We just want her home safe. If you know anything about her disappearance, we implore you to contact the police department or call the Manchester hotline using the information on your screen. You can make an anonymous report, no questions asked. I have Detective John here to issue a statement."

Detective John, who stood on the other side of Mr. Manchester, cleared his throat. "Having been missing for more than seventy-two hours now, we consider thirteen-year-old Julia Marie Manchester in danger. We have found no evidence to suggest that she left home willingly. Julia is five feet, seven inches tall, weighs approximately a hundred and twenty pounds, and has brown hair and eyes. She was last seen wearing a purple sweater, black jeans, and grey boots. She wore a black wool coat, a pink scarf, a pink hat, and carried a pink canvas backpack. Anyone with information about that should contact the police department or the hotline. Thank you."

Charlotte continued to hold her mother's hand as Detective John rattled off the contact information. She watched Vincent leave the room with a pained look on his face. Charlotte's stomach was cramping from all the stress, and Vincent hadn't been feeling well since before Julia went missing—likely from all the extra training for wrestling. As much as Vincent loved the sport, he might have to give it up for his health if his symptoms didn't improve soon.

"Please," Mr. Manchester said, his voice cracking and startling Charlotte. "We just want our little girl home safely."

With that, the cameras cut their live feeds. "Do you have everything you need?" Mr. Saks asked no one in particular. When no one answered in the negative, he shooed them out.

The crews packed up and quickly left. Charlotte's mom went back to the chair near the window with Liv and Eric by her side. Hannah came in carrying a cup of tea for Mrs. Manchester, who took it gratefully.

"Hannah, is Vincent in the kitchen?" Charlotte asked.

"No," Hannah said. "He might have gone to the restroom."

Charlotte went to the powder room off the entryway to check on her boyfriend, but the door was open a crack. She turned to go upstairs and saw Mr. Saks and her father duck into his den. She clenched her teeth. Campaign meetings during a time like this were ridiculously unnecessary. Figuring Vincent had gone to the restroom upstairs, Charlotte headed in that direction.

T he rest of the day and night had passed without any
human interaction. Now, Julia figured it was Tuesday.
She still had two granola bars left and had resorted to filling
up the water bottle in the bathroom to quench her thirst. The
water tasted different from her water at home, which ran
through a filter, but it was drinkable and hadn't made her
sick. She was hungry, though, and she felt nasty with having
no way to brush her teeth or anything to shower with or even
clean clothes to change into. The lack of pads or tampons
was also getting to her. She'd gone through a lot of the toilet
paper and paper towels already making her own.

She was just finishing a granola bar when the clanking
of keys against the door lock startled her. The masked male
figure who stood before her was larger and taller than the
woman and held a black trash bag in his hand. Julia gasped
and backed into the corner.

"No need to be scared of me, little girl," said the gruff
voice. "I ain't gonna hurtcha." He tossed the bag onto the bed
from where he stood in the middle of the room. "Should be
enough to getcha through another couple of days."

"A couple of days! I just wanna go home. Let me go!"

"Don't do nothin' stupid, and you'll get home fine." The
man left the room and locked the door behind him.

Julia waited until her heart rate had returned to normal
before getting into the trash bag. Inside, she found a travel
set that included a toothbrush and other toiletries, a small
package of toilet paper, a scratchy towel, and a washrag with

the cardboard tags still attached. Below that was a six-pack of bottled water, two boxes of protein bars, and some grey clothing. Upon further inspection, the grey items were a dollar store sweatshirt and sweatpants. Wrapped inside the clothing were socks, a sports bra, and panties still on store hangers with tags attached. The last thing in the bag was a small package of off-brand maxi pads that wouldn't have been Julia's first choice, but she was so thrilled to see them that she hugged the package to her chest.

Figuring no one would come back into the basement for a while, Julia took the items with her into the small bathroom. The door's lock was broken, but she managed to barricade herself into the room by shoving a metal folding chair from the laundry room under the doorknob. It made her feel a little safer undressing to shower, knowing that it would be hard for anyone to get to her. She thought about staying there but sleeping in the bathtub would be worse than on the old mattress.

The shower curtain hanging above the tub was just a cheap plastic liner, but it was new because it still had heavy creases in it and the chemical scent of PVC. The rust-stained tub smelled of bleach. Whoever had taken her had prepared this basement recently but hadn't thought to provide toiletries until now. Once she had the water temperature adjusted, Julia stripped out of her dirty clothes and climbed into the tub. The water wasn't hot, but it was warm and felt like heaven to her aching muscles. It was enough to make her start crying. Julia quickly washed using the items in the kit. She didn't want to take too long and end up under cold water since the basement was cold enough as it was.

After turning off the water, Julia dried with the scratchy towel and then wrapped it around her body. She took the tags off the clothing and got dressed. Everything was a bit too big except for the sports bra and the socks, but she was glad to be in something clean after wearing the same clothes for three days and having to stuff scratchy paper towels in her underwear. At least the granny panties fit better while using the gigantic, diaper-like maxi pads the man had brought to her.

Julia hung the towel over the shower rod to dry after wiping off the mirror. She'd never in her whole life been so glad to brush her teeth. Rinsing her mouth with plain water just hadn't been enough to make her feel clean—something she realized she'd always taken for granted.

She cinched up the string inside the sweatpants to keep them from falling off her hips and then slipped her feet back into her boots. Not wanting to leave the comfort of her small cave, Julia sat on the floor near her pile of dirty clothes and rested her head on her knees. She wondered what her family was doing out there to find her and take her home.

The powder room was occupied when he'd needed it, and knowing that he couldn't make it all the way upstairs without risking an accident, Vincent had ducked into Mr. Manchester's den to use the attached restroom. After his colitis episode had subsided, Vincent washed his hands and splashed some cold water on his face. He remained in the restroom for a moment to make sure the attack was over. He was just about to turn off the overhead vent when he heard the den door slam. Vincent stepped away from the wall switch.

"Just a bit longer," a male voice said. "We'll pay them, and Julia will come home by Friday at the latest."

"Byron, why did they wait two days to call, and why are they making us wait another two days for further instructions?" Mr. Manchester asked.

Byron Saks—the campaign manager. Vincent leaned against the door to hear better.

"I'll admit, that was a deviation from what we'd planned, but it's working well. The prelim reports are showing that your approval ratings are up thirty percent since news broke about Julia."

Deviation? Vincent wondered. *Plans? What plans? Were they seriously talking campaign strategy at a time like this?*

"Well, the press conference is done, so we'll have to see how public opinion looks tomorrow."

"It'll go through the roof once she's home safe."

"And you're certain she's safe?" Mr. Manchester barked. "I thought we'd have longer to prepare for this before your people jumped the gun on the whole thing."

"It was the perfect opportunity. They were staking it out, and there she was, walking alone."

Holy shit. Vincent broke out into a cold sweat. He was trapped and hoped neither of them would find him hiding in the restroom. It was bad. Really bad. And so messed up. He pulled out his phone and hit record on the voice memo button, praying it would pick up the voices.

"I still thought we were going to wait until Christmas break so she wouldn't miss school, if we even did this at all," said Mr. Manchester. "I wasn't a hundred percent sold on this whole thing to begin with, but I guess you're right. This way, it's all over the news, and the kids at school are talking about it. You're sure she's fine? They're taking care of her?"

Mr. Saks chuckled. "She's not staying in a luxury hotel or anything, but she's got food, water, clean clothes, and warm shelter. Nadia's the one taking care of her. Her and her boyfriend and his former cellmate. They're just wanting some quick money. None of them will hurt a kid."

"They're criminals, Byron. And they're not following your plan."

"*Our* plan," he retorted. "And who the hell else would agree to do this? Retired girl scout troop leaders? All three of them can only get minimum-wage jobs with their records. Nadia just fell in with a bad crowd. She's cleaned up her act, and so has that boyfriend of hers. They just need money to get a fresh start."

"That's just it. Your cousin and her boyfriend's one thing, this other guy that you didn't tell me about is in on this too. I don't know him, and neither do you. If something happens to her, God help me, Byron, you'll go down for this."

"Don't forget—you'll go down with me. You hired me for the best strategies to get you to the top of the polls. I've delivered every step of the way. You'll see when this whole thing blows over. Wait till the camera crews film the happy family all together again. The happy family stating 'no comment' as they usher their young daughter to her therapy sessions. The press will eat it up, and so will the voters."

"What am I supposed to do until then? Give more press conferences? It's another goddamn day until they're even going to call again to discuss ransom. They were supposed to call sooner."

"It's out of my hands now, Simon," Mr. Saks said. By the sound of his voice, Vincent could tell he was getting farther away.

"Just call Nadia to make sure everything is okay."

"Contacting Nadia right now is too risky. Just cooperate with the police, and make sure someone is ready to answer the phone tomorrow."

The den door opened and closed, but Vincent had a feeling that only Mr. Saks had left. He looked down at his phone and stopped the recording. He felt like a PI in one of those old crime movies; only he was the guy in danger—the one who might be holding the damning evidence in his hand. When the den door opened and closed again, Vincent risked peeking out and found the room empty. He dashed to the door and crept out, staying against the wall until he could dart up the stairs.

When he burst through the door to Charlotte's room, she jumped up from her spot on the bed and came to him. "I was just about to text you," she said. "Are you okay?"

Vincent led her back to the bed. "You should sit down," he said. "I don't know how to tell you this, Charlotte."

The color drained from her face. "Are you breaking up with me?"

"God, no. It's not that. Shit. I wish it was just about anything else..."

"You're scaring me. What's going on?"

He had to tell her. Or would it be better for her to hear it for herself? He got out his phone and pulled up the voice memos. "I overheard something I shouldn't have. I'm not sure if it recorded or not, but here." He played the audio file.

After an excruciating recording full of background noise, muffled sounds, and a loud word sporadically, the recording stopped. Vincent felt sicker than he had while overhearing Charlotte's father. Now, thanks to the shitty recording through the bathroom door, it was only his word against the two men. Charlotte's face was scrunched as she looked at Vincent.

"What exactly was that supposed to be? What did you try to record?"

"Your dad and Mr. Saks were talking in his office. About things with Julia."

"Wait...what? What things with Julia, and what were you doing in my dad's den?"

"My stomach's been crazy, so when the other bathroom was being used, I used the one in your dad's den. Before I could get out, he and Saks came in and started talking about polls and stuff."

Charlotte huffed. "Figures," she said. "Of course, he would be concerned about the polls at a time like this."

"It's more than that, Char. From what they were saying, it sounds like they're in on the kidnapping. It was planned."

Jumping up from her bed, Charlotte pushed Vincent away from her. "What are you saying? My dad! Involved in Julia's kidnapping? Do you know how crazy you sound right now? You must have misunderstood them! The whole thing's not possible. Dad would never do that!"

"Charlotte, I know what I heard. I'm sorry the recording didn't work out, but I swear to you that Saks talked about his cousin and her boyfriend having Julia hidden away. They took her earlier than what he and your dad had planned."

She shook her head and turned away. "I can't listen to this. You have to leave. Right now."

"Shit." He walked around to face Charlotte, but she turned away again. "I swear to God I wouldn't make this shit up. Why the hell would I?"

"I don't know, but you're mistaken. Go home. I don't want to talk to you right now."

"I can't leave you like this. I could text Rachel to come over. But, Charlotte, I should at least talk to the police and let them deal with it."

"Don't you dare! You can't just go around accusing people of kidnapping their own daughter."

Vincent felt like screaming, but he managed to control his temper. "Look, I don't trust Ball-Saks or your dad right now. You should be careful. I don't want you to get hurt."

Charlotte turned to him with tears in her eyes. "I'm already hurt."

With nothing else to do, Vincent left her room, slamming the door behind him. Downstairs, he passed Byron Saks in the entryway. Shooting him a glare, Vincent went through the front door and headed toward his car. Parked beside it was Detective John's car. The detective was just ending a call and looked up as Vincent approached.

"Heading home?" asked the detective.

"Yeah."

"Thanks for your help with the hotline. There's always a lot of crazies who call in that have to be sorted. People looking for their fifteen minutes of fame."

"Don't I know it." Looking around to confirm that they were alone, Vincent figured he should take his chance. "Detective, have you looked into Mr. Saks?"

"The campaign manager? Seems a bit squirrely, but he's on the up-and-up from what I've found so far."

"You sure?"

"Is there something you're not telling me, son?"

What he'd heard was bigger than Charlotte being mad at him. Julia's safety was at risk. "I don't trust the guy. I heard him talking to Mr. Manchester like he's in on this thing. Like they're both in on it."

"In on this 'thing.' You mean Julia's disappearance?"

Vincent nodded. "I can't be sure what I heard, but something about a woman named Nadia taking care of Julia—his cousin, I think. The cousin's boyfriend and a friend of his he knew from prison."

"These are serious accusations." The detective squinted at Vincent. "Especially against your girlfriend's father."

"No shit, sir—with all due respect. I said something to Charlotte just now, but she didn't or couldn't believe me. I've probably lost my girlfriend over this whole thing, but I can't just not say something. It's too important. Just promise me you'll look into it, and please, try to leave me out of it if you can. I tried to record it, but my phone didn't pick up much. I'll see if there's anything I can do with it and send it to you."

"I shouldn't even be talking to you without your parents present," Detective John said with a sigh as he handed Vincent a business card. "I know better."

"Well, technically, this is me talking to you." Vincent walked over to his car and opened the door, slipping the card into his back pocket before he plopped down into the seat. "And I'm eighteen...as of a couple of weeks ago." He slammed the door and drove off, leaving the detective standing in the driveway.

Breathing deeply to control the painful spasms in his colon, Vincent navigated through the police barricade that kept the reporters away and headed home. He'd told Charlotte and Detective John what he'd heard, but the burden of knowing sat heavy in his gut and felt like a chunk of concrete. And there was nothing he could do about it.

Detective Ernest John's Notes: 12-8-15

Missing child. Julia Marie Manchester. White female. 13 YO. BR Hair. BR Eyes. Approximately 5'7" tall, 115-125 pounds. Slim build. Last seen in purple sweater, black jeans, grey boots. Black coat. Pink hat. Pink scarf. Carries pink canvas backpack.

Backpack found in dumpster behind Marzano's Italian Restaurant downtown. Unable to get prints from backpack or dumpster—too contaminated. Family confirmed that backpack belonged to Julia Manchester.

Sheet on dishwasher at Marzano's: Parole for burglary, was working afternoon of abduction. Confirmed. No records on other employees or owner.

Simon Manchester demanded a statement from our department for press conference. Extremely concerned about public consumption of the case. Perhaps more so than his concern for his daughter?

Byron James Saks: No record. No alibi for day of abduction. Was present during phone call from kidnapper. Still behaving suspiciously. What's he hiding?

Vincent Rowlands (18)-boyfriend of Charlotte Manchester. Allegedly overheard and recorded conversation between Simon Manchester and Byron Saks. Possible ties to kidnapping. Look into Nadia Saks or kin to Byron Saks. Possible cousin of his involved in kidnapping. Has record. Look for known associates on parole. Not enough evidence to question Saks or Manchester. Yet. Get formal statement from Vincent.

Chapter 21
Liv

The press conference had drained what remained of Liv's energy, and even though the baby was smaller than a tennis ball, the pregnancy was pulling away at her independence. Just now, she'd begged Eric to fix her a cup of chamomile tea—something she would typically be capable of doing for herself if she could only manage to get up from the dining room chair. Eric was happy to oblige. He would do anything for Liv, and she knew it. He hadn't complained at all about staying with Liv in her childhood bedroom. She was already pregnant; what other objections could her parents possibly have? She would never dream of making love under her parents' roof—not that she felt like it anyway with all her stress about Julia.

"You should probably turn in early," Eric said, putting the teacup in front of Liv as he sat down beside her.

"I know," Liv said, placing her hand on top of Eric's. "I'll head up when I'm finished with this. I'm not sure I can sleep, though; I'm too exhausted."

"Now, that doesn't make any sense."

"It makes perfect sense, silly. My body is exhausted, but my brain is still wide awake."

"That's what worries me," Eric said with a sigh. "You're worried about Julia, which I can understand, but you're also wearing yourself out each day. It's not just your body right now. You need lots of rest while you're loaning it out, you know."

"I know," Liv said again before sipping her tea. The warmth hit her stomach and quelled some of the mild queasiness she'd felt all evening. It had been there since the discovery of Julia's backpack. Someone had gone to great lengths to get rid of it, right behind one of the busiest restaurants downtown. It was sheer luck—or maybe the kidnappers' stupidity—that the bag had even been found. There was still one unsettling thought on Liv's mind, one that would likely plague her dreams, even with Eric sleeping beside her.

"What's on your mind?" he asked. "You're frowning so hard it looks like you're about to burst a blood vessel."

"The backpack. Something was missing."

"Like what? Her tablet or something?"

"No. Her tablet was still in her room. It's her keys. Her keys to the house weren't there. She had keys and a fob that would disable the security alarm, just like the one I still carry."

"You think the kidnappers still have it?"

"They would have to since the keys weren't found in the dumpster or in the grid search of the different paths she could have taken from the Smiths' house. It means they could get into the house."

"You shouldn't worry about that. There's always a squad car parked out front now."

Liv took another drink, followed by a deep breath. "Yeah, but for how long? How long will this last? When will they call, and when will my baby sister come home?" Tears filled her eyes. She was much more emotional as a pregnant woman than she'd ever been before—not that her sister's disappearance wasn't worthy of her tears. Liv was used to being strong for her younger sisters.

Eric stood up to rub Liv's shoulders. "I wish I could fix this for you, babe, but I can't. If you'd feel safer, we can go home or go to a hotel to sleep."

Liv shook her head and grabbed one of Eric's hands. "No, I can't leave Charlotte."

"She can come with us."

"And my mother? What about her?"

"Bring your mom if it would make you feel better. You just need to rest. You and the baby, Livy." It had been forever since he'd used that nickname.

Liv stood and fell against Eric, letting him envelop her in his arms. "You're right. I'm worrying too much. There are police here, and you're here, and my parents are here. I'll go check on Charlotte and then go to bed."

"Good idea," Eric said. "I'm going to stay down here and work a shift on the hotline again just in case something else comes up. I'll be upstairs later."

Liv knocked on Charlotte's door and was immediately greeted with a cross reply from her sister.

"Go away, Vinny!"

"It's Liv," she said, opening the door. She found Charlotte lying on her bed, her face red and blotchy from heavy crying. "Charlotte, are you okay?" Liv went to her sister and pulled her into a hug.

"Vincent said the most horrible things, and I made him leave. I think it's over for me and him."

"Oh, Charlotte. I'm so sorry. We can talk about it if you want."

"I don't want to upset you with the baby and all…"

"Geez, Lottie, I'm pregnant, not fatally ill." Using Charlotte's childhood nickname had gotten her sister's attention. It was one thing letting Eric baby her, but Liv didn't want her sister to view pregnancy as a disability for a healthy woman. "I'm fine. You can talk to me."

"He overhead Dad and Mr. Saks talking in the den, and now he thinks they're behind the kidnapping."

Liv wasn't sure she'd heard her sister correctly. "What did you just say?"

"Vincent thinks he heard Dad and Mr. Saks talking about Julia's kidnapping like they're in on it, Liv. Like they planned it. It's the craziest thing I've ever heard."

Standing up, Liv began to pace in front of the window as Charlotte watched her. "You're right that the whole thing sounds crazy. How could Dad put any of us in danger?"

"I know, right? I mean, sure, he's preoccupied with all things campaign right now, but there've been other times in between elections where he's been great and involved. Showing up at your softball games, my debate matches, and Julia's ballet recitals. Surely that couldn't have been all for the press."

"It would be a lot of faking for anyone to pull off." Liv was sure their father loved them. He'd never given any indication that he didn't. He was still upset about the baby, but Liv truly believed he'd come around and accept his grandchild the moment the baby arrived. "I don't know about Mr. Saks, though. I have to be honest and say that he gives me the creeps."

"Me too," Charlotte said. "But there's no way Dad would let that creepy man talk him into doing something harmful to his daughter, right? Especially Julia. She's so young."

"What did Vincent say, exactly?"

After listening to her sister recount Vincent's story, Liv felt ill. The details were disturbing but accusing their father would only cause problems in their family.

"There's got to be an explanation for this, Charlotte. Vincent had to have heard something or he wouldn't have said something to you, right? You guys didn't seem to be having any problems."

Charlotte shook her head. "No problems. We were closer than ever." She put her head in her hands and mumbled, "We slept together for the first time just a few weeks ago."

"Oh, Charlotte…please tell me you were careful."

"We've been careful, but I guess that doesn't matter now."

"Eric and I were careful, too, little sister. You just have to be prepared for what could happen. And you know Vincent much better than I do. I know you're hurting right now but think about how he must feel after telling you something like this. He told you because he loves you so much that he can't keep secrets from you."

"Even if he's wrong because he misunderstood them?"

"Especially then," Liv said. "Vincent obviously doesn't think he's wrong or he wouldn't have told you, but aren't you just killing the messenger no matter what?"

"I not sure of anything anymore."

Eventually, Liv was able to convince Charlotte to wash her face and get ready for bed. It would be another long, fretful night as they waited to hear from Julia's kidnapper with further instructions. Someone was staffing the hotline and main landline around the clock, so there was no danger of missing the call.

She had to talk things over with Eric. He'd know exactly what to do.

When Eric slipped into the room later, Liv leapt up so quickly she startled him. "Geez, Liv," he said, grabbing his chest. "I thought you'd be asleep already."

"I told you I was too hyped up. Even more so now." She told Eric about what Charlotte had shared with her.

"That's crazy, but it's not the craziest thing I've ever heard, unfortunately," Eric said, joining Liv in her bed. "I only just met Saks, and the guy's shady. I don't know much about him, but I don't trust him for some reason. Do you?"

"No. And Charlotte says he gives her the creeps, too, so we all feel it, but I can't believe that Dad would be involved in something like this."

"What if Saks is blackmailing him?"

"I didn't think about that...but for what?"

"Your dad's pretty powerful. If Saks knows something your dad's hiding..."

Now things were making even less sense. "But Dad's the one running for president. Saks is just a hired campaign manager. He could go to the tabloids and get more money than trying to blackmail my parents."

"But it wouldn't be about the money, then, would it?" Eric countered. "It would be about power. If your Dad takes office—he brings Saks with him as press secretary or some other high-up position."

Liv shook her head. "That makes sense—Saks going with him—but Julia's kidnapping is the part that doesn't fit."

"What doesn't make sense to me is why Vincent would make this shit up. Livy, that kid is so in love with your sister—why the hell would he tell her something like that if it wasn't true? Especially knowing that it would hurt Charlotte."

"And it hurt her...she kicked him out."

"You have his number?"

"Yeah. Why?"

"I want to text him to make sure he's all right."

Liv gave Eric the number and waited while he texted Vincent. In less than a minute, there was a reply. Evidently, Vincent couldn't sleep either.

"He says he told Detective John. Off the record."

"Does that mean that nothing can be done?" Liv asked.

"I think it means that John will protect Vincent's identity when investigating."

Liv gripped her comforter tightly in her fists, torn on what to believe. "What if the investigation of Dad and Saks causes their attention to be away from the real kidnappers?"

Eric rubbed Liv's neck and shoulders. "Everything's going to be okay. Detective John knows what he's doing—he won't just come out and ask Saks or your dad. He'll do whatever sleuthing he does without raising any suspicion until he's sure."

"Or even worse, what if Vincent's right about what he thinks he heard? What if my dad is guilty?"

"Julia will be found or released soon, and whoever did this to her will be caught and brought to justice. I just know it. I have a good feeling she'll come home safely."

But it was late at night—when she should have been sleeping—that Liv's mind wandered into that dark place where Julia didn't come home safely. A worry too horrible to voice aloud.

Chapter 22
Wednesday, December 9
Julia

When morning light shined through the paper-covered window, Julia was relieved to have made it through another night. She'd worried that one of the kidnappers would visit her in the darkness to hurt her. Julia was devasted to be spending another day away from home and the warmth of her own bed. Even with the rattling heater and the doubled-up blanket, her mattress bed was cold against the concrete floor and cinder block walls. She'd worn extra socks to keep her feet as warm as possible and had slept in her boots and coat to keep in some of the heat.

Breakfast was another protein bar with a bottle of water. Before this ordeal, Julia had enjoyed caramel and chocolate chip protein bars many nights after ballet class. Now, she hoped to never see another protein bar after going home. She would go home, wouldn't she? Since the men had grabbed her on Saturday, they hadn't touched her again. She'd only seen one man and the woman, but she was certain there'd been two men that first day.

After she finished eating, Julia went to the bathroom to brush her teeth. There was no hairbrush in the bag from the kidnapper, so Julia did the best she could to comb her hair with her fingers—not that she cared what she looked like at the moment. She doubted she'd see anyone at all today, and that was fine by her since the only people who knew where she was were people she didn't care to see. All she wanted was to get out of the basement and go home.

Her only significant find in the basement had been the metal folding chair. She hadn't noticed anything else that she might use to try to escape. She climbed on top of the dryer again to get a better look at the high window. It was tall, but not so tall that she couldn't try to escape through it if the opportunity arose. It had been screwed closed—and pretty recently, judging by the shiny new screws that stood out against the old window frame. She looked around again and noticed something metal on the floor, poking out from under the dryer.

As she knelt to look at it, she realized it was a small flathead screwdriver with different colors of dried paint on the handle. Grabbing her prize, Julia hopped back up on the dryer and went to work on the screws, which—just her bad luck—didn't take a flathead. Using the screwdriver at an angle gave her just enough traction to turn the tight screws. After several frustrating moments of repositioning her tool, Julia was on her way to having one screw loosened.

Only three more to go, she told herself. Then she could find a way to get the bars off the outside to escape. With the chair on top of the dryer, Julia figured she might be able to get out the window to ground level. If she could just get a head start without getting caught, she could run to a neighbor's house to call the police. Those thoughts kept her grounded as she struggled with the remaining screws—while stopping every few minutes listening for footsteps above her or any sounds to indicate that someone might be coming back downstairs for her.

Trying to get away sounded less scary than just sitting around waiting for nothing to happen. It had been three days, and no one had rescued her. Either Josiah had forgotten about the tracker on her keys, or the kidnappers had dumped her bag somewhere far away. Her family could even think she was dead if her backpack and keys were found somewhere—like in a river or a dark alleyway somewhere.

Josiah had told her when installing the tracker that it updated based on the locations of other people's trackers. Someone nearby would have to have the same type of device for hers to register an accurate location. Otherwise, the tracker would show the last known place, which wouldn't help if the keys were nowhere near Julia. The whole thing went over her head a little, but listening to Josiah explain the technology had made Julia feel something for him she'd never considered before—that she could like him as more than a friend and maybe even fall in love with him someday. She giggled as she recalled the memory and hoped Josiah would get taller since she currently towered over him. That would undoubtedly make slow dancing together less awkward.

Just as she finished removing the last screw, Julia heard footsteps overhead. She rolled the screws under the dryer and hid the screwdriver under the crinkled, silver vent hose attached to the wall before running back to the mattress. She sat down only seconds before the doorknob jiggled from the sounds of someone unlocking it. Closing her eyes to pray that it was the woman again and not the man, Julia waited until she heard the door lock click before backing into the corner to await her visitor.

As she lay in bed, Charlotte replayed moments of her conversation with her boyfriend the night before. Each replay of his words made her stomach hurt. She knew the stress wasn't good for her, but avoiding it was impossible. Not only was her sister missing, but she'd had a major fight with Vincent, who actually thought her father was involved in Julia's kidnapping. The absurdity of the whole mess was enough to make her want to cry. Or punch something. Or both.

Picking up her phone, she found that she'd missed two calls from Vincent during the night and a handful of text messages from both him and Rachel. Fury overtook her crying as she pulled up the messages from Rachel. Had Vincent contacted her best friend for backup? The fist she felt clenching her heart released a bit as she read Rachel's messages.

Hey Char-girl. Saw the press conf. Brutal. RU OK?

An hour later, she'd texted again.

I know UR busy. Here if U need me. Anytime.

Next, she read Vincent's messages.

Charlotte, I'm sorry.

I would never intentionally hurt you. I hope you know that.

I love you. We should talk about this.

Opening her voicemail from Vincent, Charlotte prepared herself for more of the same.

"Charlotte, look, I'm really sorry I hurt you. I hope you know me and love me enough to trust me on this. I know what I heard, and I couldn't just keep it to myself. Please, please, call me back or text me. We have to talk about this. I love you."

"I love you too," Charlotte whispered as she deleted his message and started crying again. She loved Vincent and knew he loved her. But she also loved her father and couldn't believe that he'd do anything to hurt Julia. It didn't make any sense at all; nothing did anymore. But doubt trickled in. Charlotte's father had seemed to care more about his campaign than anything else the last year. He'd missed Julia's main dance recital over the summer and almost all of Charlotte's debate tournament last spring except the day that included a photo opportunity for local politicians during the opening ceremony. Liv hadn't requested their father's presence for any events, but if she had, Charlotte doubted their father could have pulled himself away from the campaign to attend.

But was that enough? Sure, their father was distant, but would wanting to win a presidential bid be enough to push someone over the edge to do something so bold as to have his own daughter kidnapped for press attention? Maybe in novels and movies, but did that happen in real life? Did it? In her life no less?

After a shower, Charlotte felt somewhat more human as she joined her sister and Eric to eat in the dining room since the breakfast room had been taken over by the police. She didn't feel much like eating with all the stress her body was under, so she tried to go light with just some oatmeal with half a banana mixed in. It was one of her favorite breakfasts, but today it tasted like cardboard and turmoil. Only managing to eat half of what was in her bowl, Charlotte dropped her spoon onto the table and sighed.

"Today's the day," Liv said, wiping her mouth with a napkin. "I wonder what time the ransom call will come in. The lines have been silent all morning."

Charlotte glanced at the clock. "All morning? How long have you been up?"

"Neither of us could sleep very well, so we've been manning the phones since five," Eric said. "Not a single call has come through in the last four hours."

"I'm surprised I slept at all," Charlotte admitted. "Did Liv tell you what I told her?"

Eric nodded and then drank the rest of his cereal milk right out of the bowl, and Charlotte cracked a smile at watching a grown man do such a thing. "Go easy on him," he said. "I'm sure it wasn't easy to tell you that."

"Like it was easy for me to hear that?"

"I'm sure the police will catch whoever did this," Eric said to Liv and Charlotte. "We just have to keep the faith and do what we can by answering the phone and staying out of the way of the investigation."

Staying out of the way? Did Eric actually think Charlotte would do something that might interfere with the investigation? Well, she would do some rogue sleuthing, but Charlotte wouldn't get in anyone's way.

As soon as her dad had left for another meeting and she was sure everyone else was occupied with other tasks, Charlotte slipped into her father's den. She closed the door behind her and used her phone's flashlight to look around on his desk. She thumbed through the neat stacks of papers on the desk without finding anything of interest.

Next, she opened the desk drawers. The middle drawer was full of boring "Vote for the Man-Chester" pens and highlighters and some spare campaign buttons. The other drawers held old tax records and what seemed to be campaign expense reports. Boring.

"What the hell do I expect?" Charlotte asked herself. "A giant confession letter laying on his desk?" She reached for the last drawer, which was locked. Giving up, she turned to the credenza behind her and looked through her father's books. Nothing of great interest there, either. Just a bunch of reference books that she'd never seen her father open during all the years the books had occupied the shelves. Moving the last book, she found a small key tucked underneath it. The key looked to be the right size for the lock on the desk.

Turning back to the desk, Charlotte used the key to unlock it. As she pulled open the drawer, Charlotte sat down hard on the floor. Beside a handgun were several clear freezer bags filled with bundles of money. Hundreds from the look of things. It was way too much money just to have sitting in a desk drawer instead of a safe—or better yet, a bank. And a gun? Since when did her father keep a gun in the house? He'd always supported lawful owners having guns, sure, but he'd never cared for having one himself. Afraid to touch anything, Charlotte quickly snapped a photo with her phone and then closed and locked the drawer. She returned the key to its hiding place and stood still for a minute to slow her pounding heart.

Cold sweat beaded up on her forehead as she left her father's den and stepped into the hallway. Seconds later, the main phone line rang, and Charlotte ran toward the kitchen. She arrived just in time to hear Hannah answer the phone on speaker.

"Good morning, Manchester residence, house manager speaking."

The police officers in the kitchen stood like statues as they all waited for the caller's response.

"Good morning, Mrs. Manchester," the male caller said. "How are you this fine day?"

Everyone let out a collective sigh as Hannah picked up the receiver. "As I stated, this is the house manager. I'm afraid Mrs. Manchester isn't available for any calls, but I'd be happy to deliver a message to her."

Charlotte stayed in the doorway, watching Hannah become annoyed with the caller.

"No, sir, I can assure you she's not interested. Good day." Hannah hung up the phone, shaking her head. "It's not unusual for me to take three or four cold sales calls a day. That one was for retractable awnings to put on our dog's house; I kid you not. You don't even have a dog!"

Hannah's outburst was met with chuckles from the young police officers, but Charlotte wasn't amused. When the phone rang again so suddenly, she jumped and grabbed the door frame.

"Here we go again," Hannah said, clicking the speakerphone button. "Good morning, Manchester residence, house manager speaking."

Electronic feedback filled the room, and the technician who was recording the call lifted the headphones from her ears. Charlotte's mother came up behind her and squeezed her shoulder.

"Hello?" Hannah said.

Crackling began, and then the electronically-altered voice spoke. "Julia is still alive for now. One million will get her back to you safely. Get it. At five o'clock, I'll call back with instructions."

The line went dead, and the whole room came alive. Mrs. Manchester collapsed into Charlotte's arms, crying. It was all Charlotte could do to keep her mother upright as she helped her into the living room and onto the sofa. Liv and Eric followed and sat with her. Charlotte could hear the policemen and the technician in the kitchen cursing about not having enough time for a trace.

"I need Simon…" Mrs. Manchester said, her voice barely audible in all the chaos. "We need to reach him."

"On it," Eric said, leaving the room with his phone.

"Dad will figure this out," Liv said, taking her mother's hand. "Everything's gonna be over soon. We'll pay them and get Julia back." Liv looked at Charlotte. "Then the police will catch whoever did this and make them pay."

Mrs. Manchester looked at her daughters. "How will we get through the rest of the day waiting?"

Eric came back into the room, shaking his head. "I reached Saks on Simon's phone. They'll be here within the hour. He's almost finished with a meeting."

"God forbid Saks interrupt Dad for something as unimportant as a ransom demand," muttered Charlotte.

Eric shrugged his shoulders. "That's what I thought too."

Mrs. Manchester held out her hand. "Give me a phone," she ordered to no one in particular. Eric unlocked his phone and dropped it into her hand. She pressed something on the screen and put the phone to her ear. "Byron, it's Gina. Put Simon on the phone...no...not in five minutes. Right. Now. Well, interrupt the damn meeting! This is an emergency!"

Liv raised her eyebrows at Charlotte. Their fragile mother was anything but.

"Simon, thank God. The kidnapper wants a million dollars. We're supposed to get another call at five this evening. You've got to get home so we can figure out how to get that much money. We'll have to cash in CDs and get into the girls' college funds...okay...I know. Just come home." She ended the call and handed the phone back to Eric. "Thank you. He thinks we can get the money together in time and said not to worry. But I'm still worried."

Charlotte's gut clenched. Her father already had at least that much, if not more, in his desk. Evidently, her mother knew nothing about it, or she wouldn't be so worried about getting the money in time.

Hannah shuffled into the room with hot tea for Mrs. Manchester. Her hands were shaking as she tried to serve it, so Liv took the tea kettle from her to avoid any scalding. Charlotte glanced at the clock and thought about Vincent, who would be starting his lunch break soon. Maybe she'd been too hasty with sending him away last night.

Chapter 24
Vincent

He'd gone through the motions for the first half of the day, and by lunch, Vincent knew he'd retained nothing from his classes. All he could think about was the hurt in Charlotte's eyes and the fact that she hadn't called or texted him back. Causing her pain was never his intention, but he couldn't in good conscience keep what he'd overheard to himself. It wasn't fair for Charlotte to hate the messenger, but he could understand her not wanting to believe something so terrible about her father. Vincent acknowledged that he, too, would have trouble believing that one of his parents was involved in something so sinister.

He was sure about what he'd heard and hoped that Detective John would find the truth without letting anything happen to Julia. Charlotte already blamed herself for not being with Julia when there was no possible way she was at fault. He looked down at his phone again to check for messages from her. Still nothing since the last ten times he'd checked. He wandered into the cafeteria and took his usual table. As he pulled out his lunch bag, he thought about sending another text to Charlotte but decided against it. He would just stop by her house on the way home and plead with her to forgive him.

Talking to Detective John had been the right thing to do; that much was clear to Vincent. If the roles were reversed and he had a sibling missing under the same circumstances, he'd want Charlotte to do everything in her power to help the investigation. Even if it hurt. And that's what had happened. By overhearing what he did and telling her about it, Vincent had hurt Charlotte deeply. He could have spoken to the detective without telling Charlotte, but that would have felt like lying to her.

Who was he kidding? He couldn't have lied to Charlotte. If she'd see him again, he wouldn't be able to keep it from her that he'd spoken to Detective John. Charlotte deserved to know that Vincent loved her enough to do the right thing for Julia. Eventually, Charlotte would forgive him (he hoped), but her family might never recover. Vincent knew he'd never trust Simon Manchester again after what he'd heard.

LaShawn and Rachel came and sat with him as he munched on his peanut butter sandwich. Neither of them said anything at first. They just sat and silently ate their lunches, but after a while, it was clear that Rachel could no longer contain herself.

"Have you heard from Char at all today?" she asked Vincent while looking at her phone. "Usually, she texts me right back, but I didn't hear from her last night. It looks like she read my messages this morning, though."

"I saw her last night," Vincent said. "She's not talking to me right now."

"What?" Rachel dropped her phone on the table, causing a loud slam.

"We had an argument, and she asked me to leave."

"Dude, that's harsh," LaShawn said. Rachel elbowed him. "Ouch. Watch it, girl, with those bony elbows."

"She's just emotional right now," Rachel said, dismissing the severity. "She's probably just PMS-ing. It'll be okay. Julia will be found soon. There's a ton of media coverage now since Julia fits the sweetheart profile."

"The what?" Vincent had no idea what she was talking about.

"Pretty white girl," Rachel said. "It's just how it is. Pretty white girls—especially rich ones—get more media coverage than kids of other colors who are kidnapped."

"Is that really how it is? That shouldn't matter when someone's kid's missing."

"It shouldn't, but it does," LaShawn said. "If it were me, there wouldn't be news trucks parked on my lawn. I'd be just another black kid who ran off to join a gang or something. It's different when white kids go missing, especially white girls."

Vincent shook his head. "LaShawn, your mom's white..."

"Dude, she passes for white—though she's mixed like me—but that don't matter. My dad's dark, and so am I. As far as the world's concerned, I'm a black man. It don't matter what mix of it. Both of Rachel's parents are black, and I'm darker skinned than she is. One parent with black in them makes you black. Look at Obama. He's known as the first black president, not the first mixed-race president."

"I'm sorry," Vincent said. "I just don't think about that kind of stuff."

"It's your white privilege. You don't have to think about it. Not saying it's your fault since you're not a racist asshole, but it's the truth." LaShawn took a chug of his milk. "Look around at the other kids in this school. You're in the majority. There's only a bit of the other races."

Vincent looked around. He'd never presumed to be color blind; it was just another characteristic he noticed, the same as someone's hair or eye color. But he realized skin color meant more to some people than others.

"Enough about politics and race," Rachel said, breaking up Vincent's thoughts. "Back to Charlotte. Just apologize to her, and she'll talk to you."

Vincent sighed. "It's not that simple. It was a big fight, and I've tried texting and calling, and she just won't talk to me."

"Damn," LaShawn said just as Rachel said, "What'd you do?"

"I didn't do anything!"

"Then what's the problem?" Rachel tossed a wadded-up napkin at Vincent's chest.

"I told her something that was difficult for her to hear, and she got mad at me."

"You probably said something stupid," Rachel said, this time tossing a celery stick.

"Dude, quit throwing shit at me!"

"What'd you say to her, dumbass?" Rachel scowled. "Was it something insensitive like trying to get her to sleep with you when all she can think about is Julia being missing?"

"Rach, God, no. What kind of creep do you think I am? I can't talk about the fight yet, and especially not here. The truth will come out sooner or later."

Rachel stood up, collecting her tray. "Well," she said, over her shoulder. "I'll just have to call Charlotte and get the deets myself."

LaShawn looked at Vincent and snickered. "Women, man."

"You're telling me." Vincent's phone buzzed in his pocket, and he almost dropped it while pulling it out to check. A text from Charlotte, thank God.

I'm sorry, Vinny. I need to talk to you. Please come over after school. I found something.

He quickly texted back.

I'll be there.

"You out of the doghouse, man?" LaShawn asked while looking at Rachel across the room.

Vincent laughed. "I always keep one foot in the door. You'll see soon enough."

Chapter 25
Julia

A tall male figure clad in black stood before Julia. Her visitor wasn't the woman as she'd hoped, and this man was taller than the one who'd given her the clothes. Just the presence of this one felt ominous.

"You'd think you'd be thrilled to have comp'ny after bein' cooped up in here for so long, sweetheart," the man said.

Julia stayed in her corner, staring up at the man. His voice sent chills up and down her spine.

"What's a matta? Cat gotcha tongue?" He moved into the room and squatted before her. "I won't bite...much."

"Just leave me alone or let me go," Julia said, her voice scratchy from not talking in a while.

"Ah, so ya can talk." He moved closer and brushed Julia's hair away from her face. "Ya sure are a pretty thang. How old ya say ya was, sweetheart?"

Julia recoiled at his touch and nearly gagged at the scent of cigarette smoke on his breath, which only made him grip her hair tighter. "I'm only thirteen," she said. "Please leave me alone or let me go home."

"I cain't just letcha go home. We're nowhere near yer home in the ritzy neighborhood with the fancy-schmancy sidewalks and shit. Ya think we'd have a place like this just tucked away next to all the four-car garages and sprinklers in the yards?"

"Then blindfold me," Julia pleaded. "Blindfold me and take me back to my neighborhood. Let me go, and I promise

I won't be able to identify you or anyone else. Just let me go."

"Yer tall for yer age," the man said, backing up a bit. "Strong legs, too, from what I can see. Legs that'll be good to wrap around those boys…someday. Ah…to be with a virgin again."

Julia gasped. *Oh, God, no,* she thought. She wanted out of this basement and to be anywhere else in the world. Anywhere would be better than sitting there at the mercy of the man in the room.

He held up something and jingled it. It was her key chain. "Don't be getting any ideas about kicking me again and or tryin' to get away," he said. "I know where ya live and have yer keys, so I'd just find ya again."

She strained her eyes to look for the tracking device, but the man put the keys back into the pocket of his cargo pants.

"I took the battery out of yer clever little tracker," he said. "No one's gonna find ya here. If yer daddy pays up, we might letcha go. If not, then maybe you'll grow up a little and learn how to please a man. I'd teach ya everything once ya growed some meat on them bones."

"Please, just leave me alone. Let me go home."

"That'd be dumb of me. I don't have my share of the money yet."

Julia gasped when the man leaned forward grabbed her by the chin. He ran his tongue up Julia's face from her jaw to her temple, leaving Julia too terrified to make a sound or even breathe. Before pulling away, the man kissed Julia on the cheek with a loud smack. After a few of the slowest seconds in Julia's life, he man finally stood and whistled "The Wedding March" as he walked to the door.

As soon as she heard the deadbolt lock and was sure he wasn't coming back, Julia got up and ran to the bathroom, cramming the metal chair under the door. She stumbled into the bathtub and curled up as tightly as she could and cried. She'd been scared before, but it was so much worse now.

Pacing the floor in front of the living room window, Liv waited for her father's car to appear in the driveway. She didn't know where in town he'd gone for his meeting, but she'd expected him to rush home after hearing the news of the ransom call. And the fact that Mr. Saks had, at first, refused to interrupt her dad's meeting made her furious. If anyone was capitalizing on Julia's kidnapping, it was Saks—not her father. She was convinced the press conference had been the brainchild of Byron Saks.

Everything she'd learned from Charlotte's conversation with Vincent plagued her thoughts. She couldn't just ask her father or Mr. Saks outright. Doing so would only hurt her family or put Julia in danger. Or both. Charlotte didn't know Vincent had talked to the detective, and Liv sure as hell wasn't going to tell her. That was between the two of them, and Liv didn't want to get in the middle of it.

Now that she was an adult, she no longer put her father on the pedestal she once had. He was human, and he made mistakes just like everyone else. While she was confident that orchestrating a kidnapping couldn't possibly be her dad's idea, she wasn't naïve enough to believe that he could never fall into something terrible to get what he wanted. And what he wanted more than his picture-perfect family was to have that coveted office in the White House. He'd wanted that position for as long as Liv could remember and had uprooted their lives time and time again to pursue it above everything else. Was he capable of breaking the law or being complicit in others breaking the law to get him there?

From the looks of her mother and sister, Liv could tell neither of them had slept very well. They could join the insomnia club with her. Liv had tossed and turned so much that she'd kept Eric awake too. Her back ached, and she felt cranky and bloated as she peered out the curtains again. It was the first day she'd gotten out of bed and been unable to fasten her jeans from the day before. An elastic hair tie looped through the hole and around the button worked for now under an oversized sweater.

"Olivia, please sit down," her mother said. "You're making me nervous."

Liv plopped down in the chair by the window. "I doubt me sitting will calm your nerves, Mom. Geez! Where the hell is Dad? Where was his meeting?"

"He's coming." Mrs. Manchester got up and peeked through the curtains beside Liv. "He might've found a way to get the money and made a stop at the bank."

Charlotte huffed. "Yeah, because everyone has access to a million in cash at the drop of a hat."

"Enough!" Mrs. Manchester yelled, startling Charlotte and Liv. "Dad and I will do whatever it takes to get your sister back. This whole situation is a nightmare."

"If it's this bad for us, think of how Julia must feel," Liv said. No one spoke after that.

An excruciating twenty minutes later, Simon Manchester burst through the front door, closely followed by Byron Saks.

"Gina," he said, going straight to his wife. "We'll get the money together and get our girl back tonight. Don't worry."

"Simon," she said, collapsing into his chest. "We don't know that...and that's a lot of cash. I don't even know if the police recommend paying the ransom—"

"We don't," said Detective John as he entered the room from the kitchen. "We don't know who we're dealing with here and if there's a hidden agenda. We have no confirmation that the caller has Julia or if she's..."

"If she's what?" asked Mrs. Manchester, pulling away from her husband.

Liv felt a lump rising in her throat. Her face must have shown her emotions because Eric walked over and embraced her.

"My wife asked you a question," Mr. Manchester said to the detective as he pulled his wife back into his arms.

Detective John looked around the room, making eye contact with Liv and Charlotte before turning back to their parents. "We don't have confirmation that Julia is alive. It would be prudent for us to ask for proof when the caller contacts you again. We haven't been able to trace the call—this could be some nutcase looking for quick cash who knows about Julia's disappearance from the news. We need confirmation."

"That's preposterous!" Mr. Manchester said. "They're not going to kill our daughter. We'll give them the money, and they'll return Julia and leave us the hell alone."

"And if they don't?" challenged Detective John. "Then what? What if they take the money and run, and we still have no idea where Julia is?"

"And you have a better idea?" Mrs. Manchester left her husband's arms and walked over to the detective. "You've been here for four days, and you still have no idea where she is. How can you be so sure that paying the ransom won't get her returned to us?"

Detective John signed. "Mr. and Mrs. Manchester, I can't begin to imagine how scared you must be right now. We need to keep the caller on the phone to try to get a trace or triangulate the phone towers to get a general location. We need to ask for time to get the money together and for proof that Julia is alive and well. You need to sit down with our investigators and go back over the list of former employees and campaign workers to see if anyone stands out as possibly holding a grudge. Help us to help you find Julia and capture this bastard. And can you seriously get ahold of a million in cash this afternoon?"

"The money is not an issue," Mr. Manchester said.

"Who's to say they won't up the ransom demand at the next call?" asked the detective.

"They won't up the ransom."

"With all due respect, sir," Detective John said. "You don't know who we're dealing with here."

Or do you? Liv thought. She locked eyes with Byron Saks, who smiled at her. Liv shuddered. Was he the bastard they were looking for? Then she looked at her father. He was flustered and sweating, but for what reason? Was he worried about Julia or worried about getting caught?

Charlotte was watching them as well. Liv wondered if Charlotte had figured out that Detective John was baiting their father and Saks. When Charlotte's eyes met hers, Liv felt her confusion. Perhaps their talk last night had changed Charlotte's mind about what Vincent told her.

Liv's thoughts were doing somersaults of believing and not believing in her father's guilt, and she imagined Charlotte felt the same way.

L iv followed Charlotte to her room after their parents argued with Detective John. She closed the door as Charlotte plopped down on the bed and hugged a pillow.

"You're right that Saks is creepy," Liv said as she sat on the bed. "Did you see the way he was acting down there?"

"I found money, Liv," Charlotte blurted. "A lot of money. In Dad's locked desk drawer. I didn't have time to count it, but I think it's for Julia's ransom. And I found it before the call."

Liv sighed. "Dad's acting suspicious right along with Saks, don't you think?"

Charlotte squeezed her pillow harder as her gut throbbed. "I asked Vinny to come over after school. With what he overheard and what I found, there might be enough to mention it to Detective John at least. What do you think?"

Liv's face turned ashen as she turned away from her sister.

"Liv…Olivia! What's going on? Are you okay?" Charlotte reached out and turned her sister's face back toward her.

"I'm fine," Liv finally said, "But you might get upset if I tell you what else I know."

"I'll be upset either way, so just tell me." Even as she said it, Charlotte wasn't sure she wanted to know.

"Vincent already talked to John. Last night. Eric and I chatted with him, and he said that he couldn't keep it to himself with Julia's life at stake, no matter how angry you were with him."

Even though Vincent was right to talk to the detective, it still felt like a betrayal to Charlotte. She wished he had talked to her about it first. But then again, he might have tried when she wasn't speaking to him. "Oh." Charlotte looked down at her hands as Liv reached out to grab them.

"If Dad's involved, the police will figure it out."

Charlotte took a deep breath. "I wanted Vincent to be wrong, but then I found that money."

"Why were you even looking in Dad's desk in the first place?"

"I guess because, deep down, I knew Vincent wouldn't lie to me. I just needed proof, you know?"

"If Dad orchestrated this whole thing—and that's a big if—or if he's at least involved, then that has to mean that Julia will be okay. We need to focus on that."

"Instead of focusing on the fact that our lives as we knew them are over?"

"Eric thinks there's a possibility that Dad's being blackmailed. Maybe by Saks."

"Eric knows about this too?"

"I don't keep secrets from him," Liv said matter-of-factly. "What do you think?"

"I don't see Dad getting blackmailed. For what?"

"I don't know. Doing something illegal? Having an affair?"

"God, an affair? And then that jumps to kidnapping? That just doesn't sound right. He's guilty, Liv. Our dad is going to prison for this. And he freakin' deserves it for having Julia kidnapped. We don't know that she's okay."

"She's gonna be okay," Liv said. "She has to be."

"She's with criminals, Liv. Criminals. Criminals who kidnap kids and hold them for ransom. Criminals who get hired out for kidnapping. This is not okay. Julia's gotta be terrified that she's never coming home. I have to tell the police, don't I?"

"I think you have to tell Detective John at some point."

With that, Charlotte could no longer hold back her tears. They were flowing faster than she could wipe them away. Crying in her older sister's arms was the only thing she could do when she felt utterly helpless. Part of her wanted to rush downstairs to confront her dad and Mr. Saks, but the tiny piece of her brain still rationally thinking convinced her it was a terrible idea. Her love for her father was breaking away to reveal anger and suspicion. If he was guilty, would hatred follow?

Before long, Vincent had arrived and joined Charlotte in her room. She embraced him and didn't let go for more than a minute. "I'm sorry," she whispered before kissing him. "I shouldn't have doubted you."

"Babe, I don't wanna be right about this...but I had to tell John...I just had to. I'm sorry."

"It's okay," Charlotte said, leading him to her bed. "I was hurt at first, but I get why you had to tell him. I believe you about what you heard. I was just angry and scared, so I lashed out. I didn't want it to be true. I found something too. After what you said, I couldn't get it out of my mind, so I snooped in my dad's desk. I found money. A lot of money. I think he's ready to pay the ransom because he's involved.

And there's a gun in there too. A handgun, Vincent. My dad has never really cared for guns."

Vincent took Charlotte's head in his hands and kissed her on the forehead. "You need to tell Detective John."

"I thought about confronting Dad first."

"No," Vincent said, still holding Charlotte's face. "Absolutely not. It's a bad idea. If he could do this to Julia, what could he do to you? We need to let the police handle this, especially since there's a gun in his office. Do you think it's loaded?"

"I don't know. I didn't touch it. I've never touched a gun before."

"My dad taught me to assume that every gun is loaded. Always."

"God, I feel sick," Charlotte said, laying her head in her boyfriend's lap. "I never thought my dad could do something like this."

"We still don't know for sure…" Vincent stroked her hair. "What if he's being blackmailed or something? Things aren't always like they seem."

"Liv said Eric mentioned that, too, but I don't think so. I can't see anyone having the guts to blackmail my dad. And he's been strangely calm and focused on press conferences and campaign meetings through this whole thing. Meanwhile, Mom and the rest of us…we're basket cases. And if that creep Saks looks at me like he does another time, I swear to God I'm gonna throat-punch him."

"I might beat you to it." Vincent leaned back on the bed and pulled Charlotte into his arms. "When do you want to talk to Detective John?"

"I don't know. The kidnapper is supposed to call back soon to give my parents instructions about the ransom. Maybe I should wait until Julia is home safe."

"I don't think you should w—" Vincent was cut off by the sound of the phone ringing downstairs. Charlotte bolted from the bed and ran down the hallway, taking the stairs two at a time to reach the kitchen where she knew Hannah would be waiting to answer.

Chapter 28
Julia

When her tears had run out, Julia stayed in the bathtub with her arms wrapped around her knees. She began shivering and grabbed the dry towel from the shower rod and pulled it around her shoulders. The cheap, scratchy towel did nothing to comfort her or warm her, but it was all she had.

She knew that she'd been gone from home four nights now, and tomorrow would make five. It was Wednesday evening unless she'd lost a day somehow. She was trapped in a basement that was either soundproofed or in an area away from the city traffic. There were three kidnappers: two men and one woman. One man was the most dangerous, and she hoped never to see him again. The other man and the woman hadn't been cruel like the dangerous man, but they were part of this thing, so neither could be trusted.

The food they gave her in sealed packages was safe since she hadn't become ill from it, and the tap water was safe to drink for the same reason. Her tracking device was broken, and the scary man had keys to her family's house and had threatened her family. Even if she could escape, she had no idea where she was. But if she could run to a neighbor's house, she could get them to call for help. The police would protect her family, and they could change the locks or move. The police would catch the kidnappers. They had to.

But if she did escape, who's to say that she wouldn't be caught again before she could get somewhere to get help? Julia got out of the tub and began pacing in the small bathroom. She didn't know where she was or if there were any other people nearby to help her. She had no idea where the kidnappers were and if they might see her if she tried to escape through the window above the washer and dryer. Would it be worth the risk?

The scary guy had mentioned ransom. He'd wanted Julia's dad to pay up, so the whole thing was about her father's campaign. Her father was a public figure more than her mother, so it was all about money. The kidnappers had to know that Julia's mom had been wealthy on her own before her marriage, so they were probably requesting a lot of money. Julia wondered if her parents would pay...if they could pay? She didn't know how much money her parents had. She just knew that if she wanted something, she could usually have it. Ballet lessons, new clothes, pretty much anything she asked for. She used her babysitting money for things like movies with her friends and milkshakes after dance so she wouldn't have to ask her parents to reload her debit card all the time.

"Julia?" the woman's voice called to her from the other room. "You in the bathroom?" The doorknob rattled, and the woman knocked. "Open the door."

"I'll be out in a second!" Julia called. Still shaking, she flushed the toilet and washed her hands. She glanced at her face in the tiny mirror above the sink and dried the remaining tears with the towel. Slowly, she walked to the door, removed the metal chair, and opened it.

"I brought you some dinner from a burger joint," the masked woman said. "Thought you might want something warm." The woman stepped into the bathroom and picked up the folding chair, taking it with her as she walked away.

"Thanks," Julia muttered as she followed her to the main room. She wouldn't have to be thankful for fast food if she were home eating one of the lovely meals Hannah would help prepare. A kale salad sounded divine. And Hannah's angel hair pasta was incredible.

"The food's on your bed." The woman pointed. "Behave yourself, and we'll get you out of here soon."

Julia scoffed. "Behave myself? I haven't done anything wrong. Neither has my family."

The lady rolled her eyes. "Girl, if you only knew. Your daddy's crooked as a three-dollar bill. They all are in politics. Nothin' but liars and criminals—the whole lot of 'em."

"You and your partners are the only criminals I know."

"Once we get the money, you'll never see us again. You can go back to living your privileged life as a spoiled little rich girl."

This angered Julia. "I didn't do anything to deserve this. I'm not spoiled, and I'm not rich. My parents are."

"And look where that got them."

"Let me go or go away," Julia said. "And keep that pervert friend of yours away from me."

The woman's eyes widened behind her mask. "What are you talking about?"

"Oh, so both men are perverts?" Julia said, feeling triumphant for having gotten under the woman's skin. "The one who came in today."

"No one should've come here today except me," the woman grumbled as she left the room. A few seconds later,

Julia heard the metal chair crash to the floor on the other side of the door.

Julia made another mental note. The kidnappers' organization was breaking down. The woman didn't know that one of the men had threatened Julia, and that was something she might be able to use to her advantage if it came to that. With turmoil between the three criminals, Julia might be able to try her luck at turning them against each other.

Her stomach rumbled in response to the scent coming from the bag on her bed. Eyeing the non-descript white paper bag, Julia wondered if it might have come from her favorite mom-and-pop burger place downtown near her ballet school. Inside the sack with its plain white wrappers around the burger and fries, she found her proof—brown paper napkins embossed with little daisies in the corners. No other place she'd seen had napkins like that. Once, she'd seen a couple of the busboys sitting in a back booth stamping each napkin with handheld presses. It was just one small way the owner, Daisy, put her personal touch on her place.

Julia inspected her burger and ate it after she was satisfied that it hadn't been tampered with. She could have done without the mayo, but her hunger superseded her preference for mustard. If the kidnapper could get a burger from Daisy's, and it was still reasonably warm, then they couldn't possibly be more than five or ten minutes away from downtown by car. That meant there were other people around.

She didn't think the first man and the woman would really hurt her, but the second man was different. He was a sick person to talk to her the way he had. Julia had no doubt he would hurt her if he got another chance. She had to get out of this place. She had to decide if she should try to escape tonight or in the morning. But it still worried her what might happen if she tried and failed. How badly would they hurt her if they caught her?

Vincent caught up with Charlotte, and they entered the kitchen as Liv burst through the door. The robo-voice filled the silent room as soon as Hannah answered.

"We're ready for the drop. Fairfield Park at seven tonight. The trashcan near the swing set. Manchester comes alone, or the deal is off. Bring the cash in a duffle bag and leave it in the trashcan. Any funny business, and you'll never see the girl again."

Grabbing Charlotte's hand, Vincent watched her father as he picked up the phone, ending the speakerphone.

"This is Simon," he barked into the phone. "I'll get you the money, but I need proof that my daughter is alive."

"Ask for time!" Detective John whispered at Simon's back. "Time to get the money."

Ignoring the detective, Mr. Manchester continued to speak. "Letting her go downtown is fine, but you better not hurt her, you bastard. Put Julia on the phone now. I'm not giving you any money until I have proof that she's alive."

Detective John threw his hands up in the air and walked over to the phone technician, who was madly punching buttons on a computer.

Vincent continued to hold Charlotte's hand. Charlotte had her other hand on her mother's shoulder. Mrs. Manchester was shaking as she twisted a used tissue in her hand while sitting in a chair at the breakfast table.

Mr. Manchester put the phone back on speaker and waited, his fists clenched.

"Get the girl!" the voice called. Noises that sounded like doors unlocking and then slamming filled the room.

"Talk to your father," the voice ordered.

Silence followed, and then Julia's tiny voice filled the air. "Daddy...please help me. I'm in a basement somewhere." A scuffle ensued, and Julia screamed, "Let me go!"

"Shut up," a male voice said in the background.

"You've heard her," the robo-voice said. "Now do your part."

The line went dead, and Charlotte's mother started wailing. "Please, God, tell me you got a trace!" she said to the technician.

"It's a cell phone," the technician said. "Working on triangulating the signal now. We should be able to narrow down the location significantly based on which towers the calls bounced off of. Just give me a few minutes."

"Why the hell didn't you ask them for more time to get the money?" Detective John said to Charlotte's father. "Our best chance of catching them is to stall them."

Simon turned to the detective. "They said they'd let Julia go downtown at eight o'clock tonight as long as I drop the money at seven, and I believe them. I have to do this."

"Simon, how will we get that much money so fast?" Mrs. Manchester asked through her tears.

He walked over and knelt in front of his wife. Charlotte backed away and turned to hug Vincent. He just held his girlfriend as he watched her father.

Mr. Manchester was calm, too calm, Vincent thought, as the man spoke again. "I've already gotten the money together. After the first ransom call, I went to the bank and pulled the money out of several CDs. There was a small penalty, but it's nothing compared to getting our girl back. Everything will be okay."

Charlotte looked up at Vincent and shook her head slightly. He led her out of the room into the living room.

"That's not true," she whispered. "I found the money before we got the call about the ransom. My dad was already prepared."

Pulling Charlotte into his arms, Vincent whispered into her ear. "We'll get Detective John alone and tell him what you found."

"I will, but I want to wait until after Julia is home safe," Charlotte whispered back. "Do you think they'll let her go tonight?"

"I hope so. I really hope so." Vincent kissed Charlotte on the forehead and held her close.

L iv and Eric helped her mother into the living room. Her mom was distraught, but her dad was cool and collected. Although she hated to believe it, the evidence was pointing to her father being guilty. Charlotte had found the money before the ransom call. It was too big of a deal to be a coincidence, especially since the money was hidden with a gun.

Soon, her dad walked into the room, carrying a black gym bag. He dropped it onto the coffee table, its thud startling his wife. "I've got it all there."

"What about a tracking device?" Eric asked as Detective John walked in. "Can't the police put a tracker in the bag?"

"No," Mr. Manchester said. "The kidnappers said that any funny business would ruin our chances of getting Julia back. I'm going to do exactly what they said. I'm going alone and making the drop."

"Don't you care that we catch these people?" Liv asked.

"I care more about getting Julia back unharmed," her father said. "Isn't that what you want most?"

"Dad, of course, it's what we want," Charlotte said. "It's more important than anything else. You should know that."

"We'll do whatever we can to help you," Detective John said. "We've got some information about where they might be keeping her—at least a place to start searching. The last location picked up by the tracker that her friend gave her was in the same area near downtown where her backpack was found. That was on the same day she was taken. One of these kidnappers may work in that area. We'll start canvassing again for more information to try to catch these people. We now know that there are at least two men based on the voices we heard during the phone call. The cell phone bounced off of towers around the same area. They're no more than a ten-mile radius from the center of downtown."

"I'm just focused on getting my daughter back," Mr. Manchester said. "We'll have her back tonight, and after she's checked out okay, you'll be able to question her to see if she can identify these people."

Liv wondered if the kidnappers would lead back to her father. Had her father hired them in-person? Surely not. But did the kidnappers know he was behind the whole thing? If they were caught, would they talk? No matter what happened, Liv would never trust her father again. This wasn't something she and Charlotte could keep to themselves. She glanced at Vincent, who was holding her sister. Charlotte was lucky to have such an amazing boyfriend at her age. One who had done the right thing about sharing what he knew about their father. Liv was glad Charlotte seemed to have forgiven him. She would need all the support she could get when everything came out.

Taking her mother's hand, Liv squeezed it. "Everything's gonna be okay, Mom. Julia will be okay."

Detective John was still talking. "We'll get property records for houses and businesses with basements. We'll figure out where these people have kept her. It's only a matter of time."

"Once they have the money and release my daughter, these people will be long gone," Mr. Manchester said. "They'll disappear."

"With a million split between the criminals?" challenged Detective John. "That isn't enough to disappear with and live on forever. These people are criminals. They'll do this again and again. And frankly, sir, we don't need your permission to pursue charges."

"Simon!" Mrs. Manchester said. "If they're not caught, who's to say they won't come back when their money runs dry? They might take her again since it's a surefire way to get money."

"That's not going to happen, Gina," he said, walking over to his wife. "I won't let that happen."

Anger boiled up inside Liv, and she had to leave the room. Eric followed her into the hallway. "It's everything I can do not to call out my father," she said quietly. "I'm just so angry."

"They'll be time for that," Eric said, cupping her chin. "Just try to stay calm for now. Julia will be home tonight, and then Charlotte can talk to the police, and I'm sure they'll investigate. They'll figure this out."

Tears filled Liv's eyes. "I just never thought my dad would do something like this. My dad and I have had our differences, but this is just too much."

Eric pulled her into his arms. "I know, baby. I know. And I know it's hard for you right now, but you've got to rest. You look exhausted."

"Because I am exhausted." Liv laughed to ease her tension. "Promise you'll wake me the moment you hear anything."

"I will," Eric said. "I'm gonna call my parents and give them an update. My mom's tried to call me a couple of times today while I was answering the phone for the hotline. The calls have slowed down. No more psychics or UFO sightings today."

"Well, that's a relief. Though I do wish a real psychic would call and tell us where Julia is right now."

A s she paced back and forth in front of her bed, Charlotte felt the time ticking away. Her father would leave soon with the ransom money and would hopefully return with her sister. Afterward, nothing would ever be the same again. There was no way her father would get away with it; he couldn't. But there was still a tiny molecule of hope that gripped her heart tightly enough to cause some doubt in her mind. What if everything Vincent had heard was misunderstood? And what if her father had taken out the money in anticipation of the ransom demand? It's not like she'd taken time to count it. And she had no idea what a million in cash would look like all stacked up.

"Charlotte," Vincent said, breaking through her thoughts. "You've got to sit down."

"I'm thinking."

"Think sitting. You're making me crazy."

"Sorry." She plopped down on her bed. "I want to be wrong, but that money was definitely there before the ransom call. Is there any way he could have anticipated it and taken out enough to cover it?"

Vincent gave a half-smile and ran his hand through his hair. "Maybe..."

"Let's go over again what you heard."

He sighed. "If you think that will help."

"It might."

"Your dad and Saks were talking about his campaign, and then they started talking about Julia and jumping the gun on the plan. Saks mentioned someone named Nadia, who is his cousin. Nadia's boyfriend and another guy—his former cellmate—are involved. Apparently, they didn't stick with the plan. Your dad was frustrated, but Saks talked him down. The key here is Saks. We need to find out about his cousin."

"And you told all that to Detective John?"

"Every bit of it. I just wish my damn phone had picked it up."

"What if it did? What if the file could be enhanced or something?"

Vincent held out his phone. "It's not the latest iPhone, and the bathroom vent was on. I don't think it's as easy as they make it look on TV."

"It's worth a shot, though…email it to me, and we'll open it in the audio program we use for debate."

With a couple of taps on the screen and the familiar swooshing sound, the file was on its way to Charlotte's inbox. Her hands were shaking as she waited for the download to complete. She opened the file in the audio software and hesitated before clicking the play button. She'd need to turn the volume up to max and minimize the background noise, but the risk of someone overhearing the sounds was too high.

"We should listen on the headphones," Charlotte said. "I've got my splitter, but I left my other headphones in my locker."

Vincent dug into his hoodie pocket and retrieved his earbuds. "I came prepared for once," he said, handing the plug to Charlotte.

She plugged in both sets of earbuds and started the playback. The background noise of the fan was lessened, and voices were audible, but not every word. She started the playback again at a slower speed, this time turning on the transcript feature to see if it could capture anything. It spit out some text that seemed to put a bit more of what she heard into context.

I...going to wait until Christmas break...miss school, if...at all

I wasn't...sold on this whole thing to begin with, but I guess...right. This way, it's all over the news and the kids at school are talking about it.

You're sure...care of her.

[laughter]...luck sorry hotel...anytime, but she got food...women shelter. Naughty uh...boyfriend fisher check mate...quid monkey. None...hurt uh kid.

Hair criminals, by Ron. And hair not following...plan. Are pan.

And who well else would agree to do this

Retired girl scout troop liters

All free...them can only get minimum-wage jobs with their records.

Naughty uh just welled with uh bad cow.

She cleaned up her rack

And so has mat boyfriend of hearse.

Well just need monkey to get...mesh star

That's jock itch.

Your cousin and her boyfriend won thing

His other buy that you didn't sell...about...this you.

[inaudible]

If something happens two fur, God help me, by Ron, who go down fur its.

Don't forget who go down with me.

You hired me for the best strategies to bet you...top of the polls.

[inaudible]

The press will eat it up and so will the voters.

What am I supposed to do till then

Give more press conference

It another rod ham day till hair...call again to this cuss man scum.

They well supposed to call sooner

It's out of my chance now...

Just tell not you to make sure ever time is OK

Contracting naughty uh right...to miss key

[Inaudible]

"Holy shit," Vincent whispered as he read through the transcript with Charlotte. "I can't believe the program picked up the voices so well...even with the 'monkeys' and 'jock itch.'"

Charlotte took a deep breath and read through everything again, trying to translate what the actual words might have been. She pulled out her earbuds and rested her head in her hands. "It's enough to prove a conversation, but is anything really incriminating?"

"I don't know...I bet they have better software than what our school provides, though. Detective John gave me his card. We could email him the file."

"Complete with the 'monkey jock itch' transcript?"

Vincent snorted. "Yep. Let him decipher it, and we'll talk to him after Julia gets home tonight."

"You staying?"

"Definitely. With everything that's going on, I don't wanna leave you tonight."

Charlotte leaned over and kissed him on the forehead. "Thank you," she whispered.

A knock on the door startled Charlotte. She got up and opened it to find Hannah standing in the hallway wearing a stern look.

"Charlotte, I know things are a bit unsettled right now, but you still need to have the door open when Vincent is here," she scolded. "Your mother would have a fit if she knew you two were up here like this."

"I'm sorry, Hannah," Vincent said from the bed. "We were listening to some stuff on the computer, and I must have closed the door by mistake. It's my fault."

"Sorry," Charlotte said. "We'll leave it open."

Hannah left them, and Charlotte turned back to her boyfriend with a laugh, "At least she didn't catch us in a compromising position."

"Yeah," he whispered. "Like listening to incriminating evidence."

Charlotte looked at the clock on her wall. Her dad would be heading out soon, and she figured they should go downstairs with the rest of her family.

Chapter 32
Julia

S tanding on top of the dryer, Julia struggled with the last screw on the window. Once it was out, she unlocked the window and eased it open to investigate the bars. To her delight, the bars were just an insert that could be removed easily. She pulled down the panel insert and placed it gently on top of the washing machine before standing up to look out the window again. Car doors slammed, and the rumble of the engine filled the silence of the air outside. Julia stopped breathing for a moment to listen, afraid to move and worried that someone might discover the open window or notice that the bars were gone.

After a few agonizing seconds, tires spun in the gravel driveway, and through the branches of the shrubbery, Julia watched the black SUV pull away. The taillights disappeared down what appeared to be a long road or driveway. She hopped down from the dryer and went back to the main room. Leaning against the door, she listened for any sounds on the other side, but there was nothing but silence. Julia knew it was now or never if she was going to get out of her prison. She grabbed her coat and took it with her to the laundry room. Once she was atop the dryer again, she pushed her coat through the window. It took every ounce of strength she had to hoist herself up and through the window.

Julia was halfway through the window when the door opening behind her chilled her even more than the cold air. She was caught but too far in to give up. As she wiggled her body through the small window, a strong hand seized her ankle.

"What the hell ya doin', girl?" yelled the angry man as he tried to pull her back down. Julia grabbed for the thick roots of the shrub and clung to it for dear life. "Get down, ya little bitch!" The man climbed on top of the dryer to pull Julia back inside.

Julia screamed and kicked. She wasn't about to go back in without a fight; she was in deep trouble anyway. With all her thrashing, the man was only able to keep hold of one of her ankles, and Julia managed to get a good solid kick to the man's face. He lost grip on her ankle and stumbled backward off the dryer and onto the concrete floor. With a sickening thud, the man landed on his head and went silent.

Now free and pumped full of adrenaline, Julia pulled herself through the window onto the ground. She pulled on her coat as she peered back into the window. The man was on the floor, not moving, and Julia couldn't tell if he was breathing or not. But she didn't have time to think about that; her heart pounded as she crawled from beneath the shrubbery and got the first look at her surroundings.

The unassuming red brick ranch house was surrounded by farmland, and it looked as if it had been deserted for a while. The shutters and gutter system barely hung, and most of the window screens were torn or missing altogether. The house hadn't seen a roofer or painter in years from what Julia could discern in the fading daylight. The carport at the side of the house had a single bulb burning in its center, illuminating its vacancy. At least the man inside couldn't give chase in a vehicle—if he could even get up at all. If he wasn't dead, he was at least going to be unconscious for a while.

Overcome with exhaustion, Julia fell to her knees. There were no other houses in sight, but there was a light far in the distance. Stifling a sob, Julia knew she had no time to waste. Following the long gravel driveway through the farmland was her best bet. Pulling herself to her unsteady legs, Julia took off, running down the driveway.

Before long, her energy had waned, and Julia slowed to a walk as she grew closer to the light. Or, at least, she prayed she was moving closer to the light. She hated being out on the creepy road so late in the darkness, but it was better than the alternative.

"Ahhhh!" She kicked a rock in the middle of the deserted gravel road. "I should've gone back in and taken his phone!"

She didn't have time to beat herself up on what she should have done; she had to keep going. After catching her breath, each one leaving a white fog in the frigid air, she took off again at a jogging pace. She hadn't been locked up long enough for her strong dancer's legs to suffer atrophy. Julia would find a way to save herself the only way she knew how—by running toward the light.

As she approached the house at the end of another long driveway, Julia saw that the property was dark except for a tall outside light shining down on the yard. The house wasn't in the same state of disrepair as the house she'd escaped from, but there were no cars in the driveway or carport. Despite that, she ran toward the front door and rang the doorbell, and began knocking frantically, begging someone, anyone, to be home.

When no one answered, Julia ran to the back of the house to try another door. After beating on the door and screaming for help with no response, Julia leaned her head against the door and cried again. Peering through the door's window, she could see a light above a stove in the kitchen. At least the house appeared to be lived in even if no one was home. Julia tried the doorknob and found it locked, but the shovel leaning against the back wall seemed like a suitable key.

Gripping the shovel in her hands, Julia swung with all her strength to break the window. After it had shattered, she threw the shovel back on the ground and carefully removed the large shards of glass so she could get her arm inside to reach the locks. In her rush, she still sliced open her arm, having missed some glass, and winced in pain as she turned the deadbolt. Once inside the house, Julia flipped the switch on the wall and breathed a sigh of relief as the light revealed a well-maintained kitchen. There were cereal and snack boxes left out on the counter, and children's backpacks hung on the backs of the chairs at the breakfast table.

Julia looked around the room wearily and noticed a cordless phone sitting on the countertop near a stack of opened mail. There didn't seem to be an alarm system to alert the police since Julia could hear no sirens, so she lunged for the phone and called for help, grabbing one of the envelopes to get the address.

All Liv could do was hold her mother's hand as her father paced the living room, preparing to leave with the ransom money. As she watched her father, Liv wanted nothing more than to blow up at him and reveal everything she knew but doing so might endanger Julia.

Saks joined them in the living room at the same time Detective John entered from the kitchen. Liv glared at the beady-eyed man, longing for the day he'd go to prison.

"You heading out?" Saks asked.

"Going now," Mr. Manchester said. He turned to his wife. "I'll be back with Julia soon."

"You're not going alone," Detective John interjected. "I'm going with you even if I have to ride in the trunk of the car. Sending a civilian into these situations is never a good idea."

Mr. Manchester turned to the detective. "And how well do these ransom situations work out if people disobey the kidnappers?" he asked. "This is my daughter we're talking about. I just want to pay them and get her back with no issues."

"The whole thing is an issue!" argued Detective John. "We have no guarantee that they'll have Julia with them or will even release her at all. All we have is a general area of where the ransom call might have come from. We're canvassing the neighborhoods, but we need more time to ensure the safety of your daughter. I don't think you're understanding me here!"

"This is a matter of money," Saks said. "Plain and simple. They know the Manchesters are high profile with resources. They won't harm the girl because that would mean no money."

"Glad to know you're such an expert on kidnapping and hostage negotiation," Detective John deadpanned. "Why aren't you working for the FBI already?"

Saks raised his hands in surrender and backed out of the room.

"I'm doing the best I can here for my family," argued Mr. Manchester. "Now, I'll wear the vest but no wire! They'll find it on me immediately. And I don't think you should go with me when the kidnapper explicitly said for me to come alone—"

"Don't you see that you can't trust criminals?" Detective John slammed his hand against the doorframe, causing Liv and her mother to startle at the same time his phone went off. "John," he said into the phone, his shoulders tense and his other hand still flat against the doorframe.

Liv watched the detective's face relax, and he broke into a smile and exhaled the weight of the world.

"Thank God," the detective said. "I'll be right there." He slipped his phone back into his pocket and chuckled. "We just got a 9-1-1 call from about ten miles outside of town. Julia is safe. She escaped and broke into a farmhouse to call for help. Officers responded immediately and are driving her to the hospital to be checked out, but she appears to be in good health. A male suspect was found unconscious in a neighboring house. We'll know more once we identify him."

"Oh, thank goodness!" Mrs. Manchester exclaimed. She jumped up and rushed into her husband's arms. "Our baby is safe."

Liv watched her parents and caught her father's eyes. Her dad didn't look relieved, and he wasn't crying like her mother; he looked scared.

Charlotte and Vincent came in from the front hallway. "What's going on?"

"Julia's safe," Liv told her.

"What? How?" Charlotte stumbled backward into Vincent, but he managed to keep her upright. "Where is she?"

"Let's go," Detective John said. "You all can follow me to the State Children's Hospital. That's where the responding officers are taking her."

The room was a frenzy of activity as Eric and the other police officers came in from the kitchen and breakfast room. Liv barely took her eyes off her dad. She watched him have an intense hushed conversation in the corner with Saks before they all piled into the vehicles to go to the hospital.

Straining her ears for sirens, Julia was surprised when the emergency dispatcher told her that officers had arrived on the scene. "What? I didn't hear them pull up."

"They don't use sirens for situations like this," the dispatcher said. "Now, don't be alarmed, but an officer is approaching the back of the house now."

"Police Department!" a male voice called. "Julia Manchester, are you there?"

"Yes!" Julia called. "Thank you. I'm hanging up now." She ended the call and sighed with relief as a uniformed officer appeared behind the broken glass with his gun drawn. Upon seeing Julia, the officer lowered his gun and opened the door.

"Julia, are you injured?" he asked.

Julia shook her head. "I'm fine—I think—just my arm is cut, but one of the kidnappers is hurt. He tried to grab me when I climbed out the basement window, and he fell and hit his head, I think." With that, Julia started crying. Her nightmare was almost over.

A female officer entered the kitchen next and escorted Julia out to a waiting police SUV. By that time, there were three other police cars there with their lights flashing. Julia sat in the SUV's front seat and told the woman and another officer what had happened. She pointed out the direction from which she'd escaped and gave them a description of the house. Two police cars, each holding two officers, left silently in that direction with their lights flashing.

Soon, after half of the officers had left, an ambulance pulled up. The EMTs took Julia over to the ambulance to check her out. She was shivering despite the blanket she was wrapped in and welcomed the second one the EMT provided. After getting an IV to treat her dehydration, Julia settled in for a ride to the hospital. The female officer, Officer Bethany French, rode in the back with Julia, which made her feel much safer.

"The whole city's been looking for you," Officer French said. "I'm so relieved you're safe. My daughter goes to school with you—Whitney—do you know her?"

Julia didn't know Whitney well, but she knew enough to know that she was a great basketball player and said so. She was relieved to be talking about something besides her kidnapping and was able to stop crying for a moment.

"Whitney's been talking about you a lot lately. She tells me you're a dancer."

"Yes. Ballet. I've been dancing since I was three. I've missed several rehearsals in the past few days—what day is it?"

"It's Wednesday. You've been gone for five days."

The EMT adjusted the IV flow and checked Julia's vitals while Officer French held her hand. "You'll feel much better with some fluids in you," the EMT said. "We'll be at the hospital soon."

"Will my parents be there? My sisters?" Julia asked the officer.

"We've already radioed the head detective, who was with your family tonight. They're going to meet us at the hospital."

"Good. I just wanna go home."

"I doubt you'll be going home tonight, Julia," Officer French said. "The doctors will likely want to keep you overnight for observation after they stitch up your arm, and there'll be an officer posted at your door for the duration of your stay. There are still two suspects at large."

Tears filled Julia's eyes again. She didn't want to spend another night away from home, but going home terrified her, too, since two of the kidnappers were still out there. They hadn't gotten their money, so would they try again? Would she always have to look over her shoulder? Maybe her nightmare wasn't over.

Following along behind Charlotte's parents was easy since they were in Detective John's vehicle. The detective drove with his lights flashing, and another police car followed Vincent as they drove to the hospital, going just a few miles over the speed limit. Charlotte was shivering in the front seat despite the heater blowing directly on her and the heated seat on the highest setting. Vincent reached over and put his hand on her thigh, squeezing it. Charlotte pulled her gloved hands from underneath her coat and grabbed Vincent's hand.

"Saks made a quick call after the news broke," Liv said. "It looked pretty heated from what I could see."

"Probably calling the kidnappers," Charlotte said.

"We'll figure out what's going on once we get to the hospital," Vincent said. "Detective John knows what we suspect—"

"And the transcript!" Charlotte said, turning in her seat to look at her sister. "Vinny and I put the audio recording through our school's transcript software and got some stuff from it. It's all wonky, but the FBI or police department probably have better software. If the school's cheap stuff could get that much…"

"Can we see it?" Eric asked. "Did you send it to Detective John?"

"Shit," Charlotte said. "I didn't get the chance to send it. Hannah came in and interrupted us."

Vincent grinned; at least that was one worry he could cease. "Hannah interrupted, but I emailed John while you were talking to her. Grab my phone and look in my messages. I copied myself."

Charlotte unlocked Vincent's phone and handed it to Eric. "I'm glad you got the chance to email. We can talk to him about it at the hospital after we make sure Julia's okay."

After a few minutes of silence, Liv finally spoke. "I don't know what to think about the transcript. I'm surprised the program was able to pick up anything at all."

"I ran the file through a noise reduction thing first that cuts out ambient noise. It cut out the fan sound of the bathroom enough that the voices were a bit clearer. It may not be enough since nothing picked up is damning."

"Yeah...no kidding. That transcript's hilarious, but there's not a lot there."

"I hope they can do more." Vincent signaled to turn, following the lead of Detective John's vehicle. "The 'naughty uhs' should be enough for them to look into the name 'Nadia' that I know I heard. They should have the resources to check her out if she's related to Saks."

The police car trailing Vincent turned into the hospital parking lot behind him and parked his car. Vincent followed Detective John around to the emergency room entrance, where he parked beside the detective. Liv and Eric got out of the car quickly to follow Mr. and Mrs. Manchester, leaving Vincent and Charlotte behind.

"Oh, God, do you think Julia's here yet?" Charlotte asked as she rested her hand on the door handle.

"Let's go find out," Vincent said. He got out of the car and went to Charlotte's side to let her out.

As Vincent and Charlotte approached the hospital door behind Liv and Eric, Detective John held back and made eye contact with each of them. "I saw the email and forwarded it to my team," he said. "Thank you for sharing that. We'll talk later after we get everything settled and the statements from Julia sorted out."

Vincent and Charlotte nodded as they entered the hospital ahead of the detective.

Rather than bombard Julia with everyone all at once, only her parents were allowed in to see her at first. Everyone else went to a private waiting room. After an hour or more of pacing the room, Vincent and Eric went to the cafeteria to get drinks for everyone and a snack for Liv.

Alone in the elevator with Eric, Vincent sighed. "Everything'll be crazy for a while."

"Yeah. Liv's freaking out. It was bad enough with Julia missing, but with what you heard, it's so much worse."

"I wish I hadn't...I don't want to be the one who blows this whole thing open if it comes to my word against two men. At least Detective John seems to believe me. He stopped Charlotte and me as we were coming in and said that his team was working on the recording and transcript. At least that's something."

Eric leaned against the handrail. "I'm glad you heard and recorded them, even if it didn't turn out the best quality. They shouldn't get away with this. With my baby coming soon, I can't even imagine doing something like that to my kid…or any kid for that matter. It's sick and twisted. I hate it for Liv and her sisters. And their mom—surely she knows nothing about it…"

"I don't think so."

"Yeah, you're right. But there's always been something off about Simon, and I haven't been able to put my finger on it. But not Gina; she's always been so kind to me. I don't think anyone could be that good of an actress so many years after retiring."

"Yeah, but who knew the biggest liar and actor of all would turn out to be the other parent?"

Eric just shook his head as the elevator doors opened, and the sick feeling from the last few days returned to Vincent's stomach as they walked to within smelling distance of the cafeteria.

"All we can do is support Liv and Charlotte to get them through this," Eric said as they approached a coffee cart. "This whole thing will be hard for everyone."

Everyone was right. Vincent dreaded the thought of having to testify against his girlfriend's father. The poorly transcribed recording probably wasn't enough to prove anything without Vincent's corroboration. Even then, there was no guarantee that anyone would believe him over a political candidate if there was no other proof.

After buying coffee, hot chocolate, and snacks, Vincent and Eric headed back upstairs to the private waiting area. Liv was asleep on the one bench seat in the room, her head resting in Charlotte's lap.

"Oh, hot chocolate," Charlotte cooed, taking the cup from Vincent. "You know exactly what to get to warm me up. It's so cold in here."

Realizing that Charlotte's wool jacket was covering Liv, Vincent slipped off his coat and wrapped it around Charlotte's shoulders. Eric sat down on the other side of Liv with his coffee and took out his phone. He swiped through a few text messages while Vincent sat down across from Charlotte.

"My parents keep texting for updates," Eric said. "I don't know what to tell them since we don't know anything either. No one's been back here at all, have they, Charlotte?"

"Hopefully, Mom will check in soon," Charlotte said, stroking Liv's hair. "We haven't heard anything at all—no doctors, nurses, candy stripers, police officers—no one has told us anything."

Vincent's phone buzzed in his back pocket, and he sent off a text message to his mother to let her know that he wouldn't be home for a while. In all the excitement, he hadn't checked in with her all evening, so she didn't know that Julia was safe. Vincent's parents also didn't know what he had overheard or that he'd spoken to the detective without them. Vincent was an adult according to the law, but he felt like a child who just wanted his mom and dad to rescue him and make the whole awful situation go away.

Getting examined, poked, and prodded was so much better than being trapped in that cold basement. Officer French stayed with Julia the whole time the doctor was ensuring her health.

"We can wait for your mom to get here for any other exams," the doctor said to Julia. "But we will need your clothing for any DNA evidence."

Julia's cheeks burned. "I don't need any more exams. I wasn't raped."

Officer French sighed. "I'm glad to hear that, Julia," she said, taking her hand. "The clothing can still be helpful to us. It could contain skin cells from one of the other kidnappers to help us identify them."

"Okay," Julia said. "When will my parents get here?"

"They're on the way now," the officer said. "A nurse is gonna come in to help collect your clothing, and then we'll get you into a room for the night."

"Why do I have to stay here?" Julia asked the doctor.

"You're dehydrated, and I want to keep an eye on that cut on your arm and update your tetanus shot."

Julia looked down at her arm, just then realizing that her right one was bandaged. In all the excitement, she hadn't even noticed that her arm had been stitched up.

She hadn't spoken much to the police officers other than to confirm her identity and point out from which direction she'd come back at the farmhouse. The officers said they'd get her official statement once one or both of her parents arrived. Julia figured this event would probably be enough to pull her father from his campaign circuit for the evening, or at least for a few hours before an inevitable press conference. She just hoped her dad didn't expect her to appear on television so soon.

When her mother walked through the hospital room door, Julia started crying in relief at seeing her again. Mrs. Manchester embraced her daughter and began sobbing loudly. Julia's dad stood at the doorway, talking to one of the doctors.

"Oh, my baby," Mrs. Manchester said. "I'm so glad you're all right...oh, my God, what happened to your arm? Are you okay? What did those awful people do to you?"

"She's going to be fine, Gina," Mr. Manchester said, approaching the other side of the bed. He patted Julia on the head. "The doctors say she's in perfect health save some dehydration and a superficial glass cut on her arm. Everything's going to be okay now."

"Daddy," Julia said, pulling away from her mother to hug her father. "Those people said some awful things about you."

"I'm sure they did, sweetheart. I'm sure they did."

Soon, two officers were in the room. The lady officer, Officer French, who had been with Julia since she'd been at the hospital, and a man named Detective John, who was in charge of the investigation. Julia recounted her story to them, and they began asking questions to clarify.

"You're certain there were three different people?" asked Detective John.

"Yes. Two men and one woman. The woman was a bit shorter than me, and the men were taller, but one was more stocky, and the other one was tall and thin—he was the one who I think would've hurt me if I hadn't ran away when I did. He's the one who licked my face and said terrible things—the one who tried to grab me and fell."

"We've got him," Officer French said. "He's regained consciousness and has a mild head injury and a broken wrist, but he's refusing to speak without a lawyer, and he won't give up his accomplices."

"What are you doing about catching these accomplices?" Julia's father asked.

"Everything we can," said Detective John. "We have officers staking out the old house where Julia was kept. It's about twenty miles outside of town. If they're stupid enough to show back up, we'll get them. I'd imagine they're trying to get in touch with you or the third guy now since you haven't shown up with the ransom."

"Ransom," Julia said. So, it was true.

"Of course," her mother said, smoothing her hair again. "We'd pay anything to get you back."

"What if they come after me again since they didn't get the money?" Julia asked, moving closer to her mother.

"We're not going to let that happen." Detective John said, turning his gaze to Julia's dad. "I assure you; I'll do everything I can to catch the people responsible for this."

After asking the same questions several times over, the detectives excused themselves and left Julia alone with her parents. She was still terrified but glad to be safe at the hospital with the armed officer at her door.

"I need to get Saks and get a press conference called immediately," Mr. Manchester said, heading toward the door. "I'll come back when I'm done unless you'd rather I go home?"

"Go home," Julia said, surprising herself. "Mom's staying, and I don't want Charlotte to be alone at home. When can I see her? Is Liv here too?"

"Charlotte won't be alone," Mrs. Manchester said. "Hannah's there, and a police car is parked out front. And of course, Charlotte is here, Liv too. With Eric and Vincent. Everyone has been worried sick about you." She cut a look at her husband, and Julia could tell an argument was coming.

"Of course, I'll go home with Charlotte once the press conference is over."

"Do you really have to do that tonight?" Mrs. Manchester asked.

"I need to thank the public for their support and let them know that Julia is safe," Mr. Manchester said. "There's no better time than right now!"

"Fine," Mrs. Manchester said, coolly. "I'll see you tomorrow."

"Bye, Dad," Julia said as he left the room. She turned back to her mother. "Can I please see Liv and Charlotte now?"

L iv stirred and sat up as Charlotte finished the last of her hot chocolate. As Liv stretched her arms above her head, their mother walked into the waiting room, looking pale with her eyes bloodshot.

Charlotte jumped up immediately and went to her mother, taking her into her arms. "Mom, is Julia okay?"

"Can we see her now?" Liv asked, squeezing in to put her arms around both of them. "We won't stay long, I promise, if we can just let her know we're here."

"Come with me," Mrs. Manchester said. "Julia's given her statement to the police, and she's resting now, but she's been asking for you both."

Charlotte turned back to Vincent, who was now standing behind her. He reached out grabbed her hand. "I'll wait right here for you."

"Me too," Eric said to Liv.

They followed their mother down the hall, where a uniformed police officer guarded Julia's room. Their father and Mr. Saks were speaking with Detective John at the end of the hallway near the window, the tops of their heads tinged red from the glowing Exit sign overhead. The detective looked away for a moment to make eye contact with Charlotte and gave a slight nod. At that moment, she knew he would do everything he could justice for Julia—but she felt ill about the drama it would cause in her family. How would Julia ever recover once she found out who was behind the whole thing, and could Charlotte bear to keep her mouth shut much longer?

A nurse was adjusting Julia's IV line as Liv and Charlotte walked into her room. "Charlotte! Liv!" Julia burst into tears as her sisters approached her bedside. "I thought I'd never see you again!"

"You're fine now, Jules," Liv cooed. "You're safe."

"That's right," Charlotte echoed. "You're safe now, and we're not letting anyone else hurt you ever again. I promise."

Julia shook her head. "I'm not safe until they catch the other two. They only have one guy, but there are two others. A woman and another man. They caught the meanest one— the one who..."

Charlotte's heart sank. What had this man done to her baby sister? She wasn't sure she wanted to know. "It'll be okay. They'll get him to give up the others. It's only a matter of time."

"He's hurt, though...it's all my fault. I kicked him, and then he fell and hit his head and broke his arm."

"No! It's his fault for kidnapping you! He got what he deserved." Mrs. Manchester stepped around Charlotte and Liv and climbed into the bed, pulling Julia into her arms. "That's enough for tonight, girls. The doctors gave Julia a sedative, and she needs her rest."

"Sure, Mom," Charlotte said, taking a step back. "I love you, Julia. I'll see you tomorrow."

"Bye," Liv said.

"You'll be safe at the house," Mrs. Manchester said, smoothing Julia's messy hair. "Detective John is leaving a police guard in our driveway tonight, and your father will probably come home later. I think he's going to give a press conference here in a few minutes—just him this time. We want to keep Julia away from the cameras for now."

Charlotte looked at Liv. "We'll be fine, Mom," she said, bile rising in her throat.

Out in the hall, Charlotte could barely contain herself. "Safe!" she hissed. "Seriously?"

Liv put her arm around her sister's shoulders and led her back toward the waiting area. "Calm down," she urged. "Mom and Julia don't know anything, and we need to keep quiet until they do."

"I'm trying, Liv. It's so hard!"

"I'm trying, too, but with all these hormones and the transcript stuff, I just want to punch someone in the throat."

"Who, exactly?

"All of them! Everyone involved. Dad, especially—and that creep Saks."

"It's gonna be okay...eventually, right?" Charlotte asked.

They found only Eric waiting in the room. "Where's Vincent?" Charlotte asked.

"John came and got him a couple of minutes ago," Eric said, walking over to Liv. "We need to get you home. You're exhausted."

"I'm not going home yet until Julia's back at home."

"I don't mean our home," Eric said. "Your parents' house again until all this is over."

Vincent walked back in, followed by Detective John. "I have to go to the station to give an official statement before anything else can be done."

"I want to go with you," Charlotte said. "I'm part of this too." She looked at Liv and Eric. "I think we're all involved now."

Detective John closed the door behind him. "It's best that it's just Vincent for now since he's the one who actually heard the conversation."

Vincent handed his keys to Charlotte. "Just take my car, and I'll get a ride back to your house after I give my statement."

Charlotte took the keys and watched her boyfriend leave with Detective John. She'd agreed to go back home, but she didn't have to like it.

Chapter 38
Vincent

By the time they arrived at the police station, Vincent's stomach was cramping. He practiced a few deep breathing exercises before stepping out of Detective John's SUV, and he felt relieved when he noticed his father's car in the parking lot. Despite having assured his parents that he was not in trouble, asking them to meet him at the police station wasn't a typical Wednesday evening phone call. At eighteen, he didn't have to include his parents; he wanted them there. Giving a formal statement against Charlotte's father was the last thing he wanted to do, but he didn't have a choice.

Once inside the station doors, Vincent's parents approached him and Detective John, who ushered them all to an interrogation room in the back.

"Is this necessary?" asked Vincent's father. "What's he done if he's telling us he's not in any trouble and doesn't need a lawyer?"

"Maybe we should call our family attorney," said Vincent's mom. "I'm sure she'd meet us here."

"Mom, Dad, just sit down, and I'll explain everything." Vincent plopped down in the uncomfortable metal chair, the cold seeping through his jeans.

"Mr. and Mrs. Rowlands," Detective John said, pointing to the chairs beside Vincent. "Your son is not in trouble and is legally an adult. Considering his age, though, he asked for you both to be here while he gives an official statement about a crime."

The color drained from Vincent's mother's face, and he reached out to take her hand. "A crime? Vinny...you witnessed a crime?"

"Let's get started," Detective John said, clicking on a recorder in the center of the table. He rattled off the date and his badge number and then turned to Vincent. "State and spell your full name, age, and date of birth for the record, and then we'll get started."

Vincent cleared his throat and let go of his mother's hand. "Vincent Matthew Rowlands. V-I-N-C-E-N-T, M-A-T-T-H-E-W, R-O-W-L-A-N-D-S. Eighteen. November 15, 1997."

"Thank you, now tell me what happened."

"I was visiting my girlfriend, Charlotte Manchester's house Tuesday. I'd been there since school ended to help answer the kidnapping hotline. Anyway, I had to use the restroom, so I went into Charlotte's dad's home office to use the attached one because it was closest..."

Detective John cut in, "To clarify, that's Mr. Simon Manchester's home office, correct?"

"Yes, sir, Simon Manchester's office. Before I could leave the bathroom, I heard Simon and Mr. Byron Saks come into the room. They were arguing, so I didn't want to interrupt them or even let them know I was there. Once I realized they were talking about Julia's kidnapping—and the conversation seemed weird—I started recording them with my phone, but the recording wasn't great because of the background noise of the vent."

"The bathroom vent?"

Vincent's cheeks burned. "Yes, the bathroom vent. I have stomach problems, and with all the nervous energy at the

Manchesters' house with Julia gone, it was bothering me a lot that day. That's why I ducked into his office bathroom so quickly—because I didn't think I could make it upstairs, and the hallway half bath was occupied. Ordinarily, I wouldn't have had a reason to go in Mr. Manchester's office. In fact— I hadn't been in there since Charlotte and I first started dating when Mr. Manchester asked me to come in and talk with him before we left on our date—but anyway, that doesn't matter really."

"It's fine, continue," Detective John said. Mr. Rowlands put his arm around his wife's shoulders, and Vincent realized his mother was crying softly into a tissue.

"Simon and Byron were arguing about the plan, with Simon saying it wasn't going well, that 'they' had jumped the gun."

"And you're certain Simon was speaking with Byron Saks, his campaign manager?"

"Yes. Simon said his name and was asking why did they have to wait two days for instructions. At first, I thought he was just worried, and Saks was reassuring him that Julia would be okay, but then Saks started talking about Simon's campaign ratings being up and that it was good, despite the deviation from their plan.

"At that point, I thought Saks was just being a jerk worrying about campaign numbers at a time like that, but then Mr. Manchester asked Saks to confirm Julia was safe since Saks' people had 'jumped the gun.' Then Saks mentioned that 'they'—meaning the kidnappers, I assume— were out staking it out and saw Julia walking alone and took the opportunity."

Dr. Rowlands gasped and turned toward her son. Behind her, Mr. Rowlands shook his head, his jaw tight. Vincent took a deep breath and continued. "At that point, I turned on the voice memo recording on my phone and stuck the microphone part as close to the crack in the door as I could get it without making any noise. I had to try to get proof. The whole thing just made me feel even sicker.

"Simon talked about how they were supposed to have waited until Christmas break so the press coverage would be better with all the kids out of school and asked again about Julia's safety. Saks made a comment about a woman named Nadia taking care of Julia and just needing some quick money to start over with her boyfriend. He mentioned the boyfriend's former cellmate but didn't mention the boyfriend or cellmate's names. Saks said Julia had food and everything she needed but wasn't staying in a luxury hotel. At that point, Mr. Manchester remarked about Nadia being Saks' cousin and having agreed to her and the boyfriend, but he hadn't known about the other guy. Mr. Manchester argued about the people being criminals and not following Saks' plan, which Saks argued was their plan. They kinda threatened each other at that point on who would go down for it if something went wrong.

"Saks basically told him to wait it out and be ready to answer the phone for the ransom call the next night. They left the room, and I waited to make sure they were gone before I left."

"What happened after that?" Detective John prompted.

"After I waited another five or ten minutes, I went upstairs to find Charlotte. I told her what I heard, and she didn't believe me. I tried to share the recording, but there was so much background noise, I thought it was useless. She kicked me out, so I left the house. That's when I bumped into you, Detective, and told you what I heard."

"How long have you known Charlotte and the Manchester family?"

"Charlotte about two and a half years, and the rest of the family a little less."

"Was Simon Manchester agreeable to you dating his daughter?"

Vincent shrugged, "I guess so since we officially met while we were both volunteering at the children's hospital. Besides the one talk I had with Simon right before my first official date with Charlotte, I can count on one hand the number of conversations I've had with the man."

"And what led to you sending me the transcript?"

"Oh, yeah, the transcript. Charlotte and I talked this afternoon. I went over to her house, and we ran the recording through the transcript software we use for debate club. It took out the background noise and gave us a rough transcript based on the voice patterns. That's what I emailed to you, Detective John, along with the original recording file. We thought you might have access to better software to see what you could do."

"Thank you, Vincent," Detective John said, shutting off the recording. "You'd think we'd have better software here, but we don't. We have a private outside agency taking a look at the files, but their software probably isn't much better than what your private school tuition bought."

"There's something else you need to know. Charlotte told me this afternoon that she'd snooped in her dad's office and found a lot of money hidden in his bottom drawer. This was before the call for ransom came in, and before we got word that Julia had escaped."

"That's interesting. I'll keep that in mind during the investigation."

Mr. Rowlands scooted his chair back and stood. "What does this mean for our son? Will he have to testify? Will this put him in danger?"

"Danger?" echoed Vincent's mother. "We can't expose him to this..."

"Mom, I'm already part of this because of what I heard, and Charlotte and Liv and Eric are involved too because they know. And what about Charlotte finding the money in her dad's desk? He had it ready for the ransom. You need to talk to her about it."

"Vincent, what you've provided is enough for us to do some investigating without having to involve Charlotte right now since that could tip off her parents if they're both involved." Detective John closed the folder in front of him.

"No—there's no way Mrs. Manchester's involved," Vincent said. "She's been out of her mind this whole time."

"I agree," said Dr. Rowlands. "A mother knows these things...Gina was genuinely distraught over Julia's kidnapping. I sat with her and held her while she cried. She's not involved."

"I assure you; we'll get to the bottom of this. Right now, the most important thing is that Julia Manchester is safe."

"But is she safe?" challenged Vincent's mother. "When she's back at home with the man who probably arranged her kidnapping? And my son...his girlfriend...can you guarantee their safety?"

"We're both concerned about our son if word gets out that he's the witness to this mess," Mr. Rowlands said, taking a step toward Detective John. "Why aren't Simon and this Byron guy in custody already? This whole thing's a shitshow, and there are innocent kids mixed up in it."

"I can't discuss this any further tonight," said the detective, turning to face Mr. Rowlands. "But I promise you; I'll do everything I can to protect the innocent in this shitshow."

Detective Ernest John's Notes: 12-9-15

RECOVERED: Julia Marie Manchester.

~~Missing child. Julia Marie Manchester. White female. 13 YO. BR Hair. BR Eyes. Approximately 5'7" tall, 115-125 pounds. Slim build. Last seen in purple sweater, black jeans, grey boots. Black coat. Pink hat. Pink scarf. Carries pink canvas backpack.~~

Julia escaped through a basement window, first injuring one of the kidnappers. No serious physical injuries. No outward signs of deception from the girl during initial questioning. First responding officer reports Julia as "terrified and crying."

Suspected Kidnapper in custody: White male age 25-35. Approx. 5'8" 200 lbs. No ID found. He was unconscious upon officer arrival. Refuses to give name now that he's awake. Waiting on prints confirmation now. Victim suffered concussion and broken collarbone and wrist.

According to Julia, there were three kidnappers total. Petite woman, tall man, shorter man—all white. They wore ski masks, but she could see their skin beside eyes and their hands sometimes.

Vincent Rowlands (18)-boyfriend of Charlotte Manchester. Gave formal statement with both parents present. Interview recorded and awaiting transcription. Observations: Young man showed no signs of deception. I believe him about what he heard. He has no reason to lie as Charlotte's dad was agreeable with their relationship.

Vincent says Charlotte found a handgun and a large amount of money in her father's home office before ransom call came in and is adamant that Gina Manchester is not involved. I still include her on my POI list, but I tend to agree that neither she nor Julia Manchester were involved in the kidnapping plan.

Vincent and Charlotte Manchester emailed a transcript and a voice recording he made with his phone. Both pieces of evidence are difficult to decipher and contain no substantial evidence. Further investigation needed after technician review. We need this evidence processed before we question Byron Saks and Simon Manchester. No known relatives named Nadia for Byron Saks. Interns checking marriage licenses and other records now. Possible hit on a Pearl Nadine Freeman, age 35. Has record for forgery.

Chapter 39
Thursday, December 10
Charlotte

Charlotte awoke to the sound of the security alarm going off, but it quickly stopped. Figuring it was her dad arriving home, she rolled over to get her phone from the nightstand. Noticing the tiny strip of light assaulting her eyes as she glanced at the blackout curtains on her windows, she realized it was morning. Charlotte figured Hannah had disarmed the system to get the newspaper. Either she'd slept through her father coming home last night, or he had gone back to the hospital after his press conference.

A text from Vincent was on her phone's home screen.

I'll get my car tomorrow. My parents are taking me home. Goodnight. I love you.

Charlotte texted back.

I'm sorry. I fell asleep as soon as I got home last night. I love you too. See you later.

He'd be at school already. Charlotte had all her schoolwork for the week and didn't think her teachers would expect her in class. She hadn't completed any assignments so far, and she doubted she could concentrate if she tried with everything going on. Charlotte crawled to the edge of her bed and got her laptop from the desk. She pulled up the transcript of her dad's conversation and read through it again.

Everything was jumbled, but based on Vincent's memory of a woman named Nadia, Charlotte figured all the references to "naughty uh" fit the bill. What the police could do with it was anybody's guess. It was already amazing to her that the school's software could pick up anything at all, considering the quality of the recording.

Charlotte shut the laptop and pulled on her fluffy robe and slippers. She left her room as quietly as possible to avoid waking Liv and Eric and padded down the stairs to the kitchen, the scent of coffee wafting around her. Expecting to find Hannah, Charlotte was surprised to find her father leaning against the kitchen counter with his back to her. He seemed to be deep in thought as he lifted a mug to take a sip.

"Dad," she said, startling him enough to make him spill some coffee. "You just now getting home?" He turned around and set the mug on the counter with a thud.

"Yes," he said. "It was late, so I stayed at the hospital. We held the press conference downstairs in the lobby, so it was convenient, and I think it made Julia feel better that Mom and I were both there with her."

Charlotte studied her father's face. He'd once been her hero, but now all she felt was anger and confusion when she looked at him. "Do the police have any leads?" She might as well test her luck.

"They're working on it. They have one man in custody and are looking for two accomplices based on Julia's statement. The man in custody won't talk, but he's a known criminal. He was out on parole for burglary according to his fingerprints."

"Seems quite ambitious to go from burglary to kidnapping."

"It's hard to understand why criminals do what they do sometimes," her dad said. He walked to the sink and placed his mug into it while he stared out the window into the backyard.

"Is it? Seems to me it's always related to money...or power." At that last word, Charlotte's dad turned around again to face her.

"I forget sometimes how smart you are," he said. "You could have a real future in politics."

"From what I've seen in politics lately, no, thank you." Charlotte crossed her arms and glared at her father. "It just seems like everyone wants to fight with each other and not make any real changes for the better for everyone."

Mr. Manchester sighed. "That's why I want to get into office to change things—to make things better for you and your sisters."

"Maybe things could have been better if you'd been around more instead of always running for office, Dad. A lot of things could be different if you'd been around more, and maybe we wouldn't be going through this now."

"Excuse me," he challenged. "How dare you insinuate that being ambitious in my career is somehow responsible for Julia's kidnapping?"

Charlotte swallowed hard. "That's not what I said, Dad. Why, do you feel responsible?"

"We were already in the public eye before I got into politics because of your mother's career, which she sacrificed to raise you girls. Being well-known and wealthy has its downfalls, but most of the time, the benefits outweigh the risks. Think of how many people this family has helped through our philanthropic activities. Criminals wanting money can sometimes view wealthy families with children as perfect targets."

"So now it's Mom's fault for being famous before?" Charlotte asked. "Are you saying that Julia could have been targeted because of that? It doesn't make any sense. Why wouldn't the criminals just break into our house to steal things to sell for money? This whole scenario doesn't make sense."

"That's not what I said, young lady, and I don't like your tone."

"I don't like that you seem to care more about politics than you do about our family."

"That's preposterous. Everything I do is for our family, and you're acting like a spoiled brat. Now, go upstairs and help Hannah get Julia's room ready. She's getting out of the hospital today, and I want everything perfect for Julia when she gets here."

Charlotte couldn't resist one more dig. "Will you even be here when she gets home, or will you be too busy giving another press conference? Why not just have it in the living room again so you can show your voters what a family man you are in a house where you're rarely home?"

Glaring at his daughter, Mr. Manchester muttered, "Get out of my sight."

Turning to leave the room, Charlotte was able to get halfway up the stairs before her tears came, though they had threatened many times while antagonizing her father. She wasn't completely sure why she'd done that but figured it had something to do with love turning into hatred and respect turning into repulsion. The idea that someone could care more about his career than his own family wasn't surprising to Charlotte, but it was surprising that it was her own father.

T he sedative the doctor had given her helped Julia get the best night's sleep she'd had in days, despite the interruptions for vital checks a couple of times during the night. Each time she woke, Julia would look over at her mother in the recliner, and she instantly felt relaxed again. Sleeping alone in her room at home might be a problem for a while, but at least she'd be warm and safe.

"Mom," she said. "When can we go home?"

Her mother stretched and looked at the clock on the wall in front of Julia's bed. "The doctor's supposed to be here to discuss that soon. You better finish your breakfast."

Julia looked at the rubbery eggs, cement-like oatmeal, and burnt toast on the tray in front of her and closed the cover. "I'd rather not, thank you. I'm not all that hungry."

"You have to eat, especially after what you've been through."

"Mom," Julia groaned. "I was just a little dehydrated last night. They didn't starve me. I had protein bars and even a burger one night."

Mrs. Manchester teared up. "A protein bar is not the same quality as the grilled chicken salad Hannah would have packed for your lunch or the baked tilapia we had planned for Monday night…"

Julia hated to see her mother cry. "Mom, I'm okay, I promise. Everything's going to be fine. I just wanna go home and put this whole thing behind us."

"Of course, sweetheart." Julia's mother got up to hug her daughter just as someone knocked on the door. "Come in."

A different doctor from the one the night before came in, followed by a woman in a suit. "Hi, Julia and Mrs. Manchester. I'm Dr. Katz, taking over for Dr. Williamson from last night. This is my colleague Dr. Cheng." The doctor was a stocky man with a bald head, a full beard, and a friendly smile. Julia couldn't place his accent, but she could understand him well.

The small, Asian woman stepped forward to shake Julia's hand. "Hi, Julia," she said. "You can call me Dr. Beth if you'd like. I'm the child psychologist on staff here at the hospital. Drs. Katz and Williamson want us to visit for a bit before they let you go home. Is that okay with you?"

"Sure, I'm good to talk now," Julia said. Based on her appearance, Julia had expected Dr. Cheng—Dr. Beth—to have a serious tone, but she sounded as enthusiastic as a preschool teacher, and Julia couldn't help but smile back at her.

"Great," said Dr. Beth, pushing her chin-length hair behind her ears. She turned to Mrs. Manchester. "If you'll go with Dr. Katz, Julia and I can visit for a little bit."

"Are you sure, Julia? I can stay." Her mother seemed to be pleading with her, but Julia wanted to talk to Dr. Beth alone.

"I'll be fine, Mom."

Dr. Beth pulled a chair up beside Julia's bed and sat down, crossing her legs. Julia watched her and admired her poise—

she seemed to have the grace of a dancer. Noticing Julia's quiet observation, Dr. Beth smiled at her.

"Hi. How are you feeling this morning?"

"Okay, I guess."

"Now that we have the pleasantries out of the way, we can get down to business."

"So…you have to make sure I'm not crazy?"

Dr. Beth's smile dropped. "No one thinks you're crazy, Julia, but you have been through a traumatic experience. That's enough to make anyone feel a bit unlike themselves, don't you think? I'm just here to help you talk about it."

"No medication, right?"

"I'm not that kind of doctor. I don't write prescriptions; I just listen and help you sort things out in your mind so they can't hurt you anymore. Make sense?"

Julia sighed. "I guess so."

"Tell me about what happened," Dr. Beth urged while giving Julia a smile that didn't quite reach her eyes. "How were you feeling while you were gone versus how you're feeling now?"

"I'm still afraid…"

"Why is that?"

"Because the police have only arrested the one man, and there were two other kidnappers—another man and a woman."

"Tell me about them."

"They were all white, but I couldn't see much of their skin because they always wore masks and gloves around me—not medical stuff, but winter ski masks and gloves. I don't know any of their names. The woman was a bit shorter than me, and she was kinda mean and cynical, but she never touched me. I think she was driving the day the two men grabbed me. One of the men put a cloth over my face, and when I tried to breathe, I blacked out…"

"That must have been frightening for you," said Dr. Beth, nodding as she leaned closer to Julia's hospital bed.

Julia leaned back against the pillow and closed her eyes, trying not to cry. "In that split second before I passed out, I thought they were gonna kill me or rape me. When I woke up later, I was in a cold, dark basement. I could tell by the walls and the high windows. I was locked in and lying on a dirty old mattress that was in the corner. There was a laundry room and a small bathroom that I had access to. That's how I escaped. I managed to climb on top of the dryer and get the screws out of the window so I could climb out— that's when the mean man tried to grab me. I kicked him pretty hard. Then he fell, and I ran."

Dr. Beth nodded and put the end of her pen to her lips. "What happened before that, Julia? Why do you refer to one of the men as 'the mean man,' and what made you decide to attempt your escape last night?"

"He was the man who made me uncomfortable and threatened me. He was disgusting." Julia could feel her face turning red. "He made ugly comments about wanting to show me things and how he wanted to be with a virgin again. I was scared that he would try to hurt me. He licked my face and kissed my cheek before he left. It was right after that when I knew I had to get out of there before something worse happened."

"What about the other two people? You described the woman as mean, but you haven't mentioned the other man."

Julia thought back about her experience. "The one man—I think he was the woman's boyfriend—he was a lot nicer. He brought me clean clothes and stuff that he'd picked up. The woman was just mean about my dad, calling him a criminal and stuff. She brought me food, too, but she didn't seem as nice as the man, if that makes sense. I didn't get the feeling that she or her boyfriend would actually hurt me. They wanted money...or at least she did, and he was going along with it.

"And when I told the woman that I needed supplies since I'd gotten my period, she sent the nice man in the next day with pads, clothing, and stuff to take a shower. He could tell I was afraid of him, so he made a point to tell me that he wasn't gonna hurt me. His friend, though...I think he would have hurt me if I'd stayed longer. That's why I left; I had to. I thought everyone was gone that night, and he surprised me. As scary as he was, I didn't mean to hurt him...do you know if he's gonna be okay?"

"I don't have information about his condition," Dr. Beth said. "But...between you and me...I know that he's not at the university hospital anymore. That means he's been transferred to the prison infirmary most likely."

"Okay, but what about the other two? What if they're not caught?"

Dr. Beth leaned back in her chair. "It's scary to dwell on those things we can't control, isn't it? While we can't control that, we can remember that the police are doing everything they can to catch the kidnappers to prevent them from hurting another child."

Julia took a deep breath, but it didn't make her feel any better. "I just don't understand why anyone could think they could get away with something like this. I mean, does anyone really get away with it?"

"I'd say not many kidnappers get away with kidnapping, asking for ransom, receiving it, and then not getting caught at some point. The fact that you escaped and that one of the men got caught is a good thing. Sooner or later, he'll identify his accomplices, and then the police can go after them. They have to be somewhere and hard up for money. They'll likely make a mistake and get caught."

"That's comforting. I just hope they don't take another kid and try this again."

"That's something you can't control," Dr. Beth said. "What you can control is telling the police every detail you can remember—no matter how small—because any little thing might be what helps them catch the criminals. When you start thinking about what happened to you, just remind yourself that you're safe now and those memories can't hurt you."

"Thanks. I'll try, even though I don't really wanna think about it again."

"You've already proven yourself to be a strong young woman, Julia. With the support of your family, I know you can get through this. I feel comfortable authorizing your release from the hospital today. And I'm only a phone call away if you'd like to talk to me again."

After the psychologist left, Julia's mom came back in, followed by a nurse. The nurse unhooked Julia's IV and told them that Julia was free to leave the hospital. Julia looked down at the hospital gown and realized that she had no clothing to wear other than what she'd escaped wearing.

Mrs. Manchester put her hands over her mouth. "Oh, honey," she said. "I'm so sorry. I didn't stop to grab you any clothes when I ran out of the house after I'd heard you were safe. I should have thought about that. I can call your father and see if he's left yet and get him to bring you something."

The door opened after a quick knock, and Julia's dad walked in. "Bring what?" he asked.

"I forgot to get Julia clothes from the house."

Mr. Manchester held up a reusable grocery bag. "Hannah pulled some things together right before I left," he said. "You should have everything you need. Mr. Saks is waiting downstairs for us. He's going to drive us home since there are reporters camped out front."

"In front of our house?" Julia asked. "Why?"

"No," he said, shaking his head. "They're out in front of the hospital. Young lady, there are a lot of people who were looking for you and are very glad that you're home safe. The least we can do is give a brief statement to thank the police and everyone who helped us."

Her father's statement didn't sit right with Julia. She just wanted to go home and didn't want to talk to any reporters. She supposed she'd have to eventually because of who her parents were, but it didn't have to be right away.

Detective Ernest John's Notes: 12-10-15, Part 1

RECOVERED: Julia Marie Manchester.

~~Missing child. Julia Marie Manchester. White female. 13 YO. BR Hair. BR Eyes. Approximately 5'7" tall, 115-125 pounds. Slim build. Last seen in purple sweater, black jeans, grey boots. Black coat. Pink hat. Pink scarf. Carries pink canvas backpack.~~

Suspected Kidnapper in custody: White male age 25-35. Approx. 5'8" 200 lbs. No ID found. He was unconscious upon officer arrival. Refuses to give name now that he's awake. Waiting on prints confirmation now. —Identified as William Elmer Mulligan, age 31. Out on parole for burglary. Still refuses to talk. Arrested for gun violation.

Known associates and suspects: Possible hit on a Pearl Nadine Freeman, age 35—Could this be Nadia? — Served time for forgery. Records show her as 5'4". Eddie Vaughn Watson, age 40. —Former cellmate of Mulligan. On parole for burglary. Records show him as approx. 6'1".

According to Julia, there were three kidnappers. Petite woman, tall man, shorter man—all white. They wore ski masks, but she could see their skin beside eyes and their hands sometimes. Will show girl photos of suspects and any hand tattoos.

House where Julia was held is owned by Wilma Kitchens, 50. Rented it out to Missy Vera two months ago. DL provided for rental determined to be fake. Renter always paid in cash. Has not missed rent payment.

Stakeout on the house showed no activity. Search of the property found no personal records. Basic food and hygiene items present as well as some clothing.

Forensic team found evidence including fingerprints to indicate that Julia Manchester occupied the basement for several days.

A s she flipped through the TV channels from her bed, Liv was surprised to see the local news stations reporting live from the front entrance to the hospital. As her parents walked out with Julia, her father stopped to talk to the reporters, who all stuck their microphones out to catch a soundbite.

"Thank you all for supporting the search for our daughter, Julia," he said, looking back and forth to make eye contact with the handful of cameras. "We're working with the police to help catch the criminals who did this to keep our great city safe. It's what I've based my whole campaign around, upholding those good old-fashioned American values and safety for our families. I never dreamed I'd have to suffer the heartache of not knowing where my youngest daughter was for the past few days. Thank God she's okay. We'll give a family interview soon, but for now, we ask for privacy so our girl can recover from her traumatic ordeal." He reached out and awkwardly pulled Julia and Mrs. Manchester into his arms. Poor Julia still looked disorientated.

Liv shook her head and turned off the TV as Eric came in with a plate of buttered toast. "I can't believe my father just mentioned his campaign!"

"Are you feeling any better?" Eric asked, setting the plate down on the bed.

Grabbing a piece of toast and shoving it in her mouth, Liv nodded. "Much better now. I'm starving." Though her morning sickness had been better the last couple of days during the distraction of everything happening within her family, it had hit her in full force that morning. "Oh…this is the best toast I've ever eaten."

Eric laughed as he sat beside her. "Careful not to eat it too fast, or it'll be for nothing."

"I'm good now," Liv said, grabbing the second piece. "I never puke again after noon."

Charlotte stuck her head in the room. "You okay now?"

"Fine," Liv said with a mouth full of toast. "Did you see the news?"

"No, what happened?" Charlotte came into the room and plopped down in Liv's desk chair. "More about Julia?"

"Dad was smiling for the cameras and mentioned his campaign, of course."

"Charlotte, have you heard anything from Vincent about the police station?" Eric asked. "I noticed his car was still here."

"No. He just texted that he would get his car today. It was late, and I was already asleep. I'm surprised they didn't want to talk to me last night." She pulled her knees to her chest and wrapped her arms around them. "I said some stuff to Dad this morning. I just couldn't stop myself."

"Charlotte…you didn't," Liv felt her stomach lurch again and took a deep breath to settle it. "He can't know that we know anything. It's not safe."

"I didn't say anything about that. I'm not a total idiot." She leaned her forehead down on her knees. "We shouldn't have to fear our own father. I don't even want to be in the same house with him."

"I don't either," Liv said. "But we have to be here for Julia. She's gonna need us to get through this. Especially once everything comes out."

"If it comes out," Eric said. "We don't know what's going on with the police investigation, and as far as we know, the other two kidnappers are still missing. What if there's not enough proof? What will we do then?"

Liv looked over at her sister. "I guess I'll talk to Mom in that case. For now, I just want to stay here until Julia's settled back in, and then I'll go talk to the detectives."

"Not without me, you're not," Charlotte said, raising her head. "I have to go with you. I'm not letting you go without me when I'm the one who found the money, and my boyfriend was the one who overheard Dad talking in the first place."

"They won't talk to you without a parent; you're still a minor," Liv argued.

"Only for another couple of months. Surely they'd make an exception."

"There's only one way to find out," Eric said. "But I still worry that there's not enough proof."

Charlotte opened her mouth but didn't say anything.

"What is it, Char?" Liv asked.

"I forgot with everything that's happened," Charlotte said. "But I took a photo of the money and the gun before the ransom call came in." She took out her phone and opened a photo, handing it to Liv. "That's proof. It's timestamped and geo-tagged. You can see the rug under Dad's desk."

The photo was damning; there was no question about it. Eric took the phone from Liv and zoomed in on the image.

"Look," he said, turning the phone screen to Liv and Charlotte. The sisters leaned in and focused on the stacks of bills. "At least two or three of these stacks have visible serial numbers, and I'd be willing to bet the police or FBI or someone can trace these."

"That's it," Liv said. "As soon as Julia is settled in, we're all going to the police station." She turned to Charlotte. "Let me know if you hear from Vincent."

Charlotte took back her phone and sent a text. "I asked him to call me ASAP."

Liv looked at the half-piece of toast left on her plate. Despite being ravenous earlier, she'd now lost her appetite.

Chapter 42
Vincent

Concentrating in class was hard enough for Vincent with winter break rapidly approaching, but without Charlotte sitting in the seat next to him, it was even worse. He'd checked the clock at the front of the classroom multiple times while he was supposed to be reading independently. The fifty minutes of class before lunch always seemed like it lasted hours, but that was especially so when they had a substitute teacher. No one wanted to do anything. Finally having had enough, Vincent closed his book and dropped it into his backpack, catching looks from several students around him. He got up and made his way to the front of the classroom.

He leaned down at the desk where the substitute teacher was sitting and spoke softly. "I'm not feeling well, so I'm going to the nurse's office."

"Okay," the young woman whispered. The teacher appeared young enough to be a student at the school. "Feel better soon."

"Thanks," Vincent mumbled as he left. Out in the hallway, he felt slightly guilty for lying, but his heart hurt for his girlfriend—so technically, that counted as not feeling well. He pulled out his phone and noticed a text from Charlotte.

Instead of texting back, he just called her, and she answered right away. "Hey."

"Are you okay? How's Julia?"

"Dad just held a press conference in front of the hospital, but at least Julia didn't have to say anything. She looked so small and scared. She's coming home. Wait, shouldn't you be in class right now?"

"I couldn't concentrate, and we had a sub anyway. I'm supposed to be on my way to the nurse's office to see if she'll let me check out, but I just remembered that you have my car."

"Are you feeling sick today?"

"No, I'm feeling fine physically. It's everything else that's crazy. I wanted to talk to you about what happened last night, but I don't want to do it over the phone."

"I would come to get you right now, but Julia's on her way home...I don't want to miss her, but I don't want to leave you stranded either. Your parents are at work, aren't they?"

Vincent should have thought through the logistics of his situation last night and insisted that his parents take him to get his car, but that didn't help him now. "I don't even know if the nurse will let me leave, and the office will still want my mom or dad's permission over the phone."

"Hey, I have an idea. Give me a sec."

While he waited, Vincent continued to make his way toward the nurse's office. She knew about his condition, so convincing her to let him leave shouldn't be a problem. He was ready to use his emergency credit card to pay for a ride to Charlotte's house if necessary.

"I'm back," Charlotte said. "Eric's here, and he says he'll come get you."

"That's awesome," Vincent said. "I'll probably be ready in fifteen. I'll call Eric if something changes."

As Vincent had expected, the nurse was easy to convince to let him go home. His mother might have been a different story since she already worried so much about his condition. Knowing this, he chose to call his father, who was fine with letting him leave with Eric since he couldn't have left work so soon without causing some issues. Despite Vincent being eighteen, the school had a strict policy about enrolled students leaving without parental permission.

By the time Vincent had checked out and sent a quick text to LaShawn, who would've been his ride to Charlotte's house later, Eric was waiting in front of the school.

"Thanks, man," Vincent said as he climbed into the front seat. "I just couldn't stay there any longer with everything that's going on."

"I understand." Eric pulled out as soon as Vincent had fastened his seat belt and thrown his backpack into the back seat. "There's no way I could've concentrated on work this week. I'm glad I had some vacation time to use. Do you usually work somewhere after school?"

"No. My parents won't let me. They want me to keep my grades up during the school year, so they'll only let me work during the summer since I volunteer so much at the hospital. I worked at the Boys and Girls Club last summer, and I'll probably go back there one more year before college."

"Figured you'd get a wrestling scholarship. Liv tells me you're pretty good."

Vincent was better than good; he was a state champion three years running. But there was always someone better, according to his father. Vincent wasn't allowed to focus on sports alone. His dad said that athletics were pointless if you weren't strengthening your mind and your character at the same time. That's why he'd chosen debate club—to get his father off his back. It's also when his life had changed for the better after meeting Charlotte.

"I can't count on wrestling, and I want to have options."

Eric chuckled as he turned onto the Manchester's street. "Meaning you want the option to go wherever Charlotte wants to go?"

"Busted. We've applied to several of the same places and other places that are close together." Of course, with the Manchester family drama—or trauma—Vincent doubted Charlotte was thinking about college at all right now.

"Well, we have that in common. We're both hopelessly in love with Manchester women."

"Yep."

"They're gonna need us a lot now as everything unfolds with the investigation."

Vincent figured it would come up sooner or later. "Yeah...the police statement was pretty intense last night. They're trying to get enough evidence without involving Charlotte, but I don't know if that's possible."

"Probably not," Eric said. "Charlotte showed a picture she took to Olivia and me earlier. She's planning to send it to Detective John. It's proof that her father had money in his desk before the ransom call came in. With that and what you heard, it's probably enough to bring him in for questioning, at least. It worries me that he's got a gun in his desk too."

Vincent's heart sped up. "But then what? Will he figure out that I'm the one who turned him in and make things harder for Charlotte?"

"Harder than having his daughter kidnapped? There's no way to make this easy for any of them. I'm just trying to keep Liv calm so it doesn't affect the baby. I'm sure you're worried about Charlotte's health too. Liv's told me about her condition and yours. I guess you get that since you have it too."

"I do," Vincent said as they passed the police car parked on the street and pulled into the driveway beside Vincent's car. "I'm worried about Charlotte and worried about how Julia's gonna handle all this. She's just a kid. No kid should have to deal with this."

As Vincent and Eric got out and started toward the front door, a black sedan pulled up with Saks behind the wheel and Mr. Manchester in the front seat beside him.

Eric turned to Vincent. "It's probably best if none of us say anything to Julia right now about what we know."

"Agreed." Vincent met Mr. Manchester's gaze and immediately felt uncomfortable. It hadn't even been twenty-four hours yet since he'd given his statement to the police.

S he never thought the sight of a house would make her tear up, but that's what happened as Julia arrived in the driveway to her home. There had been many moments over the last several days when she'd wondered if she'd ever get to go home again. She'd worried that the kidnappers might hurt her or even kill her before she'd be found. Now, the healing would start as Dr. Beth had said, but there were a lot of mixed emotions. She'd been taken in broad daylight right outside the driveway gate.

As soon as the car was parked, the front door burst open. Charlotte came running out, followed by Liv. It was then that Julia noticed Eric and Vincent standing in the driveway as well. Soon, Hannah was outside the door too. Everyone was there to welcome Julia home, and it felt a bit overwhelming. More tears threatened to break through, but Julia held them back as she got out of the car, closely guarded by her mother.

Charlotte and Liv were in front of her first, and Julia felt safe, falling into the arms of her older sisters. All three were crying by then.

"We're so glad you're home safe," Charlotte said.

"We've missed you so much," Liv said.

"I missed you both too," Julia said. "Now, let's get inside since it's freezing out here. I hope someone built a fire. I haven't felt warm in days."

"We'll make sure of that," her mother said, turning toward Eric and Vincent. "Boys, please build a fire in the living room for Julia. There's dry wood in the storage shed in the back."

"Right away," Eric said. He and Vincent went through the garage to get to the backyard.

Julia let herself be led into the house, where Charlotte and Liv plopped down beside her on the sofa and wrapped her in a fleece blanket. She felt like a guest in her own home, uncomfortable with everyone staring at her. Well, almost everyone. Julia's dad and Mr. Saks were still outside chatting; she could see them through the window, having what appeared to be a heated conversation.

"I think hot chocolate's just what the doctor ordered," said Hannah as she scurried off toward the kitchen. Julia didn't want anything, but she didn't want to hurt Hannah's feelings by refusing a drink. Hannah thrived on taking care of Julia and her sisters since Hannah's four children were adults.

Eric and Vincent came inside with their arms full of wood and got to work on the fire. Julia watched them in silence, mesmerized by the simple act of people caring enough about her to start a fire. Within minutes, it was going and had heated the living room nicely. The room looked even more formal with the fireplace lit and several flower arrangements and potted plants lining the walls and adorning any available table surface.

"What's with all the flowers?" Julia asked, knowing they were likely in response to her situation.

"Everyone's been so happy to hear that you're safe; they've been sending all sorts of things," Charlotte said. "All the neighbors, the parents of the kids we've sat for, the school, your dance teachers, your friends' parents."

"How thoughtful," their mother said. "I need to send them all notes. I hope you've saved the cards."

"We haven't touched the cards," Liv said. "We weren't sure if Julia would want to read them or not."

"I guess so," she said. Flowers seemed more appropriate for a serious illness or death in the family, not a kidnapping, but Julia wasn't sure of the protocol for showing thought to someone who'd been kidnapped. "But not right now. I just want to rest in my own bed. I'm still so tired from all the excitement." She stood up with the blanket still wrapped around her shoulders as Hannah came back with hot chocolate.

"Here you go, dear," Hannah said, handing a mug to Julia. "I put it in a travel cup to make it easier to drink."

"That's perfect," Julia said. "I'll take it with me." She turned to Eric and Vincent, who'd settled in on the love seat across the room. "I'm sorry you went to all the trouble for the fire. I'm more tired than I thought."

"It's no problem," Eric said.

At the same time, Vincent said, "Don't worry about it."

"Are you sure you want to be alone?" Charlotte asked. "I don't mind going up with you."

"It's okay," Julia said. "I'll feel more like myself after a nap, I'm sure." She left the room and everyone behind. Once out of sight, she took a deep breath, trying to slow her pounding heart. By the time she reached her room, having taken the stairs two at a time, her skin felt clammy, and she thought she might pass out. She closed her door and stumbled to her bed. After drawing the covers up to her chin and curling up in a fetal position, Julia started counting the ticking of the seconds on the pretty analog clock hanging on her wall. As always, the sound was comforting, like the metronome her favorite ballet teacher used to help with rhythm during class.

Having lost count of the clock's ticks somewhere in the early thousands, Julia could feel herself drifting off to sleep.

As soon as Julia was gone, Mrs. Manchester and Hannah went to the kitchen, leaving everyone else in the living room. Charlotte looked out the window and watched her father as he spoke with Mr. Saks. They were having an argument of some sort. She hoped it would be one that would result in the arrest of both of them. She could barely stand to look at her father, and that sat in her gut like a rock filled with lava. Vincent moved from the loveseat to the couch to sit beside Charlotte. She leaned in and let him wrap his arm around her shoulder.

"How did it go last night?" She asked, barely speaking above a whisper.

Vincent spoke softly back and told them about the questions the detective had asked. Eric moved over and stood near the coffee table so he could hear the quiet conversation.

"Did they give you any indication of what the next steps were?" Liv asked.

"And do they want to talk to me?" Charlotte added.

Vincent sighed. "They're gonna try to investigate without involving you, for now, Charlotte, but they may end up wanting to talk to you later. Right now, I've provided them with the most damning evidence if they can properly decipher the recording."

"I guess it would help if the guy they caught would talk," Eric said, glancing out the window. "Since he didn't get any money, I wonder what kind of deal the police might offer to the guy to give up his buddies."

"They couldn't talk about that, but I don't know." Vincent jumped as the front door slammed, which startled Charlotte in the process.

Mr. Manchester walked into the room and looked around. "Why's it so quiet in here?" he asked. "Where's Julia? Shouldn't we be celebrating?"

"Julia went upstairs to take a nap, Dad," Charlotte said. "We're being quiet to not disturb her."

"Apparently, being kidnapped is a 'traumatic ordeal' as you've already said in your press conference," Liv said. "You and Saks seemed to be having quite the conversation outside. What's that all about?"

Charlotte watched her father's reaction, which was subtle—his lips forming a tight line before he shoved his hands into his jacket pockets. "Just campaign stuff," he said. "My numbers are good right now. It's looking like I have a real shot in the primaries coming up."

"I think we're more concerned that Julia's home safe," Charlotte said as her dad's back stiffened. "We're anxious for the police to catch whoever's responsible."

"How can you think I don't care that Julia's home safe?" her father countered.

"All you seem to do is smile for the cameras and give press conferences!" Charlotte couldn't help but raise her voice until the doorbell ringing startled her.

Everyone looked around until Eric spoke up. "I'll get the door," he said to everyone as they all watched him walk toward the entryway.

Glancing out the window, Charlotte saw that Mr. Saks was still in the driveway looking toward the house while talking to a uniformed police officer. Parked beside his car was Detective John's vehicle. Charlotte turned back to her father, who was now glaring at her.

"I've been talking to reporters and giving statements begging for her safe return since this whole thing happened," he said. "Being part of the public eye and politics has its perks, but it's also a huge responsibility. It's not just my family I have to answer to; it's the voters."

Charlotte suppressed an angry chuckle. "What good are the voters if you have to sell your soul to get them?" She got up and left the room, leaving her father standing there with his mouth gaped open. For once, she'd left the trained public speaker speechless.

In the entryway, she found that Eric had let in Detective John. Charlotte made brief eye contact with the man before taking the stairs two at a time to get up to her room.

Chapter 45
Liv

Still red-faced from his heated conversation with Charlotte, Liv's father paled when Detective John stepped into the living room, followed by Eric. "Detective," he said. "What brings you here?"

"We have some developments, Mr. Manchester," Detective John said. "We need to speak with you and Byron Saks down at the station."

"What's this about?" Mr. Manchester asked. "Have you identified associates of the man arrested? What does this have to do with Byron or me?"

Liv watched her father closely—his usual composure was just a bit off. It was subtle, but she'd known him long enough that she could see the slight pulsing in his neck that usually happened when he was upset. Liv had seen that tell many times during arguments with her father when she was a teenager. Simon Manchester had a great poker face, but his body language always betrayed him if one knew where to look. She met Eric's eyes, which were wide and frightened as he stood behind the detective.

"Sir," said the detective. "We have identified the man in custody and his known associates, one of whom might have a connection to your campaign. It would be best if you came down to the station to answer a few questions so we can get to the bottom of this."

"Get to the bottom of what, exactly?" asked Mrs. Manchester as she came back into the room and stepped beside her husband. "What's going on?"

Liv watched as her mother looked back and forth between the detective and her husband.

"Good afternoon, Mrs. Manchester," Detective John said, extending his hand for a shake. She took his hand and didn't let go. "I'm terribly sorry to disturb you all on what must be a whirlwind of a day with Julia coming home. But, as I was telling your husband, we've identified the man in custody, and one of his known associates—who I assure you we're searching for right now—has ties to someone within the Manchester presidential campaign. I've asked Byron Saks and your husband to accompany us to the station so we can get to the bottom of this."

Mrs. Manchester stumbled backward and pulled her hand from Detective John's grip, placing it against her throat. "Oh...well...do I need to go too, or...Simon, do I need to call our attorney?"

Liv stood up to go to her mother's side since her father didn't seem to care that his wife might pass out on the floor. She took her mother's arm and steadied her.

"I don't think that's necessary, Gina," said Mr. Manchester, looking at Detective John. "It's just basic questioning, right, detective?"

"I asked two questions, Simon," she said. "Are you answering both?"

Detective John interrupted. "I just need Simon and Byron for now," he said. "I'm sure you want to be nearby for your daughter today. If I have any questions for you, I'll let you know. Per our regulations, an attorney is always welcome for questioning."

"Well, then, I will meet you at the station," Mr. Manchester said. Liv watched as he gave her mother a quick, close-mouthed kiss on the lips. "I should be home in time for dinner."

"Make sure of it," Mrs. Manchester said. "It's the first night with Julia back in our home, and I want us all to eat together tonight."

Liv took her mother's hand. "Everything will be fine, Mom," she said. She looked at Detective John and wondered how much evidence he'd uncovered.

Detective Ernest John's Notes: 12-10-15, Part 2

RECOVERED: Julia Marie Manchester.

~~Missing child. Julia Marie Manchester. White female. 13 YO. BR Hair. BR Eyes. Approximately 5'7" tall, 115-125 pounds. Slim build. Last seen in purple sweater, black jeans, grey boots. Black coat. Pink hat. Pink scarf. Carries pink canvas backpack.~~

Suspected Kidnapper in custody: William Elmer Mulligan, age 31.

Known associates and suspects: Pearl Nadine Freeman, age 35—
Eddie Vaughn Watson, age 40.

Wilma Kitchens, 50, came in for questioning and brought copy of DL from Missy Vera. Fake DL entirely, but a high-quality one. Comparing the photo to Freeman's mugshot leads us to believe this is the same person. Freeman served time for DL forgery.

Parole officers will make unscheduled visits to LKAs of Freeman and Watson. Will bring them in for questioning about Mulligan and false DL/Rental information.

No activity at rent house. Stakeout ends tonight.

Will question Byron Saks and Simon Manchester today. Transcripts to follow.

Transcript of interview with Byron Saks, Thursday, December 10, 2015

Detective Earnest John: Good afternoon. Thank you for coming in. Please state your name for the record.

Byron Saks: Byron James Saks.

John: How long have you known and worked for Simon Manchester?

Saks: I've known Simon for about two years, I guess. He hired me July 1 of this year to be his campaign manager.

John: And how did you hear about the job opening?

Saks: Mutual friends. It just went around the circles that he was looking for someone with experience in winning campaigns, and I'd known Simon from some of the charity circles my other clients have frequented. It all just fell into place.

John: Do you know a woman by the name of Wilma Kitchens?

Saks: No. I don't think so. Should I?

John: What about William Mulligan?

Saks: Doesn't ring any bells.

John: Mulligan is in custody on suspected kidnapping charges in the abduction of Julia Manchester. Mulligan is a known associate of Eddie Watson.

Saks: Eddie Watson—now him I know of. He got my cousin mixed up with some forgery business a few years back.

John: This cousin would be Pearl Nadine Freeman?

Saks: Yeah, that's Nadia to family. Last I heard, she'd dumped him. She did her time and has been doing well last I heard.

John: Last you heard? And when was that?

Saks: (inaudible)

John: What's that?

Saks: I'm wracking my brain. I guess I haven't seen her since—It was before her trial five, no six years ago. I gave her some legal help.

John: Are you a licensed attorney?

Saks: No. No—nothing like that. I paid for an attorney for her.

John: Are you and Nadia close?

Saks: My widowed aunt to whom I've always been close has been on her own since Nadia was a toddler. I was helping out family.

John: Family you haven't seen for five or six years? When's the last time you've spoken to Nadia?

Saks: I've already told you I haven't seen her in six years.

John: We have these amazing inventions called phones that allow us to speak to people without seeing them—and sometimes we can see them with video chat. Have you talked to Nadia on the phone recently?

Saks: Not that I recall. I speak to my aunt Martha on a regular basis, and she tells me Nadia is doing well.

John: But you haven't checked up on Nadia yourself?

Saks: Detective, I'm in the political circle. I had to distance myself from Nadia after she got mixed up with Watson. I'm sure you understand. It's not just my reputation, but the reputations of my clients I have to consider.

John: Will you let us know if Nadia attempts to contact you?

Saks: I don't know what you're implying, detective, but if Nadia is involved in this, I assure you that I am not. Why would I get mixed up in a kidnapping? That's absurd.
John: Mr. Saks, I wasn't accusing you of being involved. I merely asked you to let me know if Nadia attempts to contact you. She's a person of interest in this case, and her parole officer has been unable to make contact with her.
Saks: Of course.

Transcript of interview with Simon Manchester, Thursday, December 10, 2015

Detective Earnest John: *Good afternoon. Thank you for coming in. Please state your name for the record.*

Simon Manchester: *Simon Wells Manchester.*

John: *How long have you known and worked with Byron Saks?*

Manchester: *A couple of years. I hired him about six months ago.*

John: *And how did he hear about the job opening?*

Manchester: *You'd have to ask him from whom he heard it. We have many mutual business contacts, so I suppose he heard about it from one of them. I told several people I was looking for someone with experience on a winning campaign.*

John: *Do you know a Wilma Kitchens?*

Manchester: *No.*

John: *What about William Mulligan?*

Manchester: *No.*

John: *Mulligan is in the man we have in custody on suspected kidnapping charges in the abduction of your daughter. Mulligan is a known associate of Eddie Watson and Pearl Nadine Freeman, who also goes by Nadia.*

Manchester: *I don't know any of those people.*

John: *You sure you don't know Pearl Nadine Freeman? What about a Missy Vera?*

Manchester: *I don't recall ever meeting a Nadia Freeman or a Missy Vera. If I did, I sure don't remember. Why?*

John: *Pearl Nadine Freeman is related to Byron Saks. She's his cousin.*

Manchester: *Did she have something to do with this?*
John: *We're still trying to figure that out. The house from which Julia escaped and where we apprehended Mulligan is owned by Wilma Kitchens. Wilma is just a sweet lady who rented out her house to a lady named Missy Vera. We've determined that Vera was an alias used by Nadia Freeman. The driver's license had a photo of Freeman, but the rest of the information was fake. Freeman's served time for forgery.*
Manchester: *Does Byron know about this?*
John: *You'd need to ask Byron what Byron knows. I'm asking what you know.*
Manchester: *[Expletive] (inaudible)*
John: *We have Mulligan in custody, but he's not talking. Yet. But that doesn't matter too much because we found a gun on him, which violates his parole. He's known to run in the same circles as Eddie Watson and Nadia Freeman. Julia described three kidnappers. Freeman happens to be Byron's cousin and used a fake ID to rent a house two months ago where Julia was held after her kidnapping. Parole officers can't locate Freeman or Watson right now. These seem to be pretty big coincidences. It's only a matter of time before the crime scene processing comes back with DNA evidence to confirm that Julia was in that house. We're cross-referencing other DNA samples with those of Freeman and Watson. If we get positive hits, it supports our theory that the two are involved. With Freeman being Saks' cousin, I wouldn't trust that his nose is clean in all this.*
Manchester: *I don't like what you're implying. Are you saying my campaign manager might know something about this?*

John: *I'm saying, keep your friends close and your enemies closer. Sometimes it's hard to distinguish between the two.*

Manchester: *Understood. And what is your department doing about all this? Julia's home safely, and you have a man in custody, so do you count that as a win and move on?*

John: *Oh, there's no winning in the case of child abduction and abuse, Mr. Manchester. There's justice. And I assure you that I won't rest until all the guilty parties are behind bars.*

Manchester: *And my family thanks you for that.*

John: *Oh, Simon, one more thing before I turn you loose for the evening so you can spend time with your family.*

Manchester: *What's that?*

John: *When did you secure the ransom money from your bank?*

Manchester: *After the kidnappers demanded ransom.*

John: *And have you re-secured that money?*

Manchester: *Of course. That's a ridiculous question. No one would leave that kind of money just lying around.*

John: *Just checking. The media's had a field day with this, and having that kind of money—say locked in a desk drawer or something—at your house might leave your family vulnerable to burglary.*

Manchester: *Private security starts tomorrow to ensure my family's safety, Detective John. I know you and your officers have other cases to solve.*

John: *I'm glad to hear that since one of the suspects at large has a background in burglary and breaking and entering.*

Manchester: *I appreciate your concern.*

Chapter 46
Julia

When Julia woke up, she was back in the cold, dark basement. The mattress sagged beside her with the weight of the tall man. As the man grabbed Julia's arms, she screamed at the top of her lungs and closed her eyes. Fearing for her life, she began to fight him off with violent punches and kicks. A blast of cold water hit her face, and the shock of it forced her eyes open. She was safe in her bed, with her mom holding her arms. Charlotte was standing there, too, holding an empty glass that had been on Julia's nightstand. Julia took a deep breath and tried to get her wits about her, shaking the water from her face.

"Julia," her mother said, loosening her grip on Julia's arms. "You were screaming, and we couldn't wake you. Are you okay?"

"I think so," Julia said. She turned to Charlotte, who was hugging the empty glass against her chest as if it weighed a ton.

Charlotte put the glass back on the nightstand and grabbed a sweatshirt from Julia's desk chair, handing it to her sister. "I'm so sorry," she said. "It was the only way I could think of to wake you up."

Julia took the shirt, wiped her face, and tried to soak up the water from her bed. "It's okay; it was just a nightmare, and I'm fine now."

Charlotte and her mother exchanged a look, which irritated Julia. All she wanted was to put this whole thing behind her. She could be fine; she had to be okay.

"Well," said her mother. "I'm going to let you get changed out of your wet clothes. Come downstairs when you're done. Hannah's cooking up something special tonight just for you—your favorite, grilled chicken fajitas."

"That sounds good, Mom."

Charlotte stuck around a little longer after their mother left. "I'm here for you, Jules," she said. "Anything you need at all, just let me know."

The first thing that came to Julia's mind was the school dance. She wanted to think about something other than her kidnapping. "I really wanna borrow your red dress, the one you wore to the Valentine's dance. The winter formal is next week, and Josiah and I were talking about going together. If Mom and Dad will let me go."

"Um…yeah…sure," Charlotte said, staring at Julia. "We might have to pin the waist to make it fit you, but I don't plan to wear it again anyway. Maybe Hannah can help us take it in if Mom lets you out of her sight long enough to go to the dance."

"I'd be willing to ask her to chaperone the dance if I could just go with Josiah. Will you help me convince her?"

Charlotte chuckled. "Sure," she said. "I'll try…though I think I would have died of embarrassment if she'd chaperoned any of my dances when I was your age."

"It'll be fine," Julia said, pulling her wet sweater off her head. Her undershirt just had a few spots of water on it—not enough to bother with changing it. She walked over to her dresser, got out her favorite school hoodie, and pulled it over her head. "I'm gonna run to the bathroom, and then I'll come downstairs."

"Okay." Charlotte left the room, closing the door behind her.

Once her sister was gone, Julia slipped into her bathroom, taking the wet sweatshirt with her to toss into the hamper. She locked the door—something she never did before in her own bathroom—and sat down. She leaned against the door and pulled her knees to her chest. A few tears later, she felt ready to get up and face her family.

She got up and went to her sink to wash her face. Once she'd scrubbed away the tear streaks, she pulled out her pressed powder to combat the redness the scrubbing had left behind. On a whim, she pulled out her stage makeup kit, gave her eyes a quick sweep of shadow, and dusted her cheeks with blush. A touch of light brown mascara and she was presentable. Julia didn't usually wear much makeup outside of dance recitals and competitions, but she doubted her mother would complain about it given the circumstances she'd been through. Julia figured she could just about get anything she wanted if she only asked. So maybe she didn't need her big sister to intervene about the dance. An evening with Josiah and her other friends just dancing and snacking was just what she needed away from all the press conferences, police officers, doctors, and kidnappers.

Chapter 47
Vincent

Standing in Charlotte's doorway made him feel helpless, but what else could he do? Running into Julia's room behind Charlotte wouldn't have been a good idea with all that Julia had experienced. She was probably embarrassed about her nightmare and wouldn't want more of an audience than she had already.

Mrs. Manchester came out first and gave Vincent a small smile before turning and heading for the staircase. After a few minutes, Charlotte came out and closed Julia's door behind her. She walked over to Vincent and leaned her head against his chest. "I just wish I could take it all away from her," she mumbled.

Vincent wrapped his arms around Charlotte and kissed the top of her head. "All you can do is be there for her," he said. "And I'll be here for you."

She raised her head and kissed him on the lips. "What did I ever do to deserve you?"

"Right back at you."

"Can you stay for dinner?"

Vincent pulled his phone from his pocket and sent a group text to his parents. "Sure. Whatever Hannah's cooking smells amazing. A lot better than the leftovers in my fridge at home."

The sound of the front door slamming startled them both. "What the hell?" Charlotte said, pulling away and starting for the stairs.

From below, Mr. Manchester yelled for his wife. "Gina! You're not going to believe that bastard John. I want him off the case...or better yet, I want him fired completely."

Charlotte stopped on the top stair and waited, and Vincent stood beside her.

"Simon!" Mrs. Manchester said. "Lower your voice. We still have guests in this house!"

"Guests! What guests?" he bellowed. "It's all family here. Hannah's been with us for years, and the two guys sleeping with our daughters might as well be considered family at this point!"

Vincent gulped back the bile that had risen in his throat. Charlotte raised her eyebrows and opened her mouth when she turned to Vincent and grabbed his hand. "Did you tell your parents?" he mouthed. Charlotte shook her head and mouthed back, "No!"

"What the hell has gotten into you?" Mrs. Manchester asked her husband.

"You wanna know what the hell has gotten into me? That no-good excuse for a detective implied that Byron set up Julia's kidnapping—that's what! Can you believe the nerve of that guy? I'll have his badge, I tell you. He'll never work in law enforcement again!"

"Holy shit," Vincent whispered as he backed away from the top of the stairs. He stood against the hallway wall and put his head in his hands. Soon, Charlotte was in front of him, rubbing his arms. When he raised his head to look at her, he saw that Julia was now standing in her doorway. From the paleness of her face, Vincent was sure that she'd heard the exchange happening downstairs. Vincent turned Charlotte around to face her sister, and she rushed to Julia.

"Let's slow down here," Mrs. Manchester said. From the closeness of her voice, it was evident to Vincent that the couple had moved to the downstairs hallway, which was directly below the open landing near the staircase. Their tense voices carried and filled the space above them. "Why would Detective John say something like that?"

"He seems to think that having a criminal in your family makes you guilty," Mr. Manchester said. "The guy in custody has a couple of associates, and the woman is Byron's distant cousin, whom he hasn't even seen in years—some Nadia character."

Vincent took a deep breath and avoided looking at Charlotte, who was still standing near Julia a few steps away. He stared at the girls' socked feet.

"Wow," Mrs. Manchester said. "I'll admit that it's a strange coincidence. Nadia probably kept up with Byron and came up with the idea because of who we are. We've been in the news a lot lately."

"Oh, so you're blaming me for this!" Mr. Manchester said. "You've had press in the past too! It's not just my fault for trying to run for president and make this country better."

"That's not what I said! Watch your tone with me, Simon. I'm on your side here, but we've got to let the police do their jobs to figure out who's responsible for this. If his cousin is involved, I'm sure Byron can prove that he wasn't. It's only a matter of time. Now, have they questioned her yet?"

"No, they haven't. Get this; they can't even find this woman!"

"Then they don't have any proof at all that she was involved," Mrs. Manchester said. "Just because she was associated with the one in custody at one point doesn't mean she did anything wrong this time. Especially if there's nothing tying her to the case."

There was a long pause, and Vincent worried that the Manchesters had figured out they were being overheard.

"Simon…is there evidence that ties Nadia to the case?" asked Mrs. Manchester, breaking the silence to Vincent's relief.

"Nothing conclusive," Mr. Manchester said. "I'm sorry. You're right. I shouldn't get so worked up about this. I'm just so angry."

"I'm angry too, Simon. Someone hurt our family, and I want justice. We just have to stay calm and wait this out. Let's go get some dinner."

"I have a quick phone call to make, and then I'll be in," Mr. Manchester said. Vincent heard him walk away and close the door to his den.

"Charlotte, Julia, come downstairs for dinner!" called Mrs. Manchester.

Vincent looked at Charlotte, who seemed to be holding Julia up. "Be right down, Mom!" Charlotte called. "Julia, are you okay?"

"Have they been fighting like that the whole time I was gone?" she asked.

"No. No, not at all," Charlotte said. "They've both been so worried about you; I think it all just came out just then. I haven't heard them argue even once since you were gone. Everything's gonna be okay."

Julia shook her head and turned back toward her bedroom. "Just tell Mom that I don't feel like eating right now."

"Are you sure?" Charlotte asked her.

"The pain meds I took for my arm are upsetting my stomach. I'll eat later." Julia pulled away and closed her door.

Vincent remained in his spot, watching Charlotte. "Maybe it's best if I eat those leftovers in my fridge after all," he said.

"Yeah," Charlotte said, walking over to him. She lowered her voice. "With the recording you have—if they can use it, and your memory of a woman named Nadia, it's probably enough evidence to convict my dad, too, if they can catch her."

"I wish I'd never heard," Vincent said.

Charlotte's eyes filled with tears that she quickly wiped away. "Don't say that," she whispered. "The truth will come out, and I needed some time to prepare."

Vincent kissed her quickly on the lips. "I'm so sorry," he said. "I love you, and I'll call you later, okay?" Charlotte nodded and then started down the stairs. Vincent followed and kissed her once more before heading outside to his car. His gut burned with anger toward Simon Manchester.

Transcript of interview with William Mulligan, Thursday, December 10, 2015
Questioned in presence of public defender Reynard Satchel.

Detective Earnest John: Good evening. Thank you for agreeing to speak with me. Please state your name for the record.

William Mulligan: *William.*

Reynard Satchel: Full name please, William.

Mulligan: William Elmer Mulligan.

John: Thank you. Mr. Mulligan, do you know a woman by the name of Wilma Kitchens?

Mulligan: Never heard of her.

John: We picked you up in Kitchens' home.

Mulligan: I don't know nothing 'bout that.

John: Do you know a Missy Vera?

Mulligan: Nope.

John: Well, what do you know about?

Satchel: Please stick with specific questions that aren't so open for interpretation, Detective John. William, don't answer that question.

John: My apologies. Mr. Mulligan, do you recall how you came to be in the basement of the home on Woodward Drive yesterday evening?

Mulligan: Can I answer that?

Satchel: Yes, you may give your statement now.

Mulligan: I was crashing with my friends Nadia and Eddie. They left to go run some errands in town, and I heard this crashing noise in the basement. I went downstairs to check it out, and I catch this kid breaking in. So I tried to stop her and lost my balance before I hit my head and blacked out.

John: Okay, so you were staying with your friends, Nadia Freeman and Eddie Watson, right?

Mulligan: Yeah, that's them.

John: And you tried to be a hero by stopping a burglar?

Satchel: My client's already answered that question.

John: Describe this burglar, Mr. Mulligan.

Mulligan: It happened so fast that I barely saw her.

John: It happened fast, but you're sure it was a her?

Mulligan: I know the difference between boys and girls, and this was a girl—a young pretty one.

John: Okay. So, what was this girl doing in the basement?

Mulligan: She was going out the window, so I tried to grab her ankle to stop her.

John: And you tried to detain her.

Mulligan: To what?

John: (inaudible) You tried to stop her from leaving the basement. Why did you try to stop her from leaving the basement? Most people would call the police rather than try to stop a robbery in progress. Why didn't you call the police?

Satchel: Detective, my client couldn't very well have called the police while he was unconscious.

Mulligan: Yeah. I couldn't call the police, but it's not like I trust the police anyway.

John: Is that because of the unlicensed gun you had in your possession?

Satchel: My client was on parole for a felony. He's not allowed to possess a firearm.

John: *The first responding officers found a pistol with a filed-off serial number in the waistband of your jeans last night. You wanna tell me about that gun, Mr. Mulligan?*

Mulligan: *It weren't mine. I found it in the house and took it with me to the basement.*

John: *Where'd you find the gun?*

Mulligan: *It was in Eddie and Nadia's bedroom.*

John: *Where at in the bedroom?*

Mulligan: *Under the mattress.*

John: *Under the mattress?*

Mulligan: *Ya hard-o-hearin'? Yeah—under the mattress.*

John: *So, let's walk through this. You're crashing with your friends. They leave. You hear a noise in the basement, and you quickly go to investigate.*

Mulligan: *That's right.*

John: *How did you have time to go to their bedroom to find a concealed gun before running to the basement if it happened so fast?*

Mulligan: *I'm very fast.*

John: *Where did you get the keys to unlock the basement?*

Satchel: *What keys are we talking about here?*

John: *The CSIs found keys in the deadbolt of the basement door. I assumed that Mr. Mulligan must have also grabbed the keys to unlock the basement during his heroic efforts.*

Satchel: *Answer the question.*

Mulligan: *Those keys were in the door. I didn't know it was locked until I saw them keys hanging there. I didn't do nothing wrong.*

John: *Do you know a Simon Manchester or a Julia Manchester?*

Mulligan: Well, now I know that Julia Manchester is the daughter of that man who's gonna run for president. That's what Satchel here told me.

John: Were you aware that Julia Manchester was kidnapped and held captive in the basement of the house where you were staying with your friends?

Mulligan: I don't know nothing about that.

John: You're saying you weren't aware that your friends kidnapped a teenager and held her for ransom?

Satchel: My client has already answered the question.

John: How long were you living with your friends?

Mulligan: A couple of months.

John: You mean to tell me that in a couple of months, you didn't notice them kidnapping a girl?

Satchel: Move on, Detective. He's already answered.

John: Do you know the current whereabouts of Eddie Watson or Nadia Freeman?

Mulligan: Well, they ain't here, so I guess not.

John: A witness described three kidnappers who took Julia Manchester, with one of the men fitting your description.

Mulligan: There ain't no way witnesses could pick me out in a lineup.

John: Oh, and why is that?

Satchel: Because my client already said he had no knowledge of a kidnapping.

Mulligan: Anybody could have looked like me wearing a mask to take that girl. You can't prove nothing.

Satchel: Don't say anything else, Mr. Mulligan. This interview is over.

John: *There are other ways to identify people, Mr. Mulligan. DNA from hair follicles left on clothing and in spaces, tattoo descriptions, fingerprints. Lots of ways to make positive identifications. For example, our forensics team found your fingerprints around a mattress in the basement along with evidence to support that Julia Manchester was held for several days. And by the way, we've never said publicly that the kidnappers were wearing masks. The only way you'd know that, Mr. Mulligan, would be if you were there or had insider knowledge about it.*

Mulligan: *No. I never said that.*

Satchel: *Shut up, Mr. Mulligan. Again, Detective John, this interview is over.*

Charlotte took a moment to compose herself after Vincent left. She glanced at her reflection in the hallway mirror and took a deep breath while smoothing her hair. As she walked past her father's closed office door, she could hear him having a tense phone conversation, but she couldn't allow herself to stop and listen out of fear of him discovering her. With what he'd already done to Julia, what would he do if he knew that Charlotte was willing to help the police put him in jail for his crimes?

Liv and Eric were already sitting in the dining room when Charlotte entered from the hallway. She took her usual seat across from her sister and raised her eyebrows. Liv nodded and raised her eyebrows in return, part of their silent sister communication to share that they'd overheard their parents' fight. Their mom came in, carrying a serving platter, and she placed it in the center of the table.

"Where's Julia?" she asked Charlotte.

"Julia said she'd eat later. The pain meds are upsetting her stomach, so she wants to stay in bed a bit longer."

"I'll take her a tray up after we get finished." With a sigh, Mrs. Manchester sat down hard in her chair. "I was hoping for a nice family meal tonight with all of us together."

"I know, Mom," Liv said, placing her hand on top of her mother's arm. "Julia will feel better soon, I'm sure."

"What's wrong with Julia?" asked Mr. Manchester as he barged into the room and took his seat at the end of the table.

Charlotte shuddered. *Wasn't it obvious what was wrong with Julia? Her father had her kidnapped.* She looked at Eric to avoid staring death daggers into her father.

"Julia's stomach is bothering her from the pain meds," Mrs. Manchester said. "She doesn't feel like joining us."

"I don't know why she needs heavy pain meds in the first place," Mr. Manchester said. "She ought to be fine with ibuprofen."

"Dad, she has a really deep cut on her arm," Liv interjected. "It's a bit much for regular meds."

"But the doctor said the cut would be fine," he argued. "Fine isn't usually treated with narcotics."

"Enough," Mrs. Manchester said. "She took her last dose of pain meds with lunch before we left the hospital, and tonight she's supposed to switch over to over-the-counter stuff. She will be fine. I'm just glad she's home safely."

"I think we're all glad of that," Mr. Manchester said. "Now, let's eat."

Charlotte had to bite her tongue to keep from saying something to her father. How could he just sit there and pretend to be innocent? Had he lost his conscience, or was it never there?

After listening to twenty minutes of chatter about upcoming campaign events that he and Saks were planning, Charlotte determined that her father had sold out his family for politics a long time ago.

When dinner was over, Charlotte retreated to her room. She couldn't remain silent any longer, and she had just the platform to send a message. Charlotte went through her standard motions of turning on her webcam, launching the voice-altering software, and concealing her identity. It wasn't her regular broadcast time, but her followers would get a notification.

YouTube Video transcript:

"Hi everyone, I know it's not my regular time or my planned topic, but I'm gonna get started anyway. I can't stop thinking about the Manchester family. If you haven't heard, a thirteen-year-old girl, Julia Manchester, was kidnapped last weekend on a Saturday evening. Her father, Simon Manchester, is running for president, and her mother is a former Broadway star. The media assumed the kidnappers wanted ransom money because the family is wealthy and well-known in their area, and the world, I guess.

"Well, anyway, that story gripped me, and I really feel for the girl, Julia. To think of what she must have gone through. It's good news that she's safe now; I guess I should have mentioned that from the beginning. I'm sorry for rambling on. I saw Julia's family during several press conferences in the past, and it looked like she and her sisters didn't really want to be there. That must be hard for kids to grow up with famous parents, I guess.

"Simon Manchester was falling behind his opponent in the primaries until his daughter was kidnapped, and now he's ahead in the polls. I find that curious. He also has a newer campaign manager Byron Saks who has ties to a convicted felon. The police are looking for this felon in connection with *the case. Even more curious. So that begs the question, just how much does Simon Manchester know? He pleaded for the safe return of his daughter for the cameras with no tears or breaks in his voice while his family fell apart beside him, but did Simon—and does he—know more than he's letting on?*

"What I think is that Simon Manchester and Byron Saks planned this whole kidnapping together for exactly what it's accomplished—to get ahead in the polls. Maybe the police can prove it now. If it's true, then there must be evidence somewhere. Only time will tell."

Charlotte shut off her recording and closed her laptop. Her phone buzzed beside her—most likely with texts from Rachel and Vincent.

Seconds later, Liv burst through the door and shut it behind her. "Charlotte," she said. "What the hell have you done?"

Detective Ernest John's Notes: 12-10-15, Part 3

RECOVERED: Julia Marie Manchester.

~~Missing child. Julia Marie Manchester. White female. 13~~ ~~YO. BR Hair. BR Eyes. Approximately 5'7" tall, 115-~~ ~~125 pounds. Slim build. Last seen in purple sweater,~~ ~~black jeans, grey boots. Black coat. Pink hat. Pink scarf.~~ ~~Carries pink canvas backpack.~~

Suspected Kidnapper in custody: William Elmer Mulligan, age 31. He claims to have stopped a burglary at his friends' rent house and to have had no knowledge of a kidnapping. He's lying. My gut and his stupidity tell me he's guilty as hell.

Known associates and suspects: Pearl Nadine Freeman, age 35. Eddie Vaughn Watson, age 40, now in custody. Both arrested for parole violations—attempting to cross state lines, drug possession, forgery, and suspected kidnapping.

Will question Freeman and Watson first thing in the A.M. Transcripts to follow.

Transcript of interview with Pearl Nadine Freeman, Friday, December 11, 2015 Questioned in presence of public defender Betsy Jones.

Detective Earnest John: *Good morning. Please state your name for the record.*

Pearl Freeman: *Pearl Nadine Freeman.*

Betsy Jones: *My client is willing to testify in exchange for reduced charges.*

John: *Thank you, and the charges are up to the DA, but I can certainly let their office know that your client cooperated with a police investigation.*

Jones: *Go ahead and answer the questions for now, and I'll let you know if the question is inappropriate.*

John: *Ms. Freeman, when officers picked you up near the state line, you were carrying an ID that said you were Missy Vera. Do you know a woman by the name of Missy Vera?*

Freeman: *No. I just used that name to rent a house.*

John: *Are you admitting to forging an ID in the name of Missy Vera?*

Freeman: *Yes. A lot of people won't rent to people on parole or probation, so I used a fake ID.*

John: *You used this fake ID to rent a house on Woodward Drive a couple of months ago?*

Freeman: *Yes.*

John: *You forged an ID while out on parole and still on probation for forgery?*

Jones: *Detective, let's move on. My client has a statement to make.*

John: She can make her statement when I'm finished with my questions. Ms. Freeman, what is your relationship with Eddie Watson and William Mulligan?

Freeman: Eddie's my boyfriend, and Will is his friend.

John: Did Eddie and William live with you in the house you rented on Woodward Drive?

Freeman: Yes.

John: Were any of you employed?

Freeman: Eddie drove a garbage truck, and I did some online sales. Will worked nights at a factory until he got fired a few weeks back.

John: What type of online work Ms. Freeman?

Freeman: I had my own Etsy shop to sell graphic design stuff like invitations.

John: Ms. Freeman, do you know Simon or Gina Manchester?

Freeman: I've never met them, but I know who they are.

John: Have you met their daughter, Julia Manchester?

Freeman: Yes. We got paid to keep her at my rent house for a few days.

John: Who was paid and paid by whom?

Freeman: (inaudible)(laughter) Me, Eddie, and Will were paid by my cousin and the girl's crooked daddy.

John: I need the names of the men who paid you.

Jones: Answer his question.

Freeman: Byron Saks and Simon Manchester paid me.

John: Did you meet with both men?

Freeman: Only Byron, but he said the money came from Simon. He gave me two hundred and fifty thousand dollars as a down payment and said we'd get a million in cash once the job was done.

John: And was Julia Manchester complicit in staying at your house?

Freeman: No, she wasn't. We kept her there against her will.

John: And how did she arrive at your house?

Freeman: We took her.

John: When and how did you take her?

Freeman: On Saturday afternoon—Eddie, Will, and me saw the girl Julia walking on her street by herself while we were driving around to check everything out and make plans to take her. We already had ski masks and our supplies, so they jumped out and got her, and then I drove us to my house.

John: So, you're telling me that you took her earlier than you'd planned, and that Eddie Watson and William Mulligan were both involved, is that correct?

Freeman: Yeah, we were supposed to take her during Christmas break in a couple of weeks—Byron was gonna let us know exactly when—but we decided to seize the opportunity.

John: And what did Saks and Manchester think about you changing the plans?

Freeman: Byron said Simon was pissed, but Byron agreed that it was genius. It made it easier since we didn't have to wait around for the opportunity. Less likely for us to get caught without any witnesses around.

John: Yeah, well, not getting caught didn't work out for you.

Freeman: Guess not (expletive).

John: How am I supposed to know you're telling me the truth? How do I know you're not just making up this whole thing about Byron Saks and Simon Manchester paying you? What if this whole thing was your idea?

Jones: Detective, my client is willing to take a lie detector test.

John: Ms. Jones, you and I both know that lie detector tests aren't one hundred percent foolproof.

Jones: But a passed one along with Ms. Freeman's statement might help with asking for a reduced sentence. My client is aware of her crimes and the time she's facing in prison for kidnapping, forgery, and parole violation. She's prepared to plead guilty and will testify against Byron Saks and Simon Manchester.

Freeman: I'm telling the truth. I wanted some easy money, and Byron knew I was looking for a better job. He came to me with the offer, and I thought it sounded like a sure deal.

John: I'm gonna need proof.

Jones: My client has given me an audio recording of her meeting with Byron Saks that she's willing to share with you and the DA.

John: You could have led with that. I'll need to hear this recording before I can make any recommendations to the DA.

Jones: We'll send you a copy.

John: I think that concludes our questioning for the day. We'll be in touch.

Transcript of interview with Eddie Vaughn Watson, Friday, December 11, 2015 Questioned in presence of public defender Sabrina Rowes.

Detective Earnest John: *Good morning. Please state your name for the record.*

Eddie Watson: *Eddie Vaughn Watson.*

Sabrina Rowes: *My client is willing to testify against Byron Saks.*

John: *Thank you, and the charges are up to the DA, but I can make a recommendation based on how well Watson cooperates with the investigation.*

Rowes: *I think we're ready to proceed.*

John: *Mr. Watson, what is your relationship with Pearl Freeman?*

Watson: *She'd hate hearing you call her that. She's…Nadia's my girlfriend.*

John: *What about William Mulligan?*

Watson: *Will shared a cell with me. He's been down on his luck, so he lived with me and Nadia at our rent house.*

John: *Would this be the rent house on Woodward Drive?*

Watson: *Yeah. We lived there a couple of months.*

John: *That address doesn't match the one you provided to your parole officer.*

Watson: *No, it doesn't. I also have an apartment downtown.*

John: *Are you aware that it's a crime to lie to your parole officer about your place of residence?*

Watson: *I'm aware.*

John: *Are you also aware that it's illegal to possess a firearm as part of your parole.*

Watson: *Yes.*

John: *Mr. Watson, whose idea was it to kidnap Julia Manchester?*

Watson: *Nadia told me about the job. Said her cousin Byron was setting it up. The kid's old man wanted her taken to get some public outcry ahead of the election. Nadia and I were good with making some easy money holding the kid for a few days. We never planned on hurting her. We would've released her to her dad.*

John: *Do you admit to participating in the kidnapping of Julia Manchester and holding her against her will for several days?*

Watson: *I do, but I never hurt that girl.*

John: *You drugged her and forced her into a car, held her captive in a cold basement, but you never hurt her. How kind of you.*

Watson: *None of this was my idea.*

John: *Did you ever meet with Byron Saks or Simon Manchester about this job?*

Watson: *No. Nadia did all the meeting with Saks. She took the down payment and set up the job.*

John: *She never met with Simon Manchester, to your knowledge?*

Watson: *No. Not to my knowledge.*

John: *What were the terms of this deal.*

Watson: *Two-fifty to start and a million to finish.*

John: *Was William Mulligan an active participant in the kidnapping of Julia Manchester?*

Watson: *Yeah. He helped me grab the girl and get her into the car. He stayed at the house when Nadia had to get groceries or ship her packages or when I had to work.*

John: *Who made the ransom phone calls to the Manchester residence?*

Watson: *I did with a voice box.*

John: *A voice box?*

Watson: *Yeah, one of those little boxes that messes up your voice. Nadia used it to talk to her clients all the time to deepen her voice so they'd think there was more than one person working her business.*

John: *And was this business the online sales business Nadia owned?*

Rowes: *Detective, that's not relevant. I think we're done here unless you have other questions for my client related to the kidnapping of Julia Manchester.*

John: *Just one more question. Mr. Watson, was Julia Manchester complicit in being kept in the basement of the Woodward Drive home?*

Watson: *If she was, she's a damn fine actress. She begged me to let her go every time I saw her.*

John: *Thank you, Mr. Watson and Ms. Rowes. I believe that's all I have for now. My office will be in touch if we have further questions.*

H aving given up on trying to reach Charlotte, Vincent finally crashed around one in the morning. His parents had already said he could miss school due to the colitis-related issues he'd used as an excuse to leave school early yesterday. Of course, the stress of not knowing what was happening with Charlotte was giving his whole digestive system fits, anyway. His lie had become the truth.

His girlfriend was pretty vocal in some of her YouTube posts, but never had she been so bold as to flat out accuse her father. Vincent was one of only a few people who knew the real young woman behind the façade on YouTube, but it wouldn't take much for someone else to figure it out. He worried about what it could mean for her since he was sure that Simon Manchester was guilty. If Simon could have Julia kidnapped for his campaign, what might he do to Charlotte for telling the world that he was responsible for it?

Throughout the night, Charlotte's video was shared to the point where reporters described it as a "viral video." All the major news stations in the area talked about the case and video on their morning shows and had reporters camped out in front of the Manchesters' gated home. They all reported the same thing—that a spokesperson for the family had replied with "No comment" to the video's allegations.

Byron Saks was soon ready to make a statement about his cousin's potential involvement in Julia's kidnapping.

Vincent watched in disgust as the man's greasy hair and complexion filled the TV screen.

"Good morning," Saks said to the reporters. "After last night's events, I felt the need to make a statement. This statement is from me and not on behalf of the Manchester family. It is true that my cousin, Pearl Freeman, was arrested late last night as an alleged kidnapper of Julia Manchester along with a man who is alleged to have been involved. I've never spoken out about my cousin's criminal record, nor have I denied it. In fact, I helped her and my dear aunt secure legal counsel during my cousin's trial for forgery several years ago. But, in this great country in which we all live, all men and women are created equal and presumed to be innocent until proven guilty in a court of law."

"Mr. Saks," said one of the reporters. "Is it true that your cousin has accused you of hiring her to do the kidnapping?"

"That, I don't know," Saks replied. "My cousin is liable to say just about anything to reduce her sentence at this point. What she may or may not have said isn't my knowledge, as I haven't seen her."

"Did you arrange the kidnapping of Julia Manchester?" another reporter asked. "There's a video circulating that says you did."

"I'm not even going to dignify that with a response," Saks said, turning to walk away. "Good day."

"Wait, Mr. Saks!" called another reporter. "My sources tell me that one of the people arrested for the kidnapping also accused Simon Manchester of involvement. Can you speak to that?"

"No comment." Saks walked away this time, ignoring all the other questions being hurled at him by the reporters.

Vincent clicked off the TV and looked at his phone again. Still no word from Charlotte. He attempted to call her, but her phone went straight to voicemail. Worried, he texted Liv.

Vincent: *Is Charlotte okay?*

Liv: *I think she turned off her phone. It's crazy here. Charlotte's okay, but Dad's on a rampage.*

Vincent: *Does he know about the video?*

Liv: *Yes, but he doesn't know who did it.*

Vincent: *Tell Charlotte I'm here for her.*

Liv: *She knows. She'll call you later.*

Still snuggled up under the comforter in her childhood bed, Liv's thoughts were racing. Her sisters were not in good places, and all Liv could do was watch and try to help. The fact that she, herself, wasn't in the best place didn't help matters. She and Eric had stayed up late talking about what to do. He'd already gotten up and brought back toast, which he'd left beside the bed for Liv. She could hear the shower in the connected bathroom where Eric was getting ready for the day.

Liv stretched her arms over her head and reached for the toast. The nausea wasn't too bad this morning, but she ate slowly to keep her stomach settled. She had to be her best today. The same gut nourishing her growing baby was also churning with a strange concoction of love and hatred for her father. And confusion about those feelings. The police were already suspecting Saks based on the argument she'd overheard between her parents, so it was only a matter of time before someone talked and laid the blame right on her dad's feet where it belonged.

Anger also surfaced every time she thought about the impulsiveness with which Charlotte had exposed everything in her video. It didn't matter that no one knew Charlotte was behind the video or that Charlotte had the foresight to disable comments before recording it—the accusations were out there. People were talking about it everywhere. All the major news stations had run with the story, some labeling it a potential hoax, and a few tabloid sites had speculated as well. Strangely enough, the tabloid sites had a closer version of the events as far as Liv was concerned. Though, part of her heart—the part that still believed in fairies and unicorns—refused to believe it until she could hear an admission of guilt pass through her father's lips.

Of course, Saks denied everything. His motto seemed to be "lie first, deal with the consequences later." Liv's reluctance to fully believe her father's guilt in the matter didn't extend to Byron Saks, but she still didn't think that only one man should be punished if they were both guilty. Even having the three kidnappers in custody wasn't enough justice for Julia—who'd suffered such severe nightmares that their mother had crawled into bed with her after the second instance of crying out last night.

It was only a matter of time before Julia got wind of the viral video and their father's potential involvement. Liv's heart broke for her sisters. Julia was already devastated by her experience, so learning that her father had orchestrated it might cause her to break down. And Charlotte's anger was causing her to behave irrationally. Liv was doing everything in her power to convince Charlotte to keep her mouth shut for fear that their father might lash out at Charlotte for making the accusations—especially since every rational part of Liv's mind knew they were true.

Vincent had already texted her to check on Charlotte, which meant that Charlotte's phone was still turned off. Liv genuinely loved Vincent and her sister together. Not many teenage guys were as strong as Vincent was, and the fact that he understood Charlotte's condition made them perfect for each other. Liv hoped the two would go the distance and marry someday. While her high school romances hadn't panned out, she'd understood the reason once she'd met Eric—her true equal—while in college. She'd never wish so much heartache on her sisters, though. As far as Liv was concerned, she'd gladly let her sisters learn from her past pain to keep them from experiencing it. Too bad she couldn't shield them from what was to come.

Liv grabbed her phone from the nightstand and pulled up her favorite news website. The headline was bold and attention-grabbing:

Presidential Candidate Simon Manchester Accused of Involvement in Daughter's Kidnapping in Viral Anonymous Video. Three suspects now in custody.

She'd barely slept at all after getting griped at by Liv for the video. Liv's main concern was about the possible repercussions for Charlotte and Julia, not for their father or Mr. Saks. Liv was certain that it was only a matter of time before the police had enough evidence to arrest both men. Charlotte could admit that she'd been impulsive in her post, but she was tired of remaining silent while her sister was suffering. Julia had suffered from nightmares again, and their mother had stayed with her the rest of the night.

Charlotte had turned off her phone immediately after posting the video, for which she'd disabled the comments section. A quick check of the internet upon waking told her everything she needed to know. The video had gone viral during the night, and all the news networks were publicizing it. People were still sharing it and commenting about it on their own social media pages. Reporters interviewed Mr. Saks outside the Manchester home since his cousin and her boyfriend had been arrested last night. Everything was falling into place—or falling apart—something like that.

In less than a week, her entire family's world had been shredded. It would only get worse when the truth finally came out. Charlotte worried most about what it would do to Julia and her mother. At least Charlotte had Liv mostly on her side, but she still needed more support to get through this. Vincent was wonderful, but Charlotte needed her family—her mother most of all.

A small knock at the door startled Charlotte, and she was surprised when her mother came in, still wearing a silk robe over her pajamas. Mrs. Manchester was pale without her usual makeup and had dark circles under her eyes.

"Hi, Mom. Is everything okay?"

"No, it isn't," she said, sitting at the foot of Charlotte's bed. "I didn't sleep well because of Julia's nightmares, and then I wake up to reports of a video circulating that accuses your father of orchestrating her kidnapping. It was the last thing I needed this morning."

Charlotte gulped and decided to tread carefully. "We all heard you and Dad arguing last night about the police questioning him about Mr. Saks."

"I was afraid of that. But that's over with for now. There are two more suspects in custody, and Mr. Saks denies any wrongdoing. So has your father, but you're old enough to realize how the public can try and convict a man without any evidence."

Charlotte nodded.

Mrs. Manchester pressed her lips into a fine line and looked into her daughter's eyes. "So, imagine my surprise when I watch this video and recognize the diction and cadence of my own daughter despite all the software she went through to hide her identity."

Gasping, Charlotte backed away from her mother as blood rushed to her head.

"How could you?" her mother asked through gritted teeth. "This is our family; we stick together through the hard times. We don't lash out at each other and share accusations publicly that hurt everyone. Why would you do such a thing to your father and your sister? You have single-handedly ruined his campaign. This was his one shot at winning the nomination, and I can't imagine why you would be so vindictive."

Tears sprang to Charlotte's eyes, but she fought them back. She had to stay strong. "Mom, I swear to you that I would never want to hurt our family."

"Are you saying I'm wrong about the origin of the video?"

Charlotte took a deep breath. "You're not wrong." She watched her mother's face fall. "But neither am I. Dad's behind this with Mr. Saks. There's evidence, and the police have it."

Her mother struggled for words. "What are you talking about? That's insane. Your father would never…"

Cautiously moving closer, Charlotte silently begged her mother to believe her before spilling everything she knew. "Vincent overheard Dad and Mr. Saks talking about Julia's kidnapping—the plans, the money, everything, while Julia was missing. They were arguing about the kidnappers doing it earlier than the plan, and Saks reassured Dad that everything would be fine. When Vincent realized what was going on, he recorded audio on his phone. The recording's not the greatest, but some transcription software helped fill in the gaps. I emailed it to Detective John, and Vincent's been questioned by the police. Mom, I also found money in Dad's office—a lot of money—hidden in his bottom desk drawer before the ransom call came in. Mom, Dad was ready with the money. And he has a gun in there, too—a black handgun. I'm so, so sorry."

Her mother didn't speak for at least a full minute, her eyes searching the room before landing back on Charlotte. "Why would you do all this without talking to me?"

"I didn't want to hurt you, Mom. I was scared of Dad and scared for Julia and you. I was gonna tell you, I swear, but I wanted to make sure that the police had everything first. That didn't happen until right before we found out she was safe, and then here we are. Detective John wanted to try and leave me out of it, but I'm the only one who knows about the money in Dad's office—unless someone at the bank will testify when he withdrew it if there's not a record or something. Technicians are working on the recording to see what they can get from it."

"I don't even know what to say." Mrs. Manchester stood up, shaky on her feet. "I can't process this right now—all the lies and the spying. I need to talk to Detective John and Simon myself."

"Mom, don't! Don't say anything to Dad yet! I don't want him to hurt you. Let the police do their work."

"Maybe you shouldn't have posted that video. That hurt me. Your father has never laid a hand on me in anger, and we've had plenty of arguments throughout the years. I just don't believe he's that kind of person."

"Mom, I'm sorry."

"There has to be some sort of misunderstanding. I just can't imagine him doing something like this. It just doesn't make any sense that he would put any of us in harm's way."

"None of this makes any sense."

"I can't talk to you anymore right now. Do not—under any circumstances—leave this house today." Mrs.

Manchester walked to the nightstand and snatched up Charlotte's phone, which was still turned off, and then marched over to the desk and grabbed her laptop. "No visitors either."

"I just didn't want him and Saks to get away with it. It's not fair." Charlotte watched her mother leave the room, unsure of what to do next. She then buried her face in her pillow and screamed.

When she woke up for the day, her mother was no longer sleeping beside her, making Julia's queen-sized bed feel cold and lonely. Despite being thirteen years old, there was comfort in having her mother stay the night with her to help quell the nightmares. After the nightmares had ceased, Julia had dreamt of her parents' argument from the night before. In her dream, Julia had run down the stairs to stop them.

The woman kidnapper had said that politicians were dirty, but not Julia's father. The lady was wrong about that. There was no way her father's campaign manager could have set up the kidnapping. Her father wasn't the most touchy-feely type of parent, but he loved her. Julia was sure of it. Her father was also intelligent. Much too smart to hire someone who would do such a thing. It had to have happened as her mother said; Mr. Saks' cousin must have come up with the kidnapping plan after seeing the Manchester family in the news.

Still missing her phone since it had been lost and broken during her abduction, Julia picked up her tablet from the nightstand beside her bed to check in with her friends on social media. They had probably been worried about Julia while she was gone. After scrolling through several "Glad UR Back" messages, to which she replied, "Me 2," Julia stopped at a YouTube video Josiah had shared with her, along with the message, "Julia, Have U seen this?" Julia clicked on the link to watch the video.

After finishing the video, Julia wiped the tears from her face. How could someone say such a thing, and how would they even know? It didn't seem to matter that the video had to have been fabricated lies. The damage was done. A quick browser search found several articles about the viral video with tons of amateur detectives speculating in the comments. Julia was tempted to comment back to some of the posters, but she was crying too hard to type. She couldn't call Josiah or any of her other friends because they were in school.

Julia padded down the hall to Charlotte's room, but she discovered Charlotte was in the shower in her adjoining bathroom. Next, Julia went to Liv's room and knocked on the door.

"Charlotte, is that you?" Liv called. Julia slipped in, closing the door behind her. "Oh, Julia, I thought you'd still be sleeping. Come here, kiddo."

"Morning," Julia said, falling into her oldest sister's arms. "I'm glad you're back at home for a while."

"Me too," Liv said. "I just wish it was for better reasons. I'm so glad you're safe back at home too. Charlotte and I were so worried about you. Eric and Vincent too."

"What about Mom and Dad?"

"Mom was barely keeping it together, Jules. You're her baby." Liv patted her abdomen with emphasis. "We mothers love our babies pretty fiercely."

Julia lost focus as she studied Liv's midsection, unable to discern the start of a baby bump yet that housed her niece or nephew. "What about Dad?"

Liv seemed to hesitate at first. "You know how he is, Jules," she finally said. "His emotions stay locked up unless it's anger."

"Like last night when he and Mom were arguing in the hallway?"

Liv sighed. "I was hoping you hadn't heard that."

"I'm pretty sure the whole neighborhood heard Dad." Julia tried to keep her tears at bay, but she couldn't. "Have you seen the awful video that's been shared everywhere? Is that why the police are suspecting Mr. Saks—because of some dumb video where the person won't even show their face?"

"I've seen it," Liv said, hugging Julia. "It's causing a lot of people to talk about things they don't know."

"Mr. Saks wasn't involved, Liv. I mean, he's gross, but he wasn't there. I would have recognized his voice. And how could someone think that Dad would do that to me?"

"I don't know what to say, baby sister. I wish I could protect you from all this."

"I was thinking about commenting on some of the articles and social posts to set people straight."

"Maybe it's best that you stay off the grid for a while and let the police do their jobs."

"Even if they're doing a bad job? Are they gonna start suspecting Dad now with that video going around? I still don't understand why someone would make a video like that."

"Julia, you know that Dad's always been the source of criticism in the media since he's put himself in the public eye.

If there's anything to the accusations, the police will figure it out."

"If?" Julia suddenly felt sick to her stomach. "What are you not telling me, Liv? Do you know something about what Dad said last night?"

"Julia, I don't want to hurt you."

"Then don't lie to me," Julia said, staring into her sister's eyes. "I'm not a little kid."

"But you are a kid, Jules. You shouldn't have to deal with any of this right now. You should be focusing on getting better and feeling safe again."

"I won't get better or feel safe until this is all over. Please tell me what you know."

"There's evidence that Mr. Saks was involved with hiring his cousin to kidnap you…and there's also evidence that Dad was involved."

"What?" Julia's chest stung as if someone had punched her.

"Mom doesn't know, but Charlotte does. She wanted to tell you, but I didn't. I'm sorry. Vincent overheard and recorded a conversation between Dad and Saks while you were missing where they mentioned a woman named Nadia and talked about your kidnapping and money. The police have the recording."

A knock on the door startled Julia. Charlotte walked in, already talking, dressed in a bathrobe with a towel wrapped around her head. "Liv, I don't care if you agree; we have to tell her today because Mom knows it was me—"

Stopping once she saw Julia's tear-streaked face, Charlotte shut Liv's door and dropped to the floor in front of it. "Julia…God…I'm so sorry."

"I just told her some stuff," Liv said. "I had to."

Charlotte got up, tightening her bathrobe. She joined her sisters on the bed, wrapping her arm around Julia. "I'm so sorry, Jules. I never wanted this to be true."

Julia stood and moved away from her sisters. "I don't believe this. Why?" She started pacing in front of Liv's bed. "Why would Dad have me kidnapped? Why!"

Charlotte stood up and tried to stop Julia from moving, but Julia pulled away from her again. "Julia, just calm down, and I'll tell you everything I know."

"Me calm down! I can't! You weren't the one who got thrown into a car while unconscious from God knows what kind of drug they shoved in your face and held in a cold, dark basement for four nights, not knowing if you'd ever see your family again. You didn't have a creepy guy come into the room and lick your face after talking about how much he loved virgins! And you didn't think you were gonna be killed when that same creepy guy grabbed your leg while you were trying to escape, so don't you dare tell me to calm down!" Julia stopped talking when she looked at Charlotte, who was now crying with her. Liv was crying too.

Charlotte tried to approach her, but Julia held out her hand to stop her sister. "Just tell me what the hell is going on," Julia said.

"Vincent was in Dad's bathroom, and he overheard Dad and Mr. Saks talking about your kidnapping," Charlotte said. "He recorded most of the conversation on his phone. The recording wasn't very good, but he remembers most of the conversation, and we were able to get a rough transcript of the conversation and the audio to the police. Vincent gave a formal statement the night you escaped."

"What were you saying about Mom knowing it was you?" Julia watched as Charlotte shifted her gaze to the floor. "What was you? What does Mom know?"

"I released a video accusing Dad and Saks last night, and it went viral. I already had a big following on my anonymous YouTube channel under my username *Debate Debutante Ball.* It was stupid of me to do that video—I know that—but I was just so angry that Dad was lying to all of us."

"I don't want to believe it either, Julia, and I've been struggling with this the whole time," Liv said. "I'm just so confused and angry. I still don't want to believe that Dad would do such a thing, but the whole time you were missing, he seemed too calm about you and all worked up about the campaign and press conferences. It's like he orchestrated the whole thing for the approval ratings. And with what Vincent heard and what Charlotte found in his desk, there's just a lot of evidence."

"Wait...what did you find in his desk, Charlotte?"

"A shit-ton of money in Dad's locked desk drawer—the bottom one. I found a key under his legal terms dictionary, ironically. Dad had thousands of dollars in there, along with a gun. He had the ransom money before the kidnappers called, demanding a specific amount. He was prepared."

Julia sat down on the floor. "This can't be true."

"Eric and I thought maybe Saks was blackmailing Dad at first, but with what we've learned from Vincent and then everything else, it just doesn't seem likely," Liv said.

"And Mom doesn't believe me," Charlotte said. "She said she was gonna talk to Detective John and Dad, but I begged her not to. I'm scared that Dad has a gun in the house."

"Where are Mom and Dad now?" Julia asked.

"I don't know." Charlotte looked to Liv for help.

"I'll go find out." Liv got up and left the room.

"Julia, I'm so sorry about all this. Are you okay?" Charlotte watched her baby sister as she tried to process everything. Tears streamed down Julia's face and landed on her hoodie. She just shook her head side to side. Charlotte joined Julia on the floor. This time, Julia didn't pull away when Charlotte held her.

Liv came back a few minutes later and closed the door behind her. "Mom and Dad were obviously arguing when I found them in Dad's office, but I just knocked and went in," she said. "Dad's denying everything and saying that Byron's cousin has fabricated her whole story. He's planning a recorded press statement from our living room at three o'clock to formally deny the allegations put forth in the video. He says we all need to be ready to come in for some of the questioning to support him. And he doesn't want any of us leaving the house today."

"I can't do that," Charlotte said. "I can't lie to everyone about him."

"I don't wanna go on TV again," Julia mumbled, her face still buried against Charlotte's chest. "I just wanna go to sleep."

Charlotte pulled her sister to her feet and then tucked her into Liv's bed. Julia sobbed for a few minutes and then was asleep. "What are we gonna do, Liv?" she whispered. "Mom took my phone and computer."

"I've still got mine, and I'm calling Detective John. Eric had to leave this morning to do something for work. He was planning to come back tonight, so maybe Eric can go by the station to see what's going on if I can't reach Detective John. Dad's acting crazy, Charlotte, almost manic."

"I'm scared and just ready for this nightmare to be over," Charlotte said, smoothing Julia's hair. "This is so messed up."

"No kidding," Liv said as she dialed her phone. "Hi, this is Olivia Manchester. I need to speak with Detective Earnest John...oh, well, please have him call me back as soon as possible...yes, this is a good number for me. Thank you."

Charlotte looked at her older sister. "Not there?"

"No, he's there, but he's busy. The receptionist took a message for him, but he doesn't expect Detective John to be available most of the day due to interviews."

"Job interviews at a time like this?"

"I think it is interviews with Julia's case. Interrogations."

"Oh...I'm an idiot."

Liv laughed softly and wiped tears from the corners of her eyes. "You really stirred up a lot of trouble with your video." She handed her phone to Charlotte. "Call your boyfriend and Rachel. They're both freaking out and texting me now."

Back in her room, Charlotte dressed and then called Vincent during his lunch period.

"Liv," he answered. "What's wrong?"

"It's me," Charlotte said.

"Oh…Charlotte, thank God. I've been freakin' out. Are you okay?"

"Yeah, that's what Liv said. I'm not okay. My mom knows about the video and doesn't believe me. She took my phone and computer and said I couldn't leave the house or have visitors. Liv's called Detective John to get an update, but we don't know what's going on right now besides what's in the news."

"Yeah, your video's stirring up all kinds of shit on the web. Saks was on the news this morning denying everything, saying his cousin made up the whole story to try to save herself some prison time. The basic BS he's known for."

"Liv and I told Julia everything."

"God…is she okay?"

"She's pretty much broken down and is sleeping now. I don't know if she truly believes us, but I think she also knows that Liv and I would never make up all this shit to hurt her."

"I can't imagine."

"I know you need to go so you can eat. Is Rachel there with you?"

"Babe, I'm not at school. I couldn't concentrate with everything going on."

"I'm going crazy trapped in this house. Dad's making us do a video press release around three. I don't think I can do it, but I'm scared not to. Liv said Dad's acting crazy today."

"I'll bust through the door to get to you if I have to."

"I love you, Vinny, but please don't come. I want you to stay safe."

"I love you, too, Charlotte. But I want to get you out of that house."

"Vinny, please, just don't come over right now. I'll call you again when I can."

"Okay, but I swear I'll come over right now if you want me to."

"I know. Bye."

"Bye."

Next, Charlotte texted Rachel.

Charlotte: *Rach, it's Charlotte. Mom took my phone. She knows it was me who released the video and she's pissed b/c she doesn't believe me. We're talking to the police so everything's going to be okay, I think.*

Rachel: *OMG. I was so worried. Y didn't U tell me!*

Charlotte: *I wanted to, but I was scared.*

Rachel: *Do U need me? I can come right after school.*

Charlotte: *I need you, but don't come over today. Things are shitty here and Dad's making us do a press conference. I'm hoping the police will put a stop to it.*

Rachel: *Okay. Love U. Call or text me again ASAP.*

Charlotte: *I will. Love you too.*

Detective Ernest John's Notes: 12-11-15

RECOVERED: Julia Marie Manchester.

~~Missing child. Julia Marie Manchester. White female. 13 YO. BR Hair. BR Eyes. Approximately 5'7" tall, 115-125 pounds. Slim build. Last seen in purple sweater, black jeans, grey boots. Black coat. Pink hat. Pink scarf. Carries pink canvas backpack.~~

Suspected Kidnapper in custody: William Elmer Mulligan, age 31. He claims to have stopped a burglary at his friends' rent house and to have had no knowledge of a kidnapping. He's lying. My gut and his stupidity tell me he's guilty as hell.

Known associates and suspects: Pearl Nadine Freeman, age 35
Eddie Vaughn Watson, age 40, now in custody. Both arrested for parole violations—attempting to cross state lines, drug possession, forgery, and suspected kidnapping.

Questioning with Freeman and Watson: Both suspects state they were hired by Byron Saks and Simon Manchester. Mulligan was brought in for muscle. Both agreed that Julia Manchester was not complicit in her kidnapping.

Techs came back with good audio and transcripts of V.R.'s recording. The evidence is good, but not good enough without a confession. Voice matching may be a possibility.

It's come to my attention that a video has been released under the username of "Debate Debutante Ball." This user has posted previous political-themed videos but nothing with this level of anger Profiler suspects young white female. I suspect Charlotte Manchester made the videos.

Will re-interview Byron Saks today to see if he'll turn on Manchester. Transcript to follow.

Transcript of interview with Byron Saks, Friday, December 11, 2015

Detective Earnest John: Good afternoon. Thank you for coming in again. Please state your name for the record.
Byron Saks: *Byron James Saks.*
John: *I suppose you know why you're here.*
Saks: *I heard that my cousin and her boyfriend were arrested, but I'm not sure what that has to do with me. Of course, I'm willing to help close this case if you think I could be of assistance.*
John: *Well, you heard right that we have your cousin, Pearl Nadine Freeman, in custody. How long did you say it'd been since you'd last seen her?*
Saks: *Five or six years.*
John: *Well, Pearl Freeman, or Nadia as you call her, has a different story. She says you reached out to her a couple of months ago with a job opportunity—an opportunity to make some serious money kidnapping Julia Manchester for ransom.*
Saks: *That's absurd.*
John: *Do you deny those allegations?*
Saks: *You're damn right I deny those allegations. That's the most ridiculous story I've ever heard.*
John: *Well, Mr. Saks, in the words of Mark Twain, "Why shouldn't truth be stranger than fiction. Fiction, after all, has to make sense."*
Saks: *I didn't come here to discuss long-dead author quotes. Am I under arrest?*
John: *Not yet.*

Saks: *You can direct any further questioning to my attorney. I don't wish to have more of my time wasted today.*

John: *I will gladly step out for you to call your attorney, Mr. Saks, but I should also tell you that Nadia passed a lie detector test.*

Saks: *Nadia's a compulsive liar. Her word means nothing.*

John: *I hear compulsive lying runs in families.*

Saks: *No judge would even consider those test results. A good lawyer would get them thrown out in a heartbeat.*

John: *Oh, I'm sure a lousy lawyer could get it thrown out, but that's not the point.*

Saks: *Then what is the point, Detective?*

John: *You seem worried about the possibility of a trial, but you'll need to remember that not all trials play out in court.*

Saks: *What's that supposed to mean?*

John: *The public jury can be quite vicious, especially with that video circulating. You've seen it, right? The press has already gotten wind of Nadia's accusations. With that plus the video, people would love to hang this whole thing on a dirty campaign manager. But I'm not convinced you acted alone on this idea without some buy-in from Simon Manchester. Maybe you can come back soon with your attorney, and we can chat about that because Nadia didn't only accuse you of planning this whole thing. She says Simon's involved, too, even if she only met with you.*

Saks: *I'm done here until my attorney arrives.*

John: *I'll wait.*

**Part II Transcript of interview with Byron Saks,
Friday, December 11, 2015
Questioned in the presence of attorney,
Norman Wiltz**

John: Mr. Wiltz, your client Byron Saks is accused of orchestrating a kidnapping for ransom of 13-year-old Julia Manchester, daughter of Simon Manchester, who is running for his party's nomination.

Wiltz: My client has filled me in about his cousin Nadine Freeman's criminal record, Detective. I assure you that her questioning and malicious lies won't be admissible against Mr. Saks. Neither will some YouTube hack video hurling accusations against innocent people.

John: Oh, we're not relying on the statements of two felons— because Eddie Watson has also accused Byron Saks of hiring he and Pearl Nadine Freeman to kidnap Julia Manchester. I have audio evidence in police possession that also supports these accusations.

Saks: That's impossible. I've never been recorded speaking to Nadia or Eddie, but both of them have enough criminal connections to doctor a recording.

Wiltz: My client has the right to review any evidence, and my office would want to have independent technicians to examine this so-called evidence for any indication of tampering.

John: We'll gladly give you a copy, but what your client needs to understand is that this evidence is substantial. He needs to decide right now if he's gonna shoulder the whole responsibility for the crime planning or if he's planning to take down Simon Manchester with him.

Saks: *What are you talking about?*
John: *The audio recording we have is a conversation between two men we believe to be Byron Saks and Simon Manchester. Our experts will be comparing the files to known audio files to make a definitive match. Here's a copy of the transcript.*

Note: Copy of the attached transcript was provided to Mr. Norman Wiltz and Mr. Byron Saks.

Voice 1: *I still thought we were going to wait until Christmas break so she wouldn't miss school, if we even did this at all. I wasn't a hundred percent sold on this whole thing to begin with, but I guess you're right. This way, it's all over the news, and the kids at school are talking about it. You're sure she's fine? They're taking care of her.*

Voice 2: *She's not staying in a luxury hotel or anything, but she's got food, water, clean clothes, and warm shelter. Nadia's the one taking care of her. Her and her boyfriend and his former cellmate. They're just wanting some quick money. None of them will hurt a kid.*

Voice 1: *They're criminals, Byron. And they're not following your plan.*

Voice 2: *Our plan. And who the hell else would agree to do this? Retired girl scout troop leaders? All three of them can only get minimum-wage jobs with their records. Nadia just fell in with a bad crowd. She's cleaned up her act, and so has that boyfriend of hers. They just need money to get a fresh start.*

Voice 1: *That's just it. Your cousin and her boyfriend's one thing, this other guy that you didn't tell me about is in on this* too. I don't know him, and neither do you. If something happens to her, God help me, Byron, you'll go down for this.

Voice 2: Don't forget you'll go down with me. You hired me for the best strategies to get you to the top of the polls. I've delivered every step of the way. You'll see when this whole thing blows over. Wait till the camera crews film the happy family all together again. The happy family stating no comment as they usher their young daughter to her therapy sessions. The press will eat it up, and so will the voters.

Voice 1: What am I supposed to do until then? Give more press conferences? It's another goddamn day until they're even going to call again to discuss ransom. They were supposed to call sooner.

Voice 2: It's out of my hands now, Simon.

Voice 1: Just call Nadia to make sure everything is okay.

Voice 2: Contacting Nadia right now is too risky. Just stay here, cooperate with the police, and be ready to answer that phone tomorrow night.

Wiltz: My client and I need time to discuss this alleged evidence, and we still need a copy of that audio. Plus, we need a transcript and audio file of Nadia's alleged recording. Our experts will need to review this audio, which is obviously a hoax of some sort—probably made by the same individual who made that video.

John: I'll have a tech get the rest of that evidence to you as soon as possible.

Chapter 54
Julia

Her head was pounding, and her eyes felt puffy and swollen as she stretched her arms over her head and touched Liv's headboard. The room around her was dark, the blackout shades having been drawn. Liv's clock radio glowed beside the bed with a time well past Julia's usual lunchtime, but she didn't feel hungry. After hearing everything she had from her sisters earlier, Julia still felt sick to her stomach.

She crawled out of bed and steadied herself before heading toward the door. After all the crying, she was dizzy, and her whole body dragged like dead weight. Julia found the strength to dart past Charlotte's room in the hallway, where she could hear her sisters talking behind the closed door. Once in her room, Julia went into the bathroom and washed her face. She applied a bit of makeup to hide the redness on her cheeks and brushed her hair before pulling it into a loose bun. The last thing she cared about was looking cute for her father's press conference. Julia just wanted to feel more like herself, and with this style, she looked like she was on her way to ballet practice rather than to confront her father.

At the bottom of the stairs, Julia stood in the hallway, debating what to do next. After taking a deep breath, she started toward her father's office but was surprised to find the door open and the room empty. Taking the opportunity that had presented itself, Julia stepped inside and closed the door behind her. She walked over to her dad's massive, immaculate desk and studied the books on the shelf behind it. Finding the law dictionary, Julia pulled out the book, and as she did, a small key dropped to the carpet below. It was right where Charlotte said it would be. Their father hadn't even thought to move it.

Julia picked up the key and used it to unlock the bottom desk drawer. There was no money in the drawer as Charlotte had described, but there was a handgun lying at the bottom. It looked cold and menacing laid up against the natural wood of the drawer.

The doorbell rang, causing Julia to jump. She quickly closed the drawer and shoved the key into her hoodie pocket. Hearing her dad and Mr. Saks in the hallway and rapidly approaching the office door, Julia panicked and ran to her father's bathroom. Afraid to make any noise, she eased the door partially closed and sat down on the floor behind it. Seconds after she was settled, her dad's office door slammed.

"I knew I shouldn't have gone along with this," Mr. Manchester said. "It was a stupid idea."

"It was a great idea, but my stupid cousin screwed it up by accusing us," said Mr. Saks. "Her getting caught wasn't part of the plan. Julia messed everything up, too, by escaping."

"The plan was just your cousin and her boyfriend. That idiot friend of theirs let Julia escape and ruined the whole thing by touching my daughter. No one was supposed to hurt her. If I ever see that man, I'll kill him myself."

"You said that Julia would be less likely to cause trouble when I suggested Charlotte! So maybe we both screwed up here, but we have to get our stories straight."

"The police don't have any evidence that I was involved. Maybe it's you who needs to get a story straight. I'm planning to deny all allegations, and you should continue to do so too."

Julia bit her lip to keep herself from screaming. Everything her sisters had told her was true. Their father was guilty. He'd set her up to be held hostage for several days.

"Simon," Mr. Saks said. "The police somehow have a recording of us talking. The recording is messy, but they say they're doing some kind of voice recognition bullshit. My lawyer can get that thrown out easily. But if that stuff gets leaked, it's damning even if we deny it."

"What? How the hell could anyone have a recording of us? We've only spoken in person alone or with burner phones?"

"I told my lawyer that the whole conversation is a hoax probably put out there by one of your opponents, but Nadia's singing like a canary trying to implicate us and claims to have a recording of she and I speaking about the kidnapping."

"What?" barked Mr. Manchester. "How could you be so careless?"

"I'll get it discredited. If it even exists. The police didn't have a transcript ready yet."

"Where's the money?"

"It was at my place, but after the first round of police questioning, I moved it to a secure location."

"A secure location? Byron, that's a million dollars of my money. It's no longer needed to pay your cousin, but I sure as hell need it to pay for a damn good lawyer."

"I can't get it right now. Detective John is so far up my ass that he flat-out told me that I'm going down for this, Simon. He says the only question is whether I'm taking you with me."

"This whole damn thing was your idea!"

"You're not innocent, but we can still fix this. We can deny; we can say Nadia threatened us. We'll figure it out."

"You figure it out. I have a press conference to give, and you need to start doing your damn job and make this go away. Get that goddamn video discredited and the audio file too. And give me back my down payment!"

"You know what, Simon? Figure it out on your own. I'm out. I'm not staying here for your ill-advised press conference. And the down payment money is gone. You're not getting it back."

"Byron!"

The office door slammed, and two sets of footsteps walked toward the front door. Julia emerged from her hiding place. Shaking and barely noticing the tears streaming down her face, Julia dropped to the floor beside her father's desk. The bottom drawer was still unlocked, so Julia reached inside and pulled out the handgun. Feeling the weight of it in her hand, she took a deep breath and slipped it into her hoodie pocket. She tossed the key into the drawer and closed it again.

The wall clock read almost three, and Julia had a press conference to attend.

L iv answered her phone before the first ring had finished when she saw the main police office contact pop up on her screen. Charlotte indicated that Liv should put the phone on speaker, but Liv refused. She didn't want anyone else to overhear, and she could always fill Charlotte in later.

"Liv, this is Detective John, returning your call. Is everything okay?"

"No, everything's definitely not okay. Our dad's acting crazy because of that video, and he has a camera crew showing up here any minute to record a press statement denying any involvement," Liv told him in one breath. "Our mother and Julia both know that Charlotte and I suspect Dad and Mr. Saks, but I don't know if they believe us."

"Liv, are you in danger?" the detective asked.

"I don't know," Liv said. "But to be honest, my dad was acting crazy earlier today. He and my mother were arguing pretty loudly, and I'm worried that my dad has a gun in the house."

"Your mother also left a message for me to call her, but you had called first."

"Detective John, we're really worried here."

"I'm planning to drop by to check on things. I'll be on my way soon. I just have to finish up some things with the case to get a couple of warrants I'm wanting. I'll send a patrol car now."

"Detective, please tell me that one of those warrants is for my father."

"I'll see you soon, Liv," said the detective.

"Okay." Liv ended the call and looked at Charlotte.

"What'd he say?" Charlotte demanded. "Why didn't you put it on speaker?"

"Char, I didn't want the speaker to be too loud," Liv said. "John says he'll stop by soon to check on things. Now, it's almost three, so we need to get downstairs for that press conference."

"We need to get Julia," Charlotte said. "I don't know if we can get through this video. Maybe Dad won't make us if Julia's sick. She'll look like hell from all the crying anyway, so it's not a stretch."

Liv followed Charlotte down the hall to her bedroom to get Julia, but they found Liv's bed empty upon opening the door. Charlotte and Liv split up to check the other rooms upstairs but didn't find Julia. They met back in the hallway.

"Shit," Charlotte whispered. "Where is she?"

"Girls!" Mrs. Manchester called from downstairs. "Come down for the press statement. Right now!"

Liv and Charlotte shuffled out the door and met their mother in the hallway downstairs.

"Where's Julia?" Liv asked.

"She's already in the living room waiting on the sofa," Mrs. Manchester said. "Go join her. Charlotte, stick around out here for a moment."

Liv was reluctant to leave Charlotte, but she needed to check on Julia as well.

H e was losing his mind being cooped up at home, unable to see Charlotte. Vincent had grabbed his keys and was heading toward the back door when his phone rang with his father's name popping up.

"Hey, Dad, what's up?" he answered.

"Vincent, I just received the strangest call from Simon Manchester."

Vincent sat down on a barstool. "What?"

"Simon tells me that he's learned that you fabricated a conversation between him and his campaign manager as an act of revenge."

"What the hell?"

"Simon says that he heard you were on drugs, and because of that, he'd told you to stay away from Charlotte. He said he'd planned to call me sooner, but his concerns were on his own family because of Julia's kidnapping. He asked me to keep you away. Apparently, his campaign manager saw your car at a known drug hangout several times."

"Oh my God, Dad, that's the biggest bunch of bullshit. I've taken three piss tests in the last semester for wrestling that came up clean—you know that. And with my condition...that would be insane. That Saks creep took photos of my car when I took Charlotte home last week, so there's no telling what he's fabricating. Please don't tell me you believe him!"

"Son, of course, I don't believe that man, but I'm telling you to be careful. I don't know how he knows that you turned over the recording, but he might hurt you because of it. Don't go over to the Manchester house. Promise me."

"Dad, I can't promise you that. Charlotte might be in danger too."

"Vincent, stay home. I'm leaving work now, but I'm going to be talking to the police to find out how the hell Simon knows about the recording. They weren't supposed to release your name."

"Fine, Dad."

Beating his father to the punch, Vincent quickly dialed Detective John on his cell, and the detective answered on the second ring.

"John."

"Detective John, you've got to do something. I think the Manchester sisters are in danger, and maybe me too. Simon knows that I took the recording of him, and he says I created the whole thing. He called and threatened my father this morning."

"Vincent, I assure you that I never named you as a source. And I'm on my way to the Manchester house now. Liv called a bit ago with concerns about her father's behavior, so I'm gonna do a welfare check. I'll get to the bottom of this, I swear. The best thing you can do is stay away. Now, I've gotta go. I'm getting another call."

"Thank you." Vincent ended the call, but there was no way in hell he was staying home.

S tanding in the hallway after Liv had left, Charlotte felt small, even though she stood taller than her mother.

"I'm sorry about this morning," Mrs. Manchester said. "I talked to your father about what Vincent said, and I know the truth now."

"Oh, thank you, Mom." Charlotte sighed with relief. "Have you talked to the police? We need to stop this press conference and get Dad to turn himself in."

"Charlotte, your father knows about Vincent's drug use."

"What? Vincent doesn't use drugs."

"Your father told Vincent to stay away from you, and that's why Vincent made that tape—to get back at your father. It was a callous thing to do, and I don't want you seeing Vincent anymore either."

"Mom! He's lying. Vincent doesn't take drugs. He has to pass random drug tests to be on the wrestling team. He'd never screw that up. And he has ulcerative colitis, Mom!"

"Charlotte, I understand that all this hurts you. After the press conference, we can talk to your father, and you can apologize for making that video. When you're young and think you're in love, it's easy to be fooled by people."

Charlotte laughed at the absurdity of her mother's statement. "I guess it still happens when you're older. I believe Vincent, Mom. And I know what I saw in Dad's desk. Could he explain the money and the gun?"

"Yes, as a matter of fact. Your father was so worried about Julia that he was preparing to make a million-dollar cash reward available for tips that led to her safe return. He withdrew the money so he could have it ready at a moment's notice. Then when the kidnapper demanded that amount in ransom, he got it ready for that."

"And the gun?"

"Your father's had that for a long time. For protection."

"How convenient," Charlotte muttered. It was her mother who was delusional now—blinded by her husband's particular line of bullshit.

"Now, that's the end of this discussion. Get in that living room and support this family, young lady."

Charlotte watched her mother go into the living room and then turned to her reflection in the hallway mirror. "What the actual fuck?" she whispered before turning around to head into the living room.

Liv was sitting in the middle of the sofa next to Julia when Charlotte joined them. A camera crew was setting up lighting and closing the curtains and blinds for the video. Her parents were sitting in identical armchairs that usually sat by the window but were now in the center of the room near the fireplace. The whole thing looked like an elaborate Christmas concert with the decorated tree and grand piano in the background. The piano was a standard decoration since Mrs. Manchester rarely played anymore, but the tree was new. Charlotte could tell it was Hannah's quick handiwork since only the front of the tree that would face the cameras was decorated. The tree was as phony as all the bullshit that would soon spew from her father's mouth.

Charlotte glared at him from across the room, but he didn't acknowledge her.

"We're about ready here, Mr. Manchester," one of the crew members said. Charlotte recognized the man from other press conferences.

"Thank you," her dad replied. "I need you to run my tablet for the live broadcast portion of this for social media."

"Sure," the crewman said. "That's not a problem."

"Simon, I thought we were going to record this to release later," Mrs. Manchester said.

"I know, Gina, but I think it will be better if we share this on my campaign page live first, and then we can release a better video to the press later."

"Okay, so you want me to just run your tablet first and not record you with the good cameras?" the crewman asked. "That's fine if that's what you want, but I should at least get some B-roll footage while you're doing your live broadcast. Where's Byron? He usually asks you questions."

"Byron's detained this afternoon, so I'm going live with just a prepared statement," Mr. Manchester said. "Let's go."

The crewman set up the tablet on a tripod and worked on getting it started. Charlotte watched him tap at the screen a couple of times before giving up. "Mr. Manchester, I'm having trouble getting you logged in to go live. It wants your WIFI password."

Seizing her opportunity, Charlotte jumped up. "I'll help with that," she said. "I'll even start it running."

"Great," the crewman said.

Charlotte went to her father's tablet and quickly entered the WIFI password, which wasn't complicated at all since her father had insisted upon using "ManTheChester." Instead of pulling up her father's campaign page, though, she pulled up her own YouTube page and signed in, preparing to go live. It was time to end all the bullshit. "I'll even ask the questions. Let's go. We're live in five, four, three…"

Her dad looked nervous and sweaty as Charlotte ensured that her video was running. As Charlotte looked over to her sisters, she realized that Julia looked lost and far away as she fiddled with her hands inside her hoodie pockets. Liv had her arm wrapped around Julia's shoulders, trying to comfort her, but it didn't seem to be helping.

"Good afternoon, voters. Simon Manchester here. I want to take this opportunity to thank everyone for sticking with my family and me during this difficult time." He reached out for his wife's hand without taking his eyes off the tablet camera. "Now that my daughter is home safe, we've been victims of vicious rumors circulating, so I want to set the record straight. I, Simon Manchester, was not involved in the kidnapping of my daughter, Julia Manchester. A video claiming that I was involved has been traced to a disgruntled person looking for fame—a boyfriend of one of my daughters who was looking to hurt me. Now, this young man has a drug habit—"

"Dad!" Charlotte said from behind the tablet, startling him and her mother. "I think the voters want to know about the possible involvement of Byron Saks' cousin in the kidnapping."

Glaring at Charlotte, Mr. Manchester continued. "As my daughter just mentioned, we have determined that a distant cousin of my campaign manager was involved in the kidnapping. She's in police custody now, and I assure you that she'll be punished for her part in this whole fiasco. My campaign manager should not be held accountable for his family members' crimes, just as how our great country says that all men are presumed innocent until proven guilty. All the claims against Mr. Byron Saks are also completely false and a blatant attempt to discredit my campaign. But I know my voters are intelligent enough to distinguish fact from fiction and sort out these vicious attacks for what they are— an attack on American values."

Julia stood up from the sofa and started laughing as she walked into the frame. Liv tried to pull her back down, but Julia shoved her away. The crewmen in the room all stopped what they were doing, and Charlotte took a step in Julia's direction, not bothering to shut off the broadcast.

"Cut the bullshit, Dad," Julia said through laughter. "Seriously, just stop."

Charlotte stopped dead in her tracks, not believing what she was seeing as she watched her baby sister pull a gun from her hoodie pocket and aim it at their father's head.

"Holy shit," said one of the crewmen before backing out of the room.

"Julia!" Mrs. Manchester said. "What are you doing?"

"Julia," Charlotte said, this time taking a step back. "Why don't you put that down so we can all—"

"Shut up!" Julia screamed. "Everyone shut up except you, Dad!"

"J-Julia—Julia," he stammered. "Put down the gun. It's obvious that you've been through a lot of trauma, sweetheart, and we're going to get you some help, sweetheart."

Julia shook her head, not moving the gun's aim. "No. Don't you dare call me 'sweetheart' right now. No. Right now, you can start by telling me why. Why did you and Byron Saks offer money to three criminals to kidnap me?"

Mr. Manchester shook his head and tried to reach out to Julia, but she held out her other hand to stop him. "I. Heard. You."

"I don't know what you're talking about," Mr. Manchester said. "Julia—put the gun down."

Julia clicked off the safety on the gun. "I swear to God; I'll shoot you right now if you don't tell the truth. I heard you talking to Byron this afternoon! Less than a fucking hour ago!"

Charlotte backed away to stay out of Julia's peripheral vision and went to Liv's spot on the sofa. She grabbed her older sister's arm and pulled her up to a standing position. She then shoved Liv toward the hallway and mouthed to her to call 911.

Looking back at her parents, Charlotte could see the terror in her mother's eyes, but she did not pity her at the moment. Her only goal was to keep Julia from firing that gun and doing something she'd regret for the rest of her life.

"Dad," Charlotte said softly, but it was still loud enough to make Julia jump. "Tell the truth, and Julia will give me the gun, right Jules?"

"That's right!" Julia snapped. "But I'm gonna hold on to it for now until you start talking and tell us about the conversation you had in your office this afternoon. It's where

I found this gun in the first place. I was in your bathroom, so I heard everything. Don't you dare lie about it!"

Charlotte took another step closer to Julia, wondering if there was any possibility of getting the gun away from her. Judging by her father's reaction to the gun pointed at him, she knew it was loaded.

Mrs. Manchester was audibly crying now, but Julia didn't seem affected by it. Her aim was steady, despite the shaking that had started in her legs. "Talk!" she screamed at her father.

"Baby, I'm sorry. I never meant for you to get hurt. It was just supposed to be a few days, and then you'd be back. I'm so sorry." Mr. Manchester broke down. "It was all Byron's idea, but I'm just as guilty because I went along with it. I'm so sorry, Julia. And Gina. Liv, Charlotte. Can you ever forgive me?"

"Oh, my God, Simon! How could you?" Mrs. Manchester asked through her tears. She struggled to get her hand out of her husband's grip and backed away.

"I'm sorry. I'm so sorry." Mr. Manchester reached toward Julia. "Baby, please give me the gun. I'll turn myself in, I promise. Just give me the gun."

Charlotte took a final step toward Julia and placed her hand on her sister's shoulder. "Come on, Julia," she said. "Please put down the gun."

Julia let out a sob and lowered the gun for a moment. Charlotte breathed a sigh of relief as she reached for the gun, but then Julia brought it back up again. "Sorry's not good enough, Dad," Julia said. Then she pulled the trigger, firing one shot toward their father.

Everything went deafeningly silent around Charlotte as she knocked the gun from Julia's hand and tackled her to the floor. Their parents were on the ground, too, but Charlotte couldn't tell if either of them had been shot. Charlotte turned toward the hallway and saw Liv standing there screaming, but she couldn't hear her. Behind Liv, Detective John came running in, followed by other officers. Charlotte saw the detective pick up the gun with a gloved hand before running toward Mr. Manchester, who was laid out near the fireplace.

The next thing Charlotte knew, she was wrapped in a blanket with Liv on the sofa, her ears still ringing slightly from the gunshot blast. Vincent was kneeling on the floor, and when Charlotte saw him in front of her, she started crying and dropped down into his arms.

Detective Ernest John's Notes: Summary.
Case closed and turned over to DA.

RECOVERED: Julia Marie Manchester.

~~Missing child. Julia Marie Manchester. White female. 13 YO. BR Hair. BR Eyes. Approximately 5'7'' tall, 115-125 pounds. Slim build. Last seen in purple sweater, black jeans, grey boots. Black coat. Pink hat. Pink scarf. Carries pink canvas backpack.~~

In custody for kidnapping:

William Elmer Mulligan, age 31, denies involvement, will likely go to trial.

Pearl Nadine Freeman, age 35, full confession, will likely take plea agreement.

Eddie Watson, age 40, full confession, will likely take plea agreement.

In custody for conspiracy to commit kidnapping, kidnapping, fraud, money laundering:

Byron James Saks, age 47, denies involvement, will likely go to trial. Was caught at airport attempting to flee the country.

Simon Wells Manchester, age 51, full confession, will likely take plea agreement.

Cleared of wrongdoing:
Vincent Matthew Rowlands, age 18.
Gina Anne Manchester, age 48.
Julia Marie Manchester, age 13.

Julia Marie Manchester is currently hospitalized in the Psychiatric Ward of the State Children's Hospital undergoing treatment for PTSD. No charges expected to be filed for use of firearm that was registered to her father, Simon Wells Manchester.

Simon Manchester confession to follow:

Simon Manchester Written Confession:

I, Simon Wells Manchester, hereby confess to planning the kidnapping of my 13-year-old daughter, Julia Marie Manchester, in December 2015. Along with my campaign manager, Byron James Saks, we hired his cousin, Nadia Freeman, and her boyfriend, Eddie Watson, to kidnap Julia and hold her for ransom. The agreement was that the pair would receive the sum of $1,250,000 to handle this job, with the first quarter-million being paid up front. The rules of the engagement were to keep Julia at a safe location, make an untraceable ransom phone call, and to release Julia to my care after receiving said ransom. My end of the bargain was to keep quiet.

The purpose of the kidnapping scam was to gain public sympathy for my upcoming presidential primary election, for which I was falling behind in the polls. I am regretful and sorry for the pain I have caused my family and hope they can someday forgive me.

Simon Wells Manchester
December 11, 2015

Epilogue
December 23, 2015
YouTube Video transcript
Charlotte

"You already know what happened since a trial of epic proportions was avoided yesterday when the biggest player involved pleaded guilty. Spoiler alert: It's safe to say that shit's hit every single political fan now.

"And if you haven't already figured out who I am, I'm Charlotte Manchester, daughter of Simon Manchester, who was running for president.

"I won't even begin to bore you with the details of what political affiliation he represented because none of that really matters. Now that you know who I am, you already know all about my dad if you've been paying attention. The point is, he wanted to be president more than he wanted to be a good man.

"Thank God, my sister Julia escaped her abductors, who are currently in prison, but I'm worried she'll be scarred for life. I'm sure you've all read in the news that my sister is hospitalized. She'll need a lot of help to overcome this trauma that's hit our family. There are a lot of conflicting news reports out there right now. I want to tell the truth.

"One, my father has confessed to arranging Julia's kidnapping with his campaign manager Byron Saks. Two, Byron Saks is denying all charges. Three, two of the three kidnappers in custody have made full confessions, and the third is awaiting either a trial or a plea bargain if he decides to confess. Four, the allegations of a hoax audio recording implicating my father are false. The audio recording is real.

Five, the accusation of drug use by a boyfriend of one of the Manchester sisters is also false. Six, the reports that Julia Manchester shot our father are false. While Julia did fire the gun, as you all have probably seen in the video on this feed before it was deleted, she did not actually hit him. And last, it is true that my mother, Gina Manchester, has filed for divorce from my father.

"My father made the biggest mistake of his life that has cost him his family and his freedom—the very things he was supposedly fighting for. He thought it was his one shot for the chance at the highest political office in our country. I don't know if any of us will forgive my father for what he's done. I'm still having trouble comprehending it, but I'm afraid that my sister will need more than one shot to fully recover.

"I will make no further statements about this matter, and I will post no other videos on this channel. No comments will be allowed on this post because you'll believe what you want. I know the truth. I don't have anything left to say. Thanks for listening. Goodbye."

ABOUT THE AUTHOR:

Brandi Easterling Collins grew up in Arkansas where she still resides with her husband, two children, and their two dogs. When she's not writing or reading, she enjoys spending time with her family, thrift store shopping, painting, drawing, and leisurely walks outside.

One Shot is her fourth novel. Her other novels include *Caroline's Lighthouse, Jordan's Sister,* and *What I Learned That Summer.*

For more information about future publications, visit caniscareyou.com.

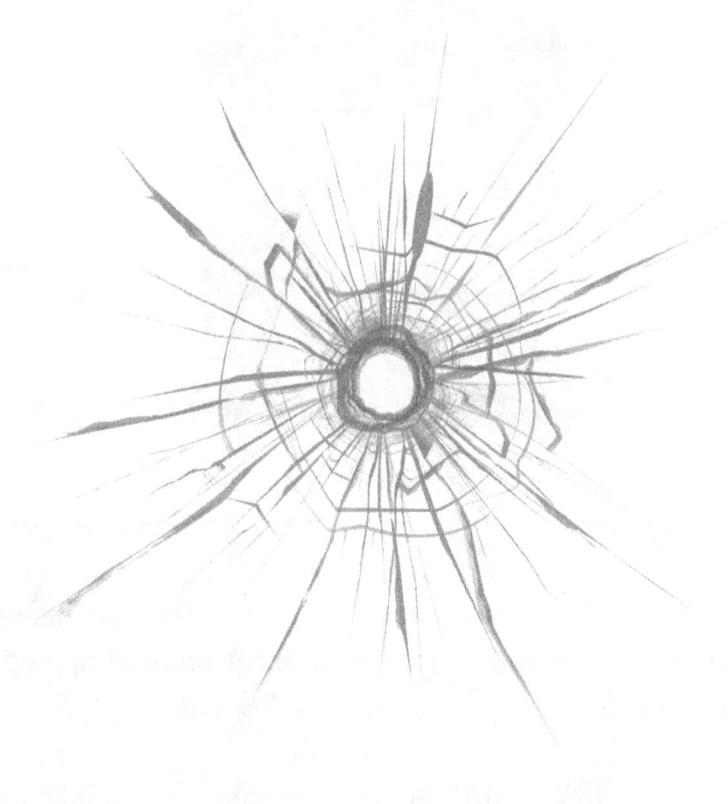

www.ingramcontent.com/pod-product-compliance
Lightning Source LLC
Chambersburg PA
CBHW051958240626
47153CB00005B/1814